COUNTERPOINT

COUNTERPOINT

IN
VINO
VERITAS

J.E. BIRK

HeartEyes Press

For all the readers who asked to see Jeremy or Aaron again: This book is for you. Thank you for giving me the chance to tell this story.

1

THAT TIME JEREMY LEARNED TO ADULT (SORT OF)

"Good morning, honey bunches!" I fling open the door of Jamie and Briar's apartment with as much flourish as I can come up with at 7:30 in the morning. Luckily, I've got skills in staying up all night and still functioning reasonably well the next day—and it's a good thing I do. I completely lost track of time last night and ended up staying out until almost 2 a.m. Whoops. I promised Jamie I would be a good boy and get a full night's rest before my first day at my new job.

At least Jamie's used to me breaking promises. Sometimes I'm amazed he's still my best friend after living in the Burlington University dorms with me. Anyone else probably would have kicked my ass to the curb after the time I came into our room at 3 a.m. drunkenly singing "We Are the Champions" at the top of my lungs. But Jamie just rolled his eyes and joined in at the chorus.

I'm still not sure how I got so lucky in the friend department.

Briar Nord, Jamie's boyfriend, looks up at me from the bowl of cereal he's pouring. He grins wryly. "Morning, Jeremy. I had a feeling we were going to regret giving you that spare key."

"Aww, sweetums, don't be like that. I brought you a treat." I whip a white paper bag out from behind my back.

Briar's eyes immediately light up. "Maple donuts? Gimme.

1

And I take it back. You can have all the keys you want if you bring me donuts in the morning."

I'm happy to pass over the bag. I had to go a little out of my way to get my morning coffee from The Maple Factory, Briar's favorite bakery, but the look on Briar's face right now makes the extra trip worth the trouble. Briar and Jamie have done a lot for me in the past month. After I got the phone call from my mom informing me that she was no longer going to "finance my playboy lifestyle," as she put it, and that there was no way she was going to pay for me to stay in Vermont during the summer once I finished my junior year, I may have panicked a little. And by "panicked," I mean I went on a drinking binge that ended with a lost wallet, a strained wrist, and a cute blond guy who kept trying to convince me we should get married.

Again: whoops.

Jamie, Briar, and our friend Lexy were not impressed. But I maintain that my reaction was proportional to the problem. My mother was insisting I move back home to Connecticut for the summer. I'm pretty sure anyone faced with three months of Delia Everett's disapproval and stern expressions would also start downing tequila shots.

Luckily, Jamie and Briar came to my rescue. Briar helped me land a sublet in the apartment above his and Jamie's, and Jamie knew a law firm in Burlington hiring a receptionist and gofer boy. It doesn't pay well, and since most of my money is going to go to rent, I'll be a little more cash-poor this summer than I'm used to. But at least I'll be in Burlington, VT, and not in Wellsford, CT, with a mom who thinks I'm wasting my life and never misses an opportunity to tell me so.

"Good morning." Jamie steps out of the bedroom and into the open living area of the apartment as he wipes sleep out of his eyes. He nods at me. "Oh, good. You're up. I was going to run upstairs and knock on your door, just in case you stayed out all night or something."

"Never," I reply innocently, but Jamie knows me well. He just shakes his head and smiles.

"Well. You're awake. And it looks like you're showered and actually going to be at work on time for your first day. Frankly, Jeremy, I'm impressed." He leans over to give Briar a good morning kiss on the cheek.

"Plus, he brought donuts," Briar replies with his mouth full.

"And . . . ." I pull another bag out from behind my back and hand it to Jamie. "Crullers. Your favorite. Just for you, best bro. See how I stuck the landing there?"

Briar applauds. "Ten points from this judge."

"Thank you." I take a bow and pull out a chair to sit down at the tiny table across from Briar and Jamie. The two of them immediately start doing this *thing* I've noticed they do in the mornings. First, Jamie rubs at Briar's hair a little while he kisses his cheek, and then Briar passes him a cup of tea that Jamie takes a sip of, and right after that, Briar nuzzles into Jamie's neck again. Next, they kiss all gently before they nod at each other. Every morning I've seen them together since they moved into this apartment looks exactly the same. And somehow, I know they're talking to each other the whole time, even though they're not saying a word.

I swore off committed relationships after my first and only real attempt at one went balls up during my freshman year at Moo U. (That's what the locals call Burlington University—because of all the cows here. Not very original, but at least it's accurate.) That choice was necessary and right, and, for the most part, I've never regretted it. Sometimes, though, Briar and Jamie make me wonder what I'm missing. They've been together for over a year now, since Jamie and I were sophomores, and they make being a couple look so *easy.* So good. Anyone who didn't know the Netflix-level drama that came with them getting together would think they've always had the perfect relationship. They even met at a romance book club Briar started. Who actually meets the love of their life at a romance book club?

Sometimes, it's hard not to look at them and remember that I'll never be able to have what they have. I can't—it's not possible. I've learned that lesson, and I mostly try not to dwell on it. But whenever I see Jamie and Briar like this, I feel a tiny twinge in my stomach . . . and I can't help wondering what life could be like if only things had worked out a little differently for me.

"I'm proud of you, Jeremy," Jamie tells me as he wipes cruller crumbs off his face. "That was a shitty bomb your mom dropped on you, but you handled it really well once we got the tequila bottle out of your hands. And maybe this will be good, you getting a real-world job and adulting with the rest of us this summer. Maybe you'll like making your own money. Maybe you'll even like working at the law firm."

I tend to doubt that. Work and I have never had a very positive relationship. It gets in the way of play, and who wants that? I'm not a total asshole: I know I'm incredibly lucky and privileged to have gone this long in life without needing a real job beyond some temporary gigs here and there. My parents' wealth isn't something I don't appreciate, especially since I spent the first two years of college watching Jamie work his ass off at multiple jobs while he was taking as many classes as I was. But there are so many beautiful things to see and experience out there in the world. Why sit behind a desk and miss out on them, I always figured, when I had the ability to enjoy them?

I'm moving forward with a new outlook, though. I've got to hold down a job and pay my rent, and I still refuse to give up on all the wonderful experiences life has to offer. I made a promise to live my life to the fullest, and I'm determined to keep that promise. So last night, I stayed out until 2 a.m. and enjoyed the hell out of myself with some grad student I met at the Vino and Veritas bar, and I still got up when my alarm went off this morning.

See Mom? I whisper in my head. *I know you think I'm a total fuck-up, but I can do this.*

At least Briar and Jamie like me the way I am. They always seem to. Even when they probably shouldn't.

Briar yawns and stretches. "Yeah. Maybe you'll like this job, Jeremy. It's cool that you get to work with Aaron."

I choke on my sip of coffee. "I'm sorry? What the fuck did you just say?"

Briar looks concerned as he passes me a napkin to wipe up the liquid I just spit all over myself. "Uh, Aaron? Jamie's brother? Who is also working at the law firm?" He and Jamie are both staring at me. I pull in a deep breath through my nose to try and quell the rising panic that's circling in my chest.

"Aaron?" I say as calmly as I can. "I thought he was in Boston. Isn't he working at the same place he worked last summer?" *Please let that be true. Please let me be misunderstanding something.*

Jamie shakes his head and pulls another cruller out of the bag I brought him. "No, everyone in our family thought that too. But then he surprised us. He said he'd rather be in Burlington this summer to be closer to us, and one of his friends at Harvard Law helped him get a clerkship here. That's how I knew there was an opening for an admin position at his firm. He mentioned it to me."

A million questions are swirling in my head. Does Aaron know I'm going to be working at his firm? Did he suggest this to Jamie? Will I have to see him a lot? Are we ever going to talk about that one night we never, ever talk about? Are things going to be as fucking awkward as they've been for the last fifteen damn months?

Oh: and does he still remember all the things I stupidly told him that night? Those things I *still* can't believe I let come out of my mouth? Those things that no one—not even his brother, my best friend—knows?

I'm stuck on that question when Briar leans over to tap me on the arm. "Dude, are you okay? Does this have something to do with how weird you and Aaron have been around each other lately?"

The panic that's been circling my lungs starts to do somersaults. "What are you talking about?" I ask, keeping my voice as even and cool as possible. "Aaron and I aren't weird around each other."

"Yeah, you are." Jamie gets up to pour himself some more hot water before dropping another tea bag into his mug. "The three of us used to hang out all the time back when you and I were freshmen and Aaron was still at Moo U. And look, I know things got weird when he got into law school early and all that drama happened with my family. But that's all been over for more than a year, and the two of you still barely even look at each other when Aaron's home from Boston. What's the deal?"

There are zero good ways to answer that question. I can't blow Jamie off and tell him he's imagining things, because he's not. Aaron and I have been weird AF since he made up with his family last spring. I spend a lot of time with Jamie's family, the Morins— partly because I'd rather be with them for holidays and weekends than deal with my mother, and partly just because I like them. They're fun and accepting, and they've adopted me the same way they've adopted Briar. Being with them reminds me of what I left behind in Connecticut. They remind me of everything I lost, but usually not in a bad way.

They remind me of the best days of my life. The days before everything went to shit and I resolved never to go back home.

But whenever Aaron comes home for a family get-together or a holiday or whatever, he and I spend the entire time trying to look polite and chill and happy to see each other without actually having to get anywhere near each other. It's a lot of work, honestly, and since work isn't really my thing, I've started avoiding Aaron. I haven't seen him since Christmas, when we both spent the day at the Morin farmhouse, and he nearly fell into the fireplace trying to get away from me during a game of charades.

I take one more breath and flash Jamie and Briar my best, most practiced smile. This is the same one I use when people ask me how my family is doing, or why I don't go home very much, or tell me how nice it must be to have a trust fund and never have to worry about anything. Sometimes I see this smile in the mirror, and I wonder how anyone could ever fall for it: it doesn't even look like it fits my face. But I've made an entire city believe it's real, including my best friends. There's no reason to believe it won't work on Jamie and Briar now.

"Aaron and I just aren't as close as we used to be," I say smoothly. "We haven't talked that much since you two made up. It's no big deal, okay? Working with him will be fine." I make a show of checking my watch. "Better get going if I don't want to be late."

Jamie's tilting one eyebrow at me, and Briar's studying me a little more closely than I like as he takes another bite of donut. "Okay," Jamie says slowly. "If you're sure. But just so you know, I think Aaron's a little nervous about this job. He tripped over the same bucket three times when we talked about it last night at the farm. And then he nearly brained himself with a milking machine."

I wince. Unfortunately, I am *very* familiar with Aaron's ability to completely lose his coordination when he's nervous. I'll never forget the incident with the lamp on The Night We Do Not Mention. "So maybe help him out if you can," Jamie adds. "I know this is your first job and all, but it's not like you're going to be nervous about work today."

"Of course not," I agree. Because he's right. Why would I get nervous about the first day at a new job? Who cares? It's just a job. Life's too short to worry about impressing people, especially people you don't know or care about. I'll show up, I'll answer phones, and I'll play fetch for everyone in the office. The only thing that matters is that the lawyers like me enough to pay me. "I'll do my best," I add as I send Jamie and Briar another beaming smile. Briar's still giving me that *look* he gives me sometimes, like he's peering deep into my soul. I always have to make sure I'm not squirming in my chair when he stares at me like that.

"Have a good day, Jeremy," Briar finally says. "Good luck."

"Thanks!" I grab a donut for the road and jet out of the apartment. My stomach's swirling, though, and I end up having to set the donut down in the passenger seat of my car.

Jamie's right: I don't get nervous about things like jobs. That's not me.

Unless I've just found out that my new job includes working with my best friend's brother, the guy I had a one night stand with fifteen months ago.

The only one night stand I've ever regretted.

Once again: whoops.

2

THAT TIME AARON ALMOST KNOCKED HIMSELF UNCONSCIOUS

"Morning, Mom." I step out onto the front porch of my family's old farmhouse, stretching as I take in the scene in front of me. Northwestern Vermont is soft and dewy this morning, the bright green grass sparkling with drops of water in the sunlight barely peeking over the horizon. Our family's cows are out in the pasture across the driveway, grazing, creating a scene straight out of a postcard. I take in a deep breath, pulling in a scent of pure, fresh sweetness that no laundry detergent can ever really recreate.

"Hi, honey." Mom pats the rocking chair next to the one she's sitting in. "Sit down with me for a moment before you have to leave for this fancy new job of yours."

There was a time when this porch was my favorite place in the world, and all I ever wanted to do was sit out here in one of these rocking chairs, joking with my brother Jamie about which one of us could milk cows faster and listening to our little sister Lissie play the guitar. I used to dream about this porch during the nine months I was estranged from my family. I quickly sink into the chair next to my mother.

"It's not that fancy," I say as I reposition my tie for the forty-seventh time. I hope I picked the right color. The other interns at

Leicester, Leicester, Holt, and Masik, the corporate law firm where I interned in Boston last summer, loved making sly comments about my suit and tie choices. Most of them seemed to have an endless supply of Armani coming from somewhere, and everything I wore came straight out of the Men's Warehouse sales rack or Goodwill.

Nope nope nope, I tell myself. *Don't think about Leicester. Don't think about last summer and the other interns, and definitely don't think about your final review.*

"I'm just so proud of you," Mom says. "You work so hard. I can't believe that next year my son will be a Harvard Law graduate!"

I have to smile. God, this woman. She's pure goodness and kindness wrapped up in a five-foot-tall package. Logically I know that if I could tell anyone about what happened at my internship last summer, it would be her. Mom's always supported me and my siblings unconditionally. I could probably tell her that I quit law school to join a heavy metal band, and she'd just ask me when my next show was so she could bring peanut butter cookies and drinks.

Mom leans over to wrap one arm around my neck. "And I was just thinking how glad I am that you came home, baby. I'm so grateful that our family is together again."

And *that's* why I can't open up to her and spill my darkest secrets about law school and how things last summer went wrong. Because when I got into law school early, and my father panicked about losing my help on the farm, the fight we had was so bad that I left home and didn't speak to anyone in my family for nearly a year. We might still not be speaking if Jamie hadn't almost overworked himself into a breakdown trying to make up for my absence.

My dad and I have buried the hatchet. He's finally hired some help, and he's apologized many times for what he said and did back then. I've apologized for leaving like I did and cutting off all contact with Jamie, Lissie, and my mom. None of them ever deserved that.

But sometimes, the guilt I feel about how I handled that whole situation keeps me up at night. That guilt spikes as I watch Lissie and Dad step out of the barn and head into the cow pasture, where Lissie stops to pet her favorite Guernsey. It's still hard to believe how tall Lissie's gotten. I missed so much during that lost year.

How can I tell my mom, my favorite person in the world, that it's possible I broke her heart and nearly destroyed our family for nothing? That I might never even practice law?

Nope, I can't do that. I can't tell her that, and I can't let that happen. This summer is my second chance. My fresh start. I'm not some wet-behind-the-ears 1L anymore. I've secured a good clerk-ship this summer, and I'm graduating next year. I've got to make the most of this opportunity. I've got to become a lawyer, the way my family, my professors, and everyone else in my life expects me to. "I have to go, Mom," I tell her as I stand up from the chair. "Don't want to be late on the first day. I love you."

"Love you too. You're coming back here tonight, right?"

"Yeah. I move into my apartment in Burlington this weekend. It'll be nice to be right across the hall from Jamie."

She pats my cheek. "My two boys, together again," she says fondly. Then she adds, "Watch out for Briar's meatloaf. He uses my recipe, but he adds about three times as much maple syrup. It's a diabetic coma waiting to happen."

My brother's boyfriend is a maple syrup fiend. "I'll be on the lookout for it. See you tonight, Mom."

"Try not to trip on anything!" she calls out as I climb into my Jeep. I grimace. I'm generally a pretty coordinated guy, but that coordination can go right out the window when my nerves get the better of me. On my first day at Harvard, I spilled an entire cup of coffee all over one of my professors. Luckily for me, she had a sense of humor about the incident and did not fail me on sight when I ended up in her torts class.

The drive to Burlington is about forty-five minutes, so I call Peter, my closest friend from Harvard, to see if he'll keep me company. He answers on the first ring.

"Hey, man. First day today, huh?"

"Yup. Thanks again for making this happen for me." Peter isn't just a friend; he's more of a mentor, really. His family is from Burlington, and he was a year ahead of me at Harvard. When we met at a coffee shop in Cambridge during my first semester at law school, we were both surprised to discover that we'd grown up less than forty minutes away from each other. Peter, who has family friends in the legal world and knew a hell of a lot more about it than I could even imagine, sort of took me under his wing. He's the one who helped me land this clerkship in Burlington; his godmother is one of the partners in the firm.

"No need to thank me. Aunt Iris and the firm are excited to have you. Her partner Tom even burned some sage in your new office last night to make sure it was cleansed for your arrival."

I nearly choke on my sip of coffee. "Say that again?"

"I should have warned you. Iris and Tom are some of the toughest lawyers in Vermont, but they're also pretty . . . new-age, I guess? They kind of do their own thing. Iris is probably the only lawyer who's ever showed up to court in Crocs. Just go with all of it. Otherwise, you'll end up in one of their dawn meditation sessions, and there's not enough coffee in the world for those things."

"Okay." I take a deep breath and remind myself that this is what I wanted when I asked Peter if he knew of any clerkships in Vermont. I wanted something as different from Leicester as I could get. And so far, it definitely sounds like I'm getting that.

"How's studying for the California bar going?" I ask. Peter's already got a corporate job lined up in Century City, which I'm told is where all the big-time firms in LA are located. I'm pretty sure Peter, who's one of the calmest and most self-assured guys I know, came out of the womb ready to kick ass and take names.

He'll never struggle in that environment the way I did at Leicester, which is one of the reasons I've never told him what happened there.

Peter's quiet for a minute. "Actually, I'm not in California."

"Really? Where are you?" After he graduated, Peter disappeared out of the Boston area fast. I just assumed he went right to the west coast.

"Well." He clears his throat. "I might spend some time in Vermont this summer. You know, get some solitude while I study."

"You're going to be in Vermont? No way!" This is great news. Maybe. On the one hand, I always enjoy spending time with Peter. He was an island of calm and a connection to home when I was alone at law school and desperately needed all of that. On the other hand, there's no way I'll be able to hide anything that goes wrong at his godmother's firm if he's right down the street.

I'm not sure I can stand to have Peter, of all people, watch me fail in real-time.

"Maybe I'll be in Vermont," Peter adds quickly. "I'm still . . . figuring some things out. I'll keep you updated. And listen, Aunt Iris's firm is lucky to have you. Have a great first day today, okay? You're going to do fantastic work. If you could make it at Leicester, you can make it anywhere."

It's a good thing I'm on Bluetooth and not Facetime. There's no way I could keep my lies about Leicester going if Peter could see my face right now. But I can't imagine ever telling Peter, who never fails at anything, just exactly what a colossal failure I was last summer.

"Thanks, Peter," I say quietly. He clicks off, and I do breathing exercises for the rest of the drive.

The Sprysky and Gentry building sits on a side street of Church Street, the hub of Burlington. It's a long, brick-covered street that's for pedestrians only. Lined with restaurants and shops, it's home to half the events in the city. Briar works at one of the bookstores there. We're supposed to have lunch later if I can get away on my first day.

My first day. And it's got to go better than the last time I had a first day at a law firm.

It has to. Peter vouched for me here. Not to mention that I lost almost an entire year with my family over my dream to become a lawyer. A whole year.

That can't have been for nothing.

"You can do this, Aaron," I whisper to myself as I step out of the car. My old Jeep used to look incredibly out of place amongst all the BMWs and Teslas at Leicester, but here it's mostly surrounded by muddy Volvos and Subarus. I hope I fit in as well as my car does.

I pull out the key card I got when I stopped by to fill out paperwork a few days ago, and I use it to open the back door of the firm's office. I step inside a quiet coatroom area, where there's a pair of rubber boots lined up next to another pair of expensive loafers. That sight immediately boosts my confidence. The boots look just like the ones I have back at the farm.

There's also a pair of bright purple Crocs, confirming Peter's stories.

"You can do this, Aaron," I whisper to myself again as I walk through the coatroom and into the reception area.

"I sure hope you can," says a cheerful voice. "Because I'm definitely not writing any legal briefs."

The familiar voice surprises me so much that I trip over the side of one of my new dress shoes and go ass-over-chest into a copying machine. I smack my head straight into the output door. For a moment all I can do is lay there, on the floor of my brand-new law firm, while the world spins around me.

"Oh no." It's that same voice. The one I know all too well. "Aaron? Are you okay? Do I need to call an ambulance or something?"

"No! No!" I pop my eyes open fast. The last thing I need is to be the guy in the office who was taken to the hospital on his first day. "I'm fine. I didn't hit my head that hard." I sit up, rubbing at a tiny bump on the side of my skull while the throbbing there slowly lessens. I really didn't hurt myself that badly. I'm a lot more shocked by the face currently swimming in front of my vision. "Jeremy Everett," I whisper.

Jeremy's dirty blond hair is bright and wild around his head, bouncing against his light blue eyes and slightly tanned skin. The small hint of beard on his chin tells me he didn't have time to shave this morning, which doesn't surprise me. Jeremy likes a good party more than anyone else I know, and he doesn't let his bed keep him away from them. His smile is wide and bright, as usual, but it's that same rehearsed smile he wears a lot. I don't know why more people don't notice how fake it looks. And what's he doing here, anyway? I guess he could need legal advice. Jeremy's family is loaded. Maybe there's an issue with his trust fund or something. "Are you meeting one of the lawyers here?" I ask.

He slowly stands from where he's been kneeling in front of me. Thank goodness he didn't try to help me up. I probably would have ended up breaking my arm or something.

Jeremy Everett didn't always turn me into a ball of nerves. The two of us used to be pretty close, actually, back when he and Jamie and I all went to Moo U together. But then that night last March happened, and, well, things have been different since then.

"Actually," says Jeremy quietly, "I'm working here too."

Oh no. No no no no no.

My heart starts pounding so loudly in my chest that I'm sure everyone in the office can hear it. "Jamie asked me if the firm was hiring," I whisper. Oh shit. This is my fault. I'm the one who told Jamie about that job. I never imagined he was planning to pass the information along to Jeremy, of all people. "You got a job here? Why?" I manage to pick myself up and stand as I rub the back of my head. "No offense, but I don't actually think of you as someone who . . . ," I trail off. I have no idea how to say the next part without sounding incredibly rude.

"Works for a living? Contributes to society in a meaningful way?" Jeremy laughs. "I'm still definitely not. If I had my way, I'd be lounging on a beach right now. Preferably in Ibiza. No, I changed my mind. St. Bart's. Have you ever been to St. Bart's? Did you know that if you're really lucky, you can get two guys and a girl to—never mind." He cuts himself off, probably because I'm openly staring at him. "Um, yeah. So, I pissed off my mom one time too many. She said I have to pay my own way this summer, Jamie mentioned this job, and here we are."

"I'm speechless," I reply in a strangled voice. Because I am.

Jeremy hesitates for a moment. "He didn't tell me you were working here too," he finally says. "Not until it was too late to get another job. I almost changed my mind. But I really can't live on Briar and Jamie's couch all summer. Those two are like bunnies, and they never let me join. Then I was thinking—"

"Aaron, you're here!" Iris Sprysky, Peter's godmother and one of the firm's founding partners, steps out of her office and into the reception area. She's a tall Black woman, a little older than my mother, and she's wearing a flowing dress covered in bright patterns. She's got on giant teal jewelry and oversized, purple-framed glasses. A pair of worn red Birkenstocks complete her look. "Oh, good, you've met Jeremy. He'll be helping us out this summer while Jen's on maternity leave. Are you all right?" She asks when she sees me rubbing my head.

"Fine! I'm fine!" I blurt out. "Totally, completely fine. Just fine."

"Umm, wonderful," my new boss says. When we talked on the phone last week, she kept telling me to call her Iris, but I know I'll feel strange calling her anything but Ms. Sprysky. This is the woman who single-handedly rewrote Vermont environmental regulations in the 90s.

"Let's meet now, please. We'll talk about what needs to be

done this week. Tom's already cleansed a space for you." She steps back into her office and closes the door.

"Guess I have to go." I brush off my suit. "It's, uh, nice seeing you again, Jeremy."

"Nice" isn't exactly the right word. There aren't many words that accurately describe how I feel when I see Jeremy Everett.

Obsessed? Horny? Anxious? Terrified? All of the above?

He hesitates again. "Yeah. You too. And you know, like I said, I was thinking—"

"I'll talk to you later," I quickly interrupt him. At some point, we're probably going to have to discuss what happened last March. But I can't handle that conversation right now. Not when my head's still throbbing, and the person who controls my destiny is waiting in her office for me.

"Oh. Okay," he says, looking slightly disappointed. "Well, I'll see you around the office then. Or at Jamie's, I guess. I'll probably run into you there a lot since I'm staying there too."

"What do you mean?" I don't even bother trying to keep the panic out of my voice as it goes up an octave. "You're staying at The Pink Monstrosity?" The Pink Monstrosity is the giant pink Victorian house in the Old North End of Burlington where Brian and Jamie have an apartment. I'm moving into it in a few days. But why would Jeremy be staying there? He's got enough money to stay in a place four times as nice.

Oh no, I think, as I remember that his mom cut him off.

"I'm staying one floor up from them. Subletting for the summer," Jeremy says.

I swallow. "Oh. Uh, well, I'm guessing Jamie didn't mention that I'm subletting the apartment across the hall from him."

Jeremy's smile stays in place, but it looks so much like the smile on a Ken doll that I want to cringe. "Then I'll definitely see you around," he says tightly. "Uh, I'll just grab you some coffee." He disappears around a corner before I can say anything else.

"You can do this, Aaron," I whisper to myself again. "This is fine. Totally fine."

Of course this will all be fine. There's no reason why it should be a problem that the one guy I haven't been able to stop thinking about for fifteen months, the one who also happens to be completely unattainable and commitment-phobic, would be working with me. Or living right above me all summer.

Nope. No reason that should be a problem at all.

3

THAT TIME JEREMY WAS FORCED TO DISCUSS FEELINGS

It turns out that this "work" thing isn't actually all that bad.

I know there are a lot of people who don't think of answering phones and fetching coffee all day as *fun*. But three days into my first real job, I'm doing what I try to do anywhere I go: I'm making my own fun. I'm talking up everyone who calls in, working to my favorite club music (with headphones, of course—I'm really not a total asshole), and chatting with the associates and partners while I grab random shit for them. I even got the number of a hot girl who came in to pick up a copy of her grandfather's will. Things this summer are looking up.

The only serious drag on the whole situation is sitting in a small office to the right of my desk while he stares intently at his computer . . . when he's not glancing over at me. Or when I'm not glancing over at him.

Most of the time, I don't *do* awkward. What's the point? Awkward isn't fun. This is why I've perfected the art of smoothly waving to the one night stand I don't want to talk to again or seamlessly winking at the other two-thirds of a former threesome when they blush as they walk by me. Working next to a guy I spent the night with shouldn't even phase me. But this isn't just any guy: this is Aaron Morin. And even I can't seem to smile over the levels of awkward that magically appear when we're in the same office together.

On Monday, he fell into the copy machine *again* when I handed him a cup of coffee in the afternoon. Yesterday I interrupted him while he was talking to Evelyn, the associate he's been working with, and he accidentally walked right into her desk. And today, he knocked an entire stack of files off a chair when I asked him how his morning was going.

It seems like it might be time for us to discuss *feelings*. Ugh. I do my best to never, ever discuss feelings. But I'm worried Aaron's going to end up in the hospital, or accidentally send me there, if something doesn't change soon.

I'm just getting off the phone with a very cute-sounding farmer who needs to talk to someone about tax law when Aaron appears by my desk. He's got that calm, collected look I've noticed he always puts on right before he talks to one of the partners or any of the clients who come in.

He's just as hot when he's walking tall and confident as when he's about to trip into a desk. But that's something I probably shouldn't be thinking about right now.

"I was wondering if you wanted to grab a drink with me after work today," he says.

"That depends. Is one of us going to end up in a body cast?"

He winces, and immediately I feel like shit. I was just trying to make him laugh. "That's kind of what I want to avoid, actually," he answers. "We need an action plan here, Jeremy. For, well, you know."

Only Aaron Morin, the guy who grocery shops with a spreadsheet, would talk about needing an "action plan" to deal with an unresolved one night stand. I can't help but smile. "Okay, fine. But can we avoid talking about feelings? You know I'm allergic to those."

He holds up his hands in surrender. "I promise to avoid discussing feelings whenever possible."

I'm definitely skeptical that we can avoid them entirely. But

I've always had trouble saying no to Aaron; that's how we ended up in this mess in the first place. So, I just shrug and say, "Sure. Let's go to Vino and Veritas."

One thing I know for sure: if you must have an epically awkward conversation, at least have it in your favorite bar.

———

At 5:02 on the dot, I find Aaron standing in the firm's parking lot with his hands in his suit pockets. He starts walking toward me and almost immediately trips over some gravel.

It's probably a good thing we're doing this.

Neither of us says much as we meander up Cherry Street, past a small specialty candle shop and a veterinarian's office owned by Emmett and Tai, some friends Briar introduced me to. Then we come to the intersection with Church Street. There's a decent amount of pedestrian traffic at this time in the evening, and the area echoes with the sounds of voices and laughter. The church at the very end of the street stands tall above everyone, as if it's guarding all the people below it. Aaron smiles wistfully. "Man, I used to love this place when I was a kid," he says softly. "Jamie and I thought Burlington was the most amazing place in the world. It was so different from the farm, you know? So many people everywhere. So many things to do and see."

Church Street is special to me too, but probably for the opposite reason. "I remember the first time I came here," I tell Aaron. "I was between Yale and Moo U for college choices. All my friends were sure I was going to choose Yale. I brought one of them with me to visit Moo U, and when we stepped onto Church Street, he started laughing. He said there was no way I could go to a school with a downtown scene that looked like it came out of a Hallmark movie."

Aaron tilts his head at me. "But you wanted the Hallmark movie."

"Yeah, I did." That's a year I don't like to think about. In fact, I actively try to avoid thinking about my senior year of high school. But that day, that moment, is still special to me. It was the first day after a lot of long, horrific, heartbreaking days when I felt any kind of real hope.

Aaron's still looking at me. "So, it was between Moo U and Yale for you? When you were picking colleges?"

Ah, shit. I didn't mean to tell him that. The last person who found out I got into Yale—some guy in my poly sci class—started laughing and made a comment about rich parents buying their kids' college admissions. To be fair, he'd seen my GPA at Moo U. Of course he thought there was no way I could ever get into Yale without my parents' help.

"Um, yeah," I say, bracing myself for some serious shade.

But Aaron just nods. "Good for you," is all he says.

We make the last block of the walk to Vino and Veritas in silence, but it's not uncomfortable silence. And that's kind of uncomfortable, because shouldn't the two of us be super uncomfortable with each other *at all times* right now? So then I start to feel uncomfortable about how not-uncomfortable I am, and I'm midway through that infinite loop and also waiting for Aaron to trip over an invisible rock and break his leg when we're suddenly in front of V and V.

"Briar's not working," Aaron says as he peers through the bookstore window past a small rainbow sticker. "Wait a minute. That isn't—"

"Isn't who?"

"I thought I saw someone at the back table. He looked just like Peter, this guy I'm friends with at school. There's no way it's him, though. He would have let me know if he was in town." Aaron frowns. "Autumn's on the cash register, though."

"Cool. We should stop by and say hi if the bookstore's still open when we're, um, done." *Discussing feelings,* I add in my head. *Sigh.* Hopefully, talking to Autumn will ease any residual awkwardness from this conversation. She's another Moo U student who works at the bookstore, and she's been hanging out with our friend group more since she and Briar started working together. I like her, even if she and Lexy do sometimes gang up on me.

They claim I make myself an easy target. It's not my fault that they're both redheads, and I've got redhead jokes for days.

We step into the vestibule at the front of the building and hang a left into the wine bar section of Vino and Veritas, one of my favorite places in Burlington. Jamie's always loved the bookstore side of V and V best, but I fell for the wine bar side long before I could even drink legally here. When I was still figuring out all my bi-ness, this inclusive and welcoming bar, filled with dark wood and good live music and plenty of people who didn't care who I was interested in or what their gender was, felt like my home-away-from-dorm. It's early enough in the evening that the bar's not very busy yet. I spot an open booth and slide into it, and Aaron slides into the other side. His eyes widen as he spots a menu—much larger than usual—sitting on the side of the table.

"That's, like, a dinner menu. Since when does Vino and Veritas serve more than bar food?" he asks.

"Since I pulled into town." A guy with a British accent and a disarming smile appears at the side of our table. "I'm Joss. If you see anything you fancy, tell Molly. She'll give me a shout. The Eton mess is as pretty as you are."

He winks at us in a way that might be sarcastic or might be hot as he taps his fingers quickly against our table. I've never been this confused two sentences into a conversation.

"Stop flirting, Joss," Tanner, the bar manager, calls from across the room.

Joss sighs. "You think matey boy would be nicer to me considering I've already made a thousand sandwiches today, but whatever. Can't complain. Who'd fucking—"

"*Joss.*" Tanner's tone is amused, but firm. "We need a swear jar out here?"

"Yeah, yeah." Joss grins and turns back to us. "Can't complain, cos I love making sandwiches. Live for it. Try Finn's fried chicken on the maple oat bread from next door. Can't say fairer than that. Be lucky, lads."

Aaron looks like he's fallen into a tornado, which maybe he has, if they even have tornadoes in Britain. I decide to answer for both of us. "We'll take the sandwiches," I tell Joss. "And two Shipley ciders?" I add, guessing Aaron's drink order. He nods, still speechless.

"Coming right up." Joss disappears, and soon Tanner slides two ciders onto the table in front of us. "You get used to Joss," he says with an air that I definitely recognize as *resigned*. People often use the very same tone when they're talking about me. He sends me a quick smirk. "Finally met someone who moves faster than you, huh?"

That seems like a real possibility. And a few minutes later, when Tanner puts plates down in front of us, I have to admit that Joss not only moves faster than me but is also *infinitely* more talented.

"Has Briar had one of these sandwiches?" Aaron asks as he swallows a giant mouthful of perfectly fried golden-brown chicken. "Because this seems like something he'd never stop talking about once he took a bite."

"Maybe he's trying to keep them all for himself. Can I have some of your fries if you're not going to finish them? They're fucking awesome."

"I think you're supposed to call them *chips*. And yeah, take some. I wish I could eat more, but I had a big lunch."

I steal some fries off his plate, and as I take a bite of one, I can't help but think about the last time something of Aaron's was in my mouth—

That night.

On my bed.

His body, laid out in front of me—

And then I slithered down it, and wrapped my lips around—

"Jeremy? Are you okay?"

Aaron's voice pulls me out of my fantasy, but not before I start to chub up downstairs. Damn it. It doesn't help that the subject of my daydreaming is staring at me hard and looking all concerned. Objectively, Aaron Morin is *hot.* He's got curly brown hair like Jamie's, but his is a little shorter and lays in tufts around his head that look perfectly styled even though I know the guy never uses anything but shampoo and conditioner in the morning. His eyes are a sharp, dark brown color that matches perfectly with his thick, dark eyebrows, and he always seems to have a hint of a five o'clock shadow even though he probably shaves on a strict schedule. Plus, he's got the body type I can never resist. He's tall and thicker around the shoulders, chest, and hips. Plenty of real estate to grab onto in bed . . . as I found out last March.

Damn it; now I'm getting hard again. *Down, boy,* I mentally scold my dick. "I'm great. Of course I'm great. I'm Jeremy Everett." I flash Aaron a wink, but his expression makes it clear he's not buying what I'm selling.

"So, about that action plan," he says quietly.

"Right. Action plan! Look, man." I take another bite because deep-fried carbs are definitely the energy I'm going to need to get through this conversation. "Let's own a few things here: you're fucking attractive, I'm fucking attractive, we spent a really good night together. But you know my life goals, Aaron. I'm here for a good time. And I know your life goals: you're probably trying to take over Sprysky and Gentry by the end of the summer. Maybe even this month."

Aaron laughs.

"So we've both got plans, and we're both going to be busy. Way too busy to worry about that night. I think we both just need to forget it ever happened. This could be a good chance to get over the whole thing, right? We used to hang out all the time, but now we don't even talk. Which kind of sucks, honestly."

Aaron nods thoughtfully. "Yeah," he says slowly. "It does."

"Exactly. So let's just let it go. Stop worrying about it, right? You can fucking stare at me all you want in the office. I'll probably do the same thing, especially when you wear your blue suit with your red tie." Aaron blushes *hard* when I say that. "And that staring doesn't have to mean anything more than you know how hot I am, and I know how hot you are. You know what I mean? That night happened, it's over, and it's never going to happen again. Let's call that night Vegas. What happens there stays there." I wave my hand in the air, as if I have the power to erase an entire twenty-four hours from existence. Because this may not be an ideal action plan, but it's honestly the best one I can come up with. Aaron Morin gets into my head way too easily, and I've got enough problems without adding "recurring fantasies about the one night I spent with my best friend's brother" to the list. "We both just move on," I tell him.

Aaron's slowly nodding. "Vegas. Okay. We can try that. But does that mean you still don't think we should tell Jamie or Briar or Lexy what happened?"

I almost spit out the sip of cider in my mouth. "Fuck no! You guys have a lot of dangerous equipment up at that farm of yours. Have you seen the giant claw Jamie attaches to your tractor to pick up hay bales? I bet that thing can crush a guy like me, no problem."

Aaron laughs again. "It definitely could. But why are you so sure Jamie would be upset? What you did that day was pretty awesome, Jeremy. It meant a lot to me that you tried to help me make up with Jamie. I think it would mean a lot to Jamie, too, if he knew about it."

"Really? Because I think he'd be pretty mad about the part where not only did the two of you *not* make up, but then I hooked up with you instead. Oh, and remember how I kicked him out of his own room to keep him from finding out?" I remind Aaron.

Aaron winces slightly.

"Anyway," I add, "Does Jamie even know you're gay? Bi? Pan? Whatever?" As far as I know, Aaron wasn't out to his family before they got in their massive tiff a few years ago.

"Gay. Confirmed that for sure." Aaron blushes slightly. "I was a late bloomer figuring it all out, but I got there eventually. And yes, my family knows. I told them last summer."

"That's cool. Great. But here's the thing: It's not like my reputation is a mystery around here, and I don't think Jamie's ever judged me for sleeping with whoever I want. It might have annoyed him sometimes when we were sharing a room and all, but he never looked down on me for it." *The way some people do,* I add silently. It doesn't matter how safe, sane, and consensual you are about your sex life: there will always be assholes who think that enjoying sex is something to be ashamed of. I frown as I rip off the crust from one side of my sandwich. "It matters to me. It matters to me that Jamie's never judged how I live my life. But if he finds out I messed around with you? Him knowing that . . . ."

I don't bother to finish the sentence because we both already know how it ends. *That could change everything.*

Aaron nods slowly. "Okay. I guess I get that. I'd rather tell him, and honestly, Jeremy, I don't think he'd look at you any differently. But I think I understand why you don't want to say anything. We can keep it to ourselves."

I swear, sometimes it's hard for me to believe that people as wholesome as Aaron Morin even exist.

"So," he says as he picks up the last bit of his sandwich, "you really think we can just forget that night happened? Move on completely?"

"It's what we both said we were going to do the next day. That was always the plan. But maybe the problem was that you went back to Boston, and we never got much practice at being around each other, right? Maybe we just need to keep practicing."

"Practice being around each other? That's the basis of your action plan?" Aaron looks at me skeptically.

I shrug. "Yeah. That's pretty much it. And like I said, look all you want while you do it. I know what I'm working with over here."

Aaron bursts out laughing. "I'll try to contain myself," he says dryly.

"Just as long as you don't walk into any more desks."

"Fair enough." Aaron grins. "And for what it's worth, I would really like to be friends with you again, Jeremy. I've missed you."

"Me too." I hold up my cider. "So. We'll be friends who've seen each other's dicks? I'll drink to that."

"Friends who've seen each other's, well, you know," Aaron agrees. He's blushing again, and he's seriously hot when he blushes. My chub *finally* just went down, and now it's taking a hike back up again. But that's okay, I guess. We agreed there was nothing wrong with looking.

"Jeremy," Aaron says hesitantly, "if we're friends again, then I want you to know . . . the stuff you told me about that night? About what's going on with your father? If you ever want to talk to anyone—"

Like hell I'm discussing any of that. "I'm great, bro. Totally great. Don't need to talk to anyone. You're moving into The Pink Monstrosity this weekend, right? Lemme know when you're getting there. I'll grab some boxes or whatever. And from now on, I'll be all 'Vegas, baby, Vegas' whenever I see you." I slam back the rest of my cider and stand up. "I'm going to go say hi to Autumn if the bookstore's still open. And then I've got plans to have dessert with some guy later. Hopefully, he likes double portions." I wiggle my eyebrows because this is what I do best: I disarm people with charm. It's always been my superpower.

But Aaron just nods slowly. He's not laughing and smiling the way people usually do when I bring out the eyebrow wiggle, though. "Okay, Jeremy," he finally says. "I won't worry about it, then. If you say so."

"I do, bro. I do."

We're both a lot better off forgetting everything that happened that night last March. Especially those things I told him about my father.

That's what I tell myself over and over on my lonely walk back to my car. *You're better off, Jeremy. You're definitely better off.*

4

THAT TIME AARON GOT HIS FIRST NEMESIS

Nothing in Jeremy's "action plan" is really rocket science, but I have to admit that it seems to be working. I managed to move into The Pink Monstrosity with him and Jamie and Briar helping, and I didn't even cause any permanent injuries to anyone. In fact, I'm back to being a mostly coordinated person since we had our conversation a week ago. It feels good to walk into Sprysky and Gentry without worrying that I'll somehow end up in traction.

If only I felt half as good about the work I was walking into every morning. This is a problem Briar reminds me of as we're eating cereal together in his and Jamie's apartment a week after my mostly-not-about-feelings conversation with Jeremy.

Briar's not a guy who pries into other people's business. All he does is ask, "How's work going?" But I immediately freeze up.

Mom asked me the same question last night, and I didn't know how to answer. The truth is that this clerkship in Burlington is a hell of a lot better than the internship I had at Leicester, that's for sure. No one seems to care that my suits are off the rack or that I have the wrong brand of shoes, and the work is challenging in exactly the way I like: filled with puzzles to be solved and pieces to put together.

But I still fall asleep every night and wake up every morning thinking about all the possible unintended consequences in the contracts I've been reviewing or all the mistakes I could have made in the briefs I've just filed. Every day feels like a ticking time bomb, and no amount of praise from Iris Sprysky or her partner, Tom Gentry, keeps me from waiting for the moment when she's going to walk into my office and announce that I've screwed up and she's really disappointed.

I'm glad school isn't like this. At law school, I've always been confident in my ability to handle my work. I know I won't ace every assignment, and I don't, but I manage to put out work I'm proud of. I don't spend every moment obsessing over all the ways I could make a mistake. I wasn't like this at Leicester, either . . . at least not when I first started working there.

But there's no way I'm telling Briar that I've been up at night obsessing over the wording in a contract about sheep ownership. "Things are fine," I finally tell him. "There's another clerk starting today. Someone from Moo U law school, in the same year as me. Should be nice to have another person to share the workload with." Sprysky and Gentry is a small firm, and they're a little understaffed right now. I definitely won't mind halving my to-do list with someone.

"That's good. How is it working with Jeremy?" Briar finishes his cereal and starts clearing the table.

"Great. Fine. Really good." And I do mean that. Everything has changed since the day of our conversation. Jeremy's coming with my family to our county's big dairy festival this weekend, and I didn't even flinch when Jamie invited him.

Briar's still *looking* at me, though. I love Briar Nord like I love my brother, but sometimes I wish he wouldn't do that: stare at me as if he's staring into my soul. "Excellent," he finally says. "That's really excellent, Aaron."

"Yup, it is." I stand up fast, mostly to get away from that stare. "Have to go. See you later?"

"Sure. Come by V and V today if you have time during lunch. Bring Jeremy."

I nod and wave at him as I leave. That's not going to happen. What Jeremy and I are doing is working right now, and I'm not going to test that by spending more time than I need to with him in small, enclosed spaces. Especially small, enclosed spaces that also contain Briar's stare.

"Aaron Morin, I'd like you to meet Benson Lewis. He'll share this space with you."

Ms. Sprysky—or Iris, as I'm finally able to call her sometimes —steps through my doorway with a guy about my age behind her. They look like a study in opposites. Iris is standing tall and thin, her curly, graying hair creating a halo around her brown skin. Meanwhile, the guy with her is short and a little chubbier, like me. He has straight blond hair cut so short it almost looks sharp and skin so pale I bet he burns just looking at sunlight. He's wearing a suit that I'm one hundred percent certain did not come off the rack and looks *very* out of place next to the orange and yellow floral-patterned dress Iris is wearing with clogs.

And he's looking at me exactly like the other interns at Leicester used to look at me: like he's had plenty of time to figure me out, and everything he sees is lacking.

But the sneering expression he's wearing disappears the moment Ms. Sprysky looks over at him, and he throws on a smile even more fakely charming than the one Jeremy wears all the time. "Great to meet you. I hear you're a Harvard guy?"

There's something in the way he says those last two words that puts me on edge, but I manage to keep my cool in front of Iris. "I am. 3L."

"Me too. Burlington U," he says smoothly.

Iris smiles. "Aaron, I'll let you show Benson the ropes. Bring him up to date on the low-income condo project, will you? That one needs all the extra hands it can get."

"Sure, no problem." We're handling all the legal work for a

31

construction firm that's trying to build more housing for lower-income residents along an area of Lake Champlain. The paperwork for that project is extensive and exhausting, full of contracts and permits and research work, and it's woken me up in the middle of the night more than once. I won't mind having an extra set of eyes on it with me.

Iris leaves, and Benson and I are left standing in our tiny office together.

"So," he says. "*You* got into Harvard?"

The smile he was wearing earlier is completely gone now, replaced with a look of something like disdain. Maybe loathing. Not that I have any idea where it came from. What did I ever do to this guy?

This whole meeting is starting to feel eerily similar to my days at Leicester. I'm trying to ignore the flashbacks cycling through my head when Jeremy knocks on the door.

"Hey, new guy! I'm Jeremy. I answer phones and do stuff at the front desk, and I brought you a new laptop. IT's got it all set up for you. Want me to show you where the coffee machine is?"

Now Benson's looking at Jeremy the exact same way he was looking at me a minute ago. I notice he pays extra attention to the sneakers Jeremy's wearing with his khakis. Iris and Tom couldn't care less about Jeremy's more casual office wear: I even heard Tom say that our clients like how approachable it is. But Benson's clearly not impressed.

"Thanks, I'd love some coffee," he finally says as he reaches over to take the laptop. "Could you bring some into me? Since you're the front desk guy and all?" He's smiling again, but it's about as genuine as a container of fake maple syrup. Jeremy isn't fooled for a second.

"Sure," he says smoothly. "I'll be right back." He shoots me a look that clearly says *what's this guy's problem?*

If only I knew.

It doesn't take me long to find out.

Benson and I spend the morning going over some paperwork for the condo project together, though "together" is definitely an overstatement of our partnership. Basically, he stares at his laptop, and I stare at mine, and he grunts out an answer whenever I ask him a question. It's not a fun working environment, but it's fine. And this is the guy's first day. I try to cut him some slack.

But then he and I get called into a meeting with Iris and Evelyn, the associate who's been taking lead on the project, to discuss a meeting they have with the contractor the next day.

That's when everything goes wrong.

Benson and I are explaining what we've reviewed, what we've proofed, and where we've made changes in some of the wording of the land acquisition contracts. "Good work," Iris says as she highlights some phrasing to look over. "You have a great eye for detail, Aaron. Benson, you helped with this?"

"I did, ma'am," he says easily. "Obviously, I've only had a few hours here, so I didn't get to look through everything. Oh." He frowns down at a page.

That *oh* echoes through the conference room, into the walls, and back into my very soul.

My heart starts to pound, and I force myself to do some of the breathing work that I had to learn when things got bad at Leicester. *In-one-two-three-four. Hold. Out-two-three-four. Hold.*

Maybe it's nothing. Maybe he just noticed something to point out to the client.

"Section 4.a definitely needs to be changed." He marks something on the page and pushes it across the table to Iris. I catch a glimpse of the paper as it goes by: it's a section of the contract dealing with indemnity, and I lose all my breathwork when I realize what Benson's noticed. It's an entire clause that could not only be very costly for our clients but also open them up to huge liability.

How did I miss that? And how did Benson just notice it now?

We both went through this section of the contract together earlier. Several times, actually.

Then I see the brief flash of triumphant smirk that moves across Benson's face while Evelyn and Iris aren't looking. He schools his look back into one of concern before they glance up again, but that one moment is all it takes for me to know exactly what happened here. Benson saw the problem with that clause earlier and purposely ignored it—just so he could "find" it during this meeting and point out my mistake in front of everyone.

"Yes, this will definitely have to be changed," Iris murmurs, and my face burns. I'm praying for a trapped door to open up below me when the intercom in the room suddenly buzzes.

"Iris?" It's Jeremy's voice. Because he's never had any problem whatsoever calling our boss *Iris.*

"Yes?" she asks.

"I'm so sorry. I just realized that the contracts you're reviewing are the wrong file. I hit print on an old version. The ones you have are only one version off, so there shouldn't be any massive differences, but I want to make sure you have the correct ones. Can you give me a minute to reprint?"

"Yes, of course. Thanks for catching that, Jeremy." Iris sets down the paper she's holding. "Aaron, are you alright?"

Everyone at the table turns to look at me. "I'm fine," I say, but that's definitely not true. My face feels like it's about a hundred degrees, and I'm still forcing myself to breathe in and out.

"Are you sure?" Evelyn leans across the table. "You look sick."

Actually, I really need some water, but Benson's wearing that disgusting smirk again, and there's no way I'm going to give him the pleasure of letting him know this whole sequence of events got to me. "I'm just a little warm," I say. "No problem."

"Okay." Iris shrugs. "Let's take a quick break while we wait for Jeremy to print us those updated pages, then. I'm assuming that clause was noted in the updated version, Aaron?"

The best part of my day comes when the "correct" file arrives with a note on section 4.a that it needs to be changed.

A note I'm very positive I didn't put there.

Jeremy's waiting for me and Benson near our office door when we get back from the meeting. "Everything go okay with those contracts?" he asks innocently.

Benson's glaring at him so hard I'm surprised Jeremy's face isn't melting. "You didn't happen to be listening to our meeting, did you?" he asks.

Jeremy spins a pencil around in his hand. "I don't know what you're talking about," he says. "I'm just a desk guy, sitting in a small office most of the day, really close to a conference room with a door open. A guy who sometimes makes mistakes and prints the wrong files."

Benson's eyes narrow as he turns on me. "This is what I hate about guys like you," he says with a hiss. "Just because you got into Harvard, you think you're better than everyone else."

Honestly, what is this guy's problem? "When did I say I was better than anyone?"

Benson ignores me. "You completely missed that clause in the contract," he says. "I had every right to call you out on it the way I did. But guys like you always get lucky." He draws himself up to his full height and crosses his arms over his chest. "I'm not worried, though. I've got the whole summer to prove to these people who the better lawyer will be. Where you go to school doesn't mean shit." He stalks into our office and all but slams the door behind him.

"What was that all about?" I ask.

Jeremy's studying the closed door with one eyebrow raised. "Well. If I had to guess, I'd say someone didn't get into Harvard Law. And I'd say someone has a chip on their shoulder about that."

"Seriously? You think he's jealous? Oh, *shit*." The last thing I need right now is Benson targeting all my work, trying to trip me up when I'm already terrified of tripping up. Because the truth is that I'm the one who screwed up today. I got really lucky that Jeremy took the fall for me by pretending he'd made the mistake.

"Listen," I tell Jeremy, "I can't thank you enough for what you just did. You didn't have to pretend you'd printed the wrong file."

Jeremy shrugs. "We both know you'd asked Benson to go over that contract already. What he did, calling you out in front of everyone like that, was seriously messed up."

"Yeah, but you didn't have to step in and take the fall for me." We're both leaning up against the wall in the quiet front office space, our heads just a foot apart. Today Jeremy's wearing a light blue shirt with a purple tie, and it makes his eyes look even brighter than they usually do. It reminds me of that night fifteen months ago, and how bright his eyes looked under the foggy light of Church Street as we walked together.

The night that never happened. I blink hard as I try to push that image out of my mind.

"No, I didn't have to do it." Jeremy smiles. "But let's face it, Aaron. You live and die by what these people think of you, and I don't give a shit what anyone thinks of me. So why wouldn't I take the fall like that? All I had to do was type up a note and hit 'print' again. No big deal. The whole fifteen minutes meant nothing to me. But it meant everything to you."

This is the side of Jeremy that I sometimes wonder if anyone else sees: the side that's thoughtful and caring and so loyal he'd lie down in the road for someone.

"Thank you," I say again. The words are entirely inadequate, and I know it, but they're all I have.

"No problem." Jeremy yawns and stretches. "I'm tired. Maybe I'll actually stay in tonight. Briar and Jamie have been bugging me to play some new board game with them. You want to join?"

"Something tells me I'm going to be working late." I glance through the window of the door Benson just slammed. He's typing intently on his laptop.

Jeremy frowns. "That dude's a tool. Try not to worry about

him. Everyone here likes you, and it seems to me you're doing fine."

"I guess," I mutter. "I just can't screw this up. Not again."

"What do you mean, again?" Jeremy takes a step toward me, his eyes narrowing in concern.

I shake my head. There's no way I could explain what happened at Leicester to someone like Jeremy. I can't even explain it to Peter, and he's always been my closest friend in Boston. "Never mind," I mumble.

Jeremy sighs. "Well, whatever's got you all freaked out, you may need to get over it quick. Because I'm sorry to tell you, bro, but I think you might just have your first nemesis."

5

THAT TIME JEREMY IGNORED IMPORTANT THINGS (AGAIN)

"What kind of grown person has a nemesis?"

Aaron is sucking at the straw of his maple milkshake like it's wronged him somehow, and I'm trying hard not to stare at his lips.

Spoiler alert: I am failing. Miserably.

"Plenty of people," I tell him. "Most comic book characters. The majority of politicians. TikTok comedians. Instagram influencers. Almost anyone who's ever had an opinion on the internet, probably."

Aaron looks up from his milkshake and glares at me. "Is that supposed to make me feel better? I don't even use TikTok. I'm not sure what people do there. Don't they all dance or something?" He's doing that thing where his lower lip drops slightly, like he's trying not to pout but definitely is. He used to make that face a lot back when he was taking this psychology class with a professor who would ding him on assignments for little mistakes. Aaron would pace his dorm room, making that face, wondering if the class was going to fuck up his GPA.

It's weird, the things you remember. I haven't thought about those days in a long time.

"How old are you?" I tease him. "C'mon, Aaron, stop stressing about Benson. It's Saturday. We're at a festival where people are running around in cow costumes throwing boxed milk at people. Your whole family is here, and you were just complaining about how you haven't seen them much since you started working at the law firm. Take a break, okay?" I throw up my arms and gesture at the scene around us.

Because if this scene won't take Aaron's mind off the law firm and that fuckwad Benson, nothing will.

We're standing in the middle of Main Street in Fairlington, Vermont, a town that's about forty-five minutes north of Burlington and near the Morin farm. The entire street and the huge park next to it have been roped off for the festival, and the place is hopping like only small-town Vermont can hop during a festival. There are booths with vendors selling everything from tarot card readings to maple-flavored cheese (yes, it's really a thing, and IMO, it's disgusting). There are people dressed up like farm animals dancing in the middle of the street to hip-hop music playing over the loudspeakers. Someone just announced that the pig race will be starting in half an hour across from the chocolate milk drinking contest.

And this is just what the festival has to offer on its surface. At last year's Dairy Festival, I hooked up with one of Jamie's old high school friends behind the cow milking contest. Let's just say I declared her the unofficial winner.

Aaron sighs. "Fine," he mutters. "I'll try not to think about Benson anymore. But I still just can't believe this is happening all over again."

"What's happening all over again?" Ever since Benson tried to low-key destroy Aaron, he's been making comments like that. It's obvious something went down at the last law firm he worked for, but he won't say exactly what. And as much as I want to bug him about it, I'm not going to.

I know the importance of burying a secret as far inside your-self as you possibly can. I know the fear of wondering how much of yourself you might have to destroy to finally dig that secret up again.

So I don't say anything when Aaron just shakes his head and shrugs, staring at the ground the whole time. He starts walking ahead of me, toward the Cow Pie Bingo contest. And yes, Cow Pie Bingo is exactly what it sounds like.

Someone draws a bunch of Bingo squares in the middle of the street.

They let a cow loose on the squares.

Everyone bets on where the cow's going to shit.

The people who bet right win the money and split the pot.

I fucking love Vermont. People in Connecticut just don't do enough stuff like this.

I've been looking forward to Cow Pie Bingo all week. I missed it last year because of my personal milking contest, and it's all Briar talked about after he won a bunch of money. This year, I'm taking the whole pot. I've got my bet down on O-71, and I'm planning to cheer that cow on as loudly as I can.

"Aaron! Jeremy!" Lissie comes running up to us and wraps her arms around Aaron. All the wrinkles in Aaron's forehead immediately soften, and the stress I've been seeing in his face since we left Burlington finally looks like it's seeping out of him. I wish I knew how to melt the stress out of him without sending Lissie in for a dive-bomb hug. He's looked miserable at work ever since Benson showed up, and I can't seem to cheer him up no matter what I do. He didn't even crack a smile when I "accidentally" put salt in Benson's coffee yesterday.

Which was funny as hell, by the way. I've never seen someone spit coffee all over their desk in real life before.

"It's so good to see you!" Lissie lets go of Aaron and turns her hug on me. "I thought I was going to see you all summer, but neither of you ever come to the farm." The pout she's wearing looks a lot like Aaron's.

"Sorry, Lis." Aaron rubs her hair affectionately. "Work's been busy. But we're here now, right? Let's go play some Cow Pie Bingo."

"C'mon, O-71!" I call out as we walk up the main street. The sun's bright and high in a cloudless sky above us, which is something I've learned not to take for granted in Vermont, even in June. This state can do clouds like they're its *job*. Next to me, Aaron's face has relaxed into a kind of half-smile. He passes me his milkshake and I take a sip, letting the sensation of the just-slightly-too-sweet coolness wash over my tongue. Lissie's pointing out the gazebo in the park where she has a guitar recital soon, and she's talking excitedly about how Aaron and I have to go. I'm sure we will. No Morin ever says no to Lissie. Even us adopted Morins.

This is one of *those* moments. One of those moments so perfect you have to grab hold of it and enjoy every sparking sensation it surrounds you with. I spend most of my life chasing moments like these, and when I find myself in one, I make sure to take in every element.

Right now, I'm focusing on Aaron's expression as he carefully listens to Lissie explain the piece she plans to play at the recital. I take a quick mental picture of the way one side of his mouth slides up when he's happy. Aaron Morin's smiles have been part of some of my best moments in life. It seems hard to imagine, now, that I went so long without seeing them.

My phone buzzes in my pocket, and Aaron and Lissie walk ahead of me while I pull it out to see who wants me. There's supposed to be a party at the Moo U hockey house tonight, and there's no way I'm missing any updates about that. Those bashes are always filled with good booze and other people looking for a good time.

But one look at my phone has me wishing I'd left it at home this morning.

Uncle J: *Jeremy, please call me. It's important. I have news.*

And then:

Your mother is threatening not to pay your tuition this fall.

And just like that, my perfect moment is gone. All the air feels like it's suddenly leaving my lungs. My mom wouldn't really do that, would she? Would she really stop me from graduating? Moo U isn't cheap for out-of-state students. Hell, it's not even cheap for in-state students. And I don't know much about how financial aid works, but I'm betting there's no way I'll qualify. My family owns three houses. I'm screwed if Mom cuts off my tuition.

If she does that, if she really cuts me off—

No. I won't think about it. I *can't* think about it. No way am I letting my family's fucked-up drama interrupt this day. No way am I letting it interrupt Cow Pie Bingo.

I hit the lock button on my phone and shove it back into my pocket as fast as I can.

If there's one thing I've gotten good at over the past three years, it's pretending my family doesn't exist.

———

"Are you okay?" My friend Lexy nudges me in the side. Hard, because she's Lexy, and everything Lexy does has force behind it. Even her bright red hair looks aggressive today against the white baseball cap she's wearing. "You're just sitting there, all quiet. And you haven't mentioned anything about getting it on with someone behind a tent here somewhere. Should I be worried?"

"Lissie's sitting like two rows below us," I remind her. "We don't need to talk about last summer. Or the milking tent. Which was actually a booth, I think." I can't really remember, to be honest. I wasn't exactly focused on categorizing temporary structures at the time.

"Since when did you care what Lissie hears you say?" Lexy laughs as she whips her hair back behind her head and starts pulling it into a ponytail. "Seriously, though, are you okay? You really are being weird today."

"He's a responsible adult now," Jamie says from the other side of her, where he's canoodling with Briar. One of them inches a little closer to the other one every five seconds. We've been on these bleachers waiting for this cow to take a shit for almost half an hour now, and if it takes too much longer, the audience is going to get a much more interesting show from Briar and Jamie than what the cow has to offer.

"It's true," Briar adds. "Jeremy and I sometimes have breakfast together in the morning before he leaves for work. He sets his own alarm and everything." He frowns. "Except yesterday he did say something about putting salt into someone's coffee. So I don't think he's completely matured."

I smirk as I think about Benson's reaction when he took his first sip of that coffee. The way his eyes widened in shock was priceless. I feel no guilt, though. The guy deserved every grain he drank after what he did to Aaron. "Well," I say laughing, "the thing is—"

My phone buzzes in my pocket. Again. Is it my imagination, or is it louder this time? And this time, it doesn't stop.

Someone's calling. And I know exactly who.

Buzz. Buzz. Buzz.

Buzz.

"Jeremy?" Lexy's nudging me again. "Is that your phone? Are you going to answer it?"

She's staring at me, I realize. They're all staring at me. Jamie and Briar in their makeshift bleacher love nest. Lexy, whose picture-perfect Vermont family is running a pancake tent just down the street from us. Mr. and Mrs. Morin, who are sitting just a few rows away with Lissie and Aaron.

And the Morins are the truly perfect family, aren't they? The family that put itself back together after it broke in half.

Too bad my family never has a chance in hell at doing that.

"Yup, going to answer it," I say cheerfully as I stand up. It's taking every ounce of energy I have to hold onto that false cheer, and I cling to it like a life raft. "Yell for my square if the cow finally gets around to taking a shit, okay?"

I hit the bottom of the bleachers in record time and take off in the opposite direction of Cow Pie Bingo, down Main Street. I pass a used clothing boutique and a coffee shop. I'm pretty sure there's a furniture store in there somewhere. My breath's coming in short gasps, and my vision feels like maybe it's blurring a little. It's been a long time since I felt like this—like I've lost control of my own body. But then again, it's been a long time since my uncle called me.

I end up in front of the high school Jamie, Lexy, and Aaron all went to. It's one of those classic New England brick buildings, complete with a clock tower and ivy crawling up the walls and everything. I sink down on the steps in front of it and stare at my phone.

I may be Burlington's favorite playboy, but I'm not an idiot. I know what the world thinks of me. And I also know it's better to be a playboy who doesn't pay attention to shit than someone who goes around all day thinking about voicemails like the one my uncle has probably just left me.

I sit there for a long time, my hands shaking. Finally, I manage to hit the voicemail button and lift the phone to my ear.

My uncle's voice is soft and low, the way I remember it. Uncle Jerry's always been a good guy, but his voice makes me cringe. Every time I hear it, I'm instantly reminded of the day he came out of my father's hospital room and told me what he'd learned from the doctor.

The worst day of my life.

"Son," he'd said, his low baritone echoing through the area of the waiting room we were in until I thought it might never stop. "It's what we've been worried about. Your dad has Alzheimer's. Early onset."

That was the day my world stopped. The day I stopped being Jeremy Everett, happy kid with a solid GPA, good test scores, and a clear future in his family's wealth management business in front of him.

That was the day I began to hate Uncle Jerry's voice with a fiery passion. Uncle Jerry, who's never shown a single symptom of the disease that's destroying my father, despite all the genes they share. I avoided him after that, and he doesn't call me much anymore. He must have noticed I never call him back.

It's clear from the first few seconds of the voicemail he just left for me that he wouldn't be calling me now if he didn't think he had to.

"Hi, kiddo. Listen, I know you and your mom are on the outs. I get that you two have your own issues, and I'm not trying to get in the middle. But your dad isn't getting any better, son. I really think you should come home and see him. Your mom says she's tried to give you space and time, but it's been years now since you were here. We both think it's time you came home."

I close my eyes against the memory of the last time I saw my father, right before I left for Vermont to start my freshman year at Moo U. The vacant look in his eyes. The confusion and fear when I tried to hug him. He was already losing me in his mind. "Have we met before?" he'd asked.

That was the last time I saw him.

Uncle Jerry's still babbling into my phone's speaker. "I think she's really serious this time, Jeremy. She really will cut off your tuition. Let's talk about this, okay? You can't keep running away from things. And I know she's pushing you to take those genetic tests. I know—"

I can't listen to him anymore. I can't. I hang up the phone and let it drop down onto the step next to me, where it's saved from certain death only by its overpriced case. I close my eyes and drop my head into my arms while Uncle Jerry's words do laps past each other in my head. *Tuition . . . isn't getting any better . . . test . . .*

.

test test test test test test
"Jeremy?"

Suddenly there's a hand on my knee, and a shadow looming over me.

Aaron. Of course.

I take in one long breath. Hold it. Let it out again. And when I look up at him, I've got it back in place: my charming, perfect smile. The one the world knows me for.

Aaron jerks away like I've slapped him. "Jeremy? Are you okay? What's going on?"

He's alone. I wonder if he told everyone else that he was coming to find me or if the cow finally took a crap and the game's over. Honestly, I don't give a fuck if it is. "Nothing's going on," I say. I'm working overtime to keep my voice from shaking. "Just got a phone call. There's a party tonight at the hockey house."

Aaron's eyes narrow. "You walked all the way to the high school to talk to someone about a party?"

I stand, carefully pocketing my phone along the way. "It's actually sunny outside, dude. In Vermont. I had to take advantage of that."

Aaron hesitates. It's obvious he's nervous, and for a minute I worry that klutz-o Aaron is about to make his return. But then he does that thing where he draws himself up to full height, like he's gathering every inch of self-confidence he has. Sometimes I imagine that this is what he must have done the day he told off his father and left the family farm for law school.

"Jeremy," he says steadily. "That was your family, wasn't it? You can talk to me, okay? I remember everything you told me that night. I want to help. If I can."

The soft kindness in his words nearly kills me. He would try to help, too. I know he would. This is a guy who once spent his entire summer building a treehouse for his little sister because she was sad that her friend had one and she didn't. Aaron's pure like that. Driven. He's a problem solver to the core.

But I'm nothing like Aaron. I'm not pure, and I'm not driven, and I'm not a problem solver. I'm here for life's perfect moments, and I don't stick around for the imperfect ones.

"Don't stress about me, Aaron," I tell him. "You don't need to, remember? I don't worry about stuff. Life's too short for that."

And then I walk away. I walk away from Fairlington. Away from cow shitting contests and maple milkshakes and perfect families that make me remember just a little too much of what I've lost sometimes.

I walk away from Aaron Morin.

I know it might take me the entire ride back to Burlington before I mean the words I just said to him. But I'll get there—I always do. Enough booze and enough good sex and enough beautiful moments and I'll be able to forget that phone call. I'll be able to forget Uncle Jerry's voice and that final expression on my father's face before I left home for the last time.

But as I drive down I-89 back to Burlington, my car inching closer and closer to the hockey party and mental freedom, there's one thing I can't seem to forget.

I can't forget the expression on Aaron's face when I left him standing there.

6

THAT TIME AARON REMEMBERED STUFF

"I wasn't even supposed to be in Vermont that day, Darla."

Darla looks from the hay I just put down in front of her and tilts her head at me questioningly. She pushes her face silently into my hand as I rub her ears.

This is what I love about cows: they're great listeners. They never talk back, and they don't try to give you unsolicited opinions. They don't tell you that you're spending waaaay too much time thinking about your brother's best friend when you're supposed to be helping your dad with the evening feeding. They don't tell you that you need to stop thinking about a guy who has YOLO tattooed on his ass because you've got to get back to Burlington and spend your Saturday night looking over research about recycled material compliance in new builds.

They don't tell you that you shouldn't be worrying about the dark, terrified look in that guy's eyes when he ran away from you earlier in the day.

Darla nudges at my hand again. "I really wasn't supposed to be here. This was last March, back when I was living in Boston, and I wasn't talking to anyone here. Did you miss me while I was gone? Back then?"

Darla uses her tongue to sweep a pile of hay into her mouth.

"I'm guessing you didn't, unless maybe it was feeding time," I mutter. "Anyway, I was in Boston. And I was lonely as fuck, and I kept writing texts to Jamie and Lissie and Mom and almost sending them. But I never did. You know why?" I slide down the metal piping that makes up part of Darla's stall to sit down next to her head. She nuzzles into my side, looking for more hay. "Because, Darla. Because I was afraid I couldn't have both places: law school and this farm. You're a lot of work, you and your pals here. Did you know that?"

Darla's stallmate, Delilah, shoves her head into my other side. "I know, I know. You both want more hay. See? You're a lot of work. And I'd finally told Dad that I couldn't do the farm work anymore and I needed to go after what I wanted in life. I was afraid if I didn't cut myself off from everything here, I wouldn't be able to do that. I was afraid I wouldn't be able to let go."

Delilah gives up on me and works on trying to steal hay from the cow on the other side of her.

"Anyway, Darla, I was lonely as fuck. And then one day I got this text from Jeremy Everett, of all people. He told me that Jamie was miserable without me here, and Lissie and Mom were miserable, and Dad was probably miserable too, and that he thought I should come home and talk to them."

Darla also gives up trying to get more feed out of me and settles in for an ear rub.

"At first, I ignored him. But then he started sending me GIFs, and he wouldn't stop. GIF after GIF after GIF. You know how annoying it is to get 50 GIFs a day? You want to guess what all those GIFs were?"

Darla tilts her head.

"Yes, exactly. Cows. Alllll day long, for almost a week straight, he sent me GIF after GIF of cows. I don't even know where he found them all."

Darla loudly swallows a mouthful of cud.

"I mean, of course he found a million cow GIFs to send me.

He's Jeremy Everett. And even then, even before anything happened, I could never say no to Jeremy Everett."

The cement floor of our barn is cold, but Darla's head is warm against my body as I sit and remember everything that happened that night. *That night.* The night Jeremy and I have promised to forget ever happened.

The night Jeremy Everett, the playboy of Burlington, permanently etched himself into my life.

Fifteen Months Earlier

"Oh, he-ey."

Jeremy's leaning on the bar, grinning widely at Molly, the bartender, and flashing his most charming half-smile. I happen to know this is the same half-smile that got him into bed with multiple art students all at the same time last year, and my Instagram account suggests that night is now slated to be chronicled in at least two gallery showings. Jeremy Everett is nothing if not memorable.

"Could I have a Shipley Cider?" he asks in the low, come-hither-ish voice he's basically trademarked. Unfortunately, it doesn't look like Molly's interested in the same thing Jeremy is. She looks up from the broken glass she's wiping off the countertop—I've been in the Vino and Veritas bar enough to make a solid guess that she's the one who dropped it—and laughs.

"You're underage," she reminds him as she accidentally brushes most of the glass onto the floor. One of the other bartenders rushes to grab a broom.

"Oh, c'mon. Help a classmate out." He keeps the voice low and the eyebrows high, and all Molly does is shake her head.

"He can have juice," Tanner calls across the noisy bar. "With a fucking straw. And feel free to give him some crackers. And nothing else until he turns twenty-one."

"I'm turning twenty-one in like a month," Jeremy mutters to

himself as Molly puts a glass of orange juice in front of him. She quickly sets a small bowl of animal crackers next to it.

"Where did you even get those? You don't serve animal crackers here!"

"Enjoy!" she calls back as she bustles off with a tray of drinks. She manages to trip on something completely invisible and nearly drops them all on top of a group of women laughing together in a booth.

It's probably a good thing I've never developed any kind of crush on Molly. Between my nerves and her general klutziness, the two of us could end up burning Vino and Veritas to the ground. But I didn't drive all the way to Burlington to think about the Vino and Veritas bartenders. I've got other things on my mind right now.

"Hi, Jeremy."

He whips around when he hears my voice, and his eyes widen the second he sees me behind his barstool. "Aaron! Aaron Fucking Morin!" He stands up and wraps his arms around me. They're familiar in a way that nothing has been for months, and I lean into them, soaking up the comfort they offer. "I couldn't believe it when you finally texted me back," he says as he ends the hug. "Sit down. Did you just get here?"

"Um, yeah. Well, kind of." I close my eyes and rub my temples as I fall onto the stool next to him. "No, actually. Not exactly."

"That cleared absolutely nothing up," Jeremy says, and I can hear the smile in his voice. "Want to try that again?"

"I got your stupid texts," I mumble. "All twenty-nine thousand of them."

"It was eighty-seven. And do you know how hard it is to find eighty-seven cow GIFs? I had to make some of those myself. You could at least be grateful."

I snort as I open my eyes again to stare at him. "Grateful? I'm supposed to be grateful that you interrupted a lecture from one of the top property law attorneys in the world with a video of a Jersey running through a kitchen?"

"Jerseys are the brown ones, right? That was one of my favorites. Especially the part where it stopped so the little kid could get some milk for his cereal. But you came! You came home! So I guess it worked."

I sigh. "Well, I came back to Vermont. So that part worked."

"Just to Vermont?" he asks hesitantly. "You didn't go out to the farm? Jamie's there, I'm pretty sure. I was supposed to be in Cabo this week, but I came back early, and he wasn't in our dorm room."

I'm on break from school this week, so I'm not surprised he and Jamie are too. I was a few days into spending the week alone in my studio apartment in Cambridge and wishing Peter wasn't in Los Angeles when one cow GIF too many appeared on my phone. I got into my Jeep and started driving.

"Jamie's at the farm," I answer softly. "I saw his truck there. I drove past it. But I couldn't pull into the driveway." I drop my arms onto the bar and let my head fall into them. Maybe if I ignore the tears at the corners of my eyes, they won't fall. "I couldn't pull into the driveway, Jeremy. I couldn't do it. I drove up and down the road eight times, and I couldn't pull in. So then I . . . ."

"You texted me instead," Jeremy says. "I mean, of course you did. I'm exactly what comes to mind when someone wonders who will offer them quiet, calm comfort in this hellacious world. I'm a balm for the soul, really."

I pull my head back up as we both start laughing. No one in the history of the world has *ever* called Jeremy Everett a "balm for the soul."

Except that he did answer right away when I texted him tonight. And he didn't hesitate to meet me here, even though I know he probably has more interesting places he could be during the middle of Moo U's spring break.

Something dawns on me. "Wait a minute. You said you were in Cabo. Why would you come back from Cabo in the middle of spring break?"

Jeremy shrugs and plucks a graham cracker from the bowl in front of him. "Three dots appeared under that last cow GIF I sent you. And then they disappeared. I thought maybe . . . ."

He came back to Vermont because of me? He left *Cabo,* one of the warmest, sunniest places on earth, to return to a gray, frigid Vermont March? All because I *almost* texted him back?

I'm still processing that information when Jeremy stands up. "C'mon. Let's go for a walk. Especially since everyone here insists on ruining my fun!" he calls loudly across the bar.

"I'll stop ruining your fun when you stop trying to get my bar closed down!" Tanner calls back to him.

I stay glued to my barstool. The reality of my situation won't stop crashing over me in waves. I can't pull into my own family's driveway. I drove all the way home for the first time in months, and I couldn't make that last turn. I couldn't bring myself to do it.

I'm making my family miserable. Jeremy basically said so. I'm hurting Jamie. And Lissie and Mom. And maybe Dad, too. Who knows how he feels? Maybe he never wants to see me again.

What if I'm never able to make that turn again? What if that day I left the farm was the last time I ever saw them? That question has every muscle in my body shaking, and I grip the edge of the bar hard to make sure I stay on the stool.

Jeremy tugs on the sleeve of my winter jacket. "Let's go," he says softly. Then, when I don't move, he adds, "Aaron. You'll figure this out. I promise." The look on his face as he says it is so earnest, so honest—I know right away this is the real Jeremy. The Jeremy behind all the smiles and the big laughter and the charm and come-hither voices.

And I believe him. "Let's go," I agree.

He throws some money down on the bar while I force myself to stand up. When he reaches for my hand, I let him take it, and I follow him out of the bar into the cold. Somehow, though, it doesn't feel nearly as cold outside as it did before I walked into Vino and Veritas. Maybe Jeremy Everett really is a balm to the soul after all.

We end up walking down Church Street together, both of us silent, and silent isn't Jeremy's normal state of being. It's a cloudy, darkly overcast night, and the streetlights are surrounded by a cold fog that makes everything around them and us look almost surreal.

"Why'd you stop talking to everyone? Why did you leave? Why did you stop coming home after you got into Harvard?" Jeremy asks somewhere between Vino and Veritas and Lissie's favorite music shop. The words are so surprising in the dulled light of the sky that I stop where I am, in the middle of the street, next to a tall lamp that's shrouded in a halo of yellow glow.

Jeremy comes to a stop of his own in front of me. The hood of his jacket is shadowing his eyes, but their soft, blue color stands out from under the jacket's pink cloth. He looks older under this light. When I first met him, I thought he looked incredibly young and old at the same time, somehow. He was still a college freshman then, all limbs and wide smiles, and yet there was always something lurking behind those smiles. Something in his eyes that shadowed everything else.

Jeremy has seen things. Hard things. I don't know what they are, but I know they sit behind every flash of joy he sends out into the world. And they're sitting behind the question he just asked me.

"Why did I leave?" I repeat the question back to him, as if I might find the answer in the words somewhere. Lissie texted me those exact same words the morning after I got to Boston. *Why did you LEAVE Aaron?!* I must have reopened that message twenty-five times just to stare at the capitalization of the word *LEAVE* as I wondered all the things, like what she was doing and what kind of day she was having.

"Why?" Jeremy asks again. "I thought you getting into one of the best law schools on the planet was kind of amazing, but then you disappeared, and now Jamie never talks about what happened with you." Jeremy's frown, which looks almost foreign on his face, deepens. "And Jamie spends most of his time back at the farm and I basically never see him anymore. It really sucks, if I'm being honest, and every time Lexy or I try to ask him about it, he blows us off. Lexy calls you Brother-Who-Shall-Not-Be-Named when we talk about you."

"She does?" I can't decide if that makes me want to laugh or cry.

"Yup," he says softly. He steps into my space, until the two of us are almost backed up against that streetlight, two shadows under the gray Vermont night. People walk by every once in a while, but I hardly notice them. It's like they're just the background in a movie scene, and the real world, the important one, is just me and Jeremy.

"It's like . . . I don't know if I can explain it, but I'll try." Jeremy nods, and I try to pull the words together.

"It's like I've always lived in two worlds. The one that made me and the one I want to live in. And I was ready to jump from one world to the other. I had it all planned, Jeremy. I got into law school and figured out how to pay for it. But then I tried to tell Dad, and he just wasn't ready for me to make that jump." I shake my head. "And now I can't figure out how to go back home. I can't figure out how to pull into the driveway of my own fucking house and tell him I made the right choice. I can't figure out how to text my own sister and brother back. Mostly because I know the minute I have to see how my leaving has made their lives harder, I might just give up. I might quit law school altogether. And I'm not ready to do that."

"Aaron." Jeremy pulls both of my cold hands into his. He's wearing soft leather gloves, and the warmth there gives me the energy to speak the words I say next.

"I don't know how to have both worlds. So, I picked one, and I gave the other up. I know it probably doesn't make sense. But that's what happened."

Jeremy's gloved hands are circling mine, rubbing them, and his eyes are fixed on me. I swear I've never seen Jeremy Everett look this serious or this real.

"It makes perfect sense," he whispers.

I've been waiting for someone to say those words for so long. Even Peter, who knows me better than almost anyone else at school, doesn't seem to really understand my family situation. He doesn't understand why I can't answer my own sister's texts when it's my dad and me who had a fight. I've been waiting for someone to tell me they understand since the day I drove my Jeep out of my family's driveway in Morse's Line. When Jeremy says those words, they're like a magnet, drawing me forward and into him, just as he pushes forward toward me.

What happens next feels as other-worldly as the scene around us.

Our lips meet in a moment of light and electricity, and then Jeremy's grabbing onto me and holding tight while I cling to him like a life raft. Our mouths move together as if they're magnetized. It's the wildest and most erratic kiss of my life, and I can't stop, I can't let go of him—

Then someone nearby laughs loudly, and the sound breaks through the stillness of the air. We pull apart at the same time, staring at each other, panting.

"Shit," he whispers.

"Shit," I whisper back.

"You want to come home with me?" he asks. He blurts out the words quickly, and his eyes go wide. I'm certain he didn't plan to say that.

There are a million reasons I should say no. The farm. Law school. The fact that this is Jeremy Fucking Everett, The Playboy of Burlington. The best friend of the brother I'm not speaking to right now.

But right now, in the middle of a cloudy night on Church Street, I let every single one of those reasons disappear into the chilly air. "Yes," I tell him.

7

THAT TIME JEREMY REMEMBERED STUFF

"Jeremy? I thought that was you." Tai, one of Briar's good friends, slides onto the barstool next to me at V and V and slaps me gently on the back. "Wouldn't have expected to see you here tonight. Aren't there better parties to be joining on a Thursday night?"

I look around at the bar. People are milling around, chatting and listening to the folk singer on stage. Somehow the drive to the hockey house for a rager brought me to V and V instead. I offer Tai a shrug. "Just felt like coming here tonight."

Tai laughs. "Is the great Jeremy Everett finally losing his party wings? Won't be long now before you're coming to our house for Friday night Clue games."

I grin back at him. "I doubt that." Tai's a great guy, and he may just understand me better than most people. He's a former club rat like me who still joins me once in a while for the rotating LGBTQ dance nights that different bars in Burlington like to host. But he's never alone at them—he brings Emmett, the veterinarian he's in love with. And he's raising Emmett's son with him. Lexy likes to get in the occasional dig about how maybe if Tai can grow up, I can too. "Who knows," she said once. "You might even one-up him and go for the full-on 2.5 kids."

If only she knew why that will never happen.

"Maybe I should have gone to the hockey house party tonight." I look around the room surrounding us and sigh. The folk singer is leaving the stage, and things at the bar are already starting to wind down. I can't even remember a single song she sang. I haven't noticed much of anything tonight, honestly. I found a spot near Auden, the bartender, and for the last three hours, I haven't really moved from it. I'm probably going to have to start paying rent here soon.

"J?" Tai's studying me with a worried expression. "Are you okay? Did you have too much?"

"Nah, I'm fine." I school my features into my perfect smile, even though it feels almost painful to pull up the corners of my mouth right now. "Did you say something?"

"I asked if you wanted another." Auden looks at me from across the bar as he picks up my empty whiskey glass. "You've been staring at that glass for ten minutes." Now he and Tai both have worried expressions.

I should say yes. I've spent the last three hours trying to erase my uncle's voice and Aaron's face from my brain, and neither will go away. Clearly, the drinks I've already had tonight weren't enough. I need another. I need a distraction. I need to lose myself in a warm body. Someone as hot and fun as Tai who hasn't found the love of their life and settled into the perfect future. Someone who knows the importance of enjoying a moment and then letting it go.

But for some reason I don't want to do any of that. I don't feel like having another drink. I don't feel like finding someone at V and V and pretending I'm up for sex tonight. I don't feel like doing any of it.

"Nah." I stand up from the bar. "Think I got too much sun today. I'm tired. Gonna head home."

Tai and Auden both nod, but they're staring at me like I just announced I'm giving up alcohol. "Okay," Tai says finally. "If you're sure."

I say goodbye to the few people who are still hanging out and take off. The air outside has a slight summer chill to it, and as I start the walk down Church Street, I can't stop thinking about another night I walked through Burlington in the cold.

The night last March. *That night.*

The night Aaron Morin, Mr. Perfect, got into my head and started living there rent-free.

Fifteen Months Earlier

I was starting to wonder if all the cow GIFs had been a mistake.

When I'd first started sending them, I hadn't thought very hard about it. When do I ever think through anything very hard? All I knew was that Jamie was miserable, snapping at me and Lexy all the time, and Aaron was gone. And it was pretty clear the two issues were connected.

What the fuck, I figured. May as well insert my own ass into the problem. I started sending Aaron the GIFs, and I didn't stop. Partly because it was fun, and partly because I missed Aaron more than I thought I'd miss my best friend's straitlaced brother.

Then those three dots appeared on my phone while I was in Cabo, and next thing I knew, I was on a plane heading back to Vermont despite the fact that it was eighty degrees in Cabo and very much *not* eighty degrees in Burlington. And now I'm walking down Church Street holding fucking hands with my best friend's brother.

Who I basically just made out with.

Except it feels wrong to call whatever we just did *making out.* That kiss was so much more than making out. Honestly? That kiss was probably the most connection I've felt with any other human being in a long-ass time. And I'm trying very, very hard not to think too much about that right now. Because if I do, I might just drop Aaron's hand and find the next plane back to Cabo.

Church Street's always quiet by this hour of the night. Only the restaurants and bars are still open, and there aren't that many crowds around. The lights catch on every brick in the street, highlighting the empty stillness of the city's busiest area. I remember when I told my high school friends that this was where I was going to college. They laughed. "I give you one semester," my friend Avi said. "That city's dead. There's no one fucking *there*."

But sometimes, I crave the quiet and stillness that Burlington is so good at offering up. So many of my perfect, favorite moments since I moved here have happened in the corners of Burlington's most silent spaces—not in frat houses or dorm parties or even beds filled with beautiful bodies.

I glance over at Aaron. Lots of my best moments in Vermont have included him. Hours of playing video games in his room or mine and Jamie's. Hours of watching him study while I studied the way the middle of his forehead creases into lines when he's concentrating hard. Dinners next to him at the Morin farmhouse, laughing and teasing him about the way he wolfs down his mom's meatloaf whenever it's within five feet of him.

We end up back in Aaron's Jeep, which is parked in a nearby garage. I should probably think about my own car, which is in the same garage somewhere, but it's the last thing on my mind right now. Neither of us says anything as he pilots the car through Burlington, the grinding gears of the old Jeep the only sound between us.

He takes my hand again when we get back to the high-rise dorm where Jamie and I live. Or maybe I take his? I'm not sure. All I know is that soon we're in the elevator together, the fluorescent lights flickering above us, and I can't keep my hands off him. I plaster myself into him, shoving him hard against the wall as I bury my tongue in his mouth. He shoves back, holding me hard, and every dip of his lips against mine feels like pure magic.

He pulls away suddenly as the elevator doors start to open. "Jamie?" he asks, the word coming out between breaths.

I shake my head. "He'll stay in Morse's Line tonight. Let's not . . . ."

Let's not fucking talk about your brother right now, I add in my head.

Aaron nods, and the next thing I know he's got me pushed up against the wall of the hallway. It's like we're two desperate, horny teenagers who haven't ever gotten off before. And I can't speak for Aaron, but it's been less than thirty hours for me.

What the fuck is going on here? The words drift through my head, but I shove them away and let myself focus on Aaron's hands. He's clinging to the cloth of my parka while we kiss. Somehow I manage to get my key card out of my wallet and open the door to the dorm room I share with Jamie—*don't fucking think about Jamie right now, don't do it*—and then we're inside.

Inside a room.

With a couch.

And a bed.

Clothes come off like they were never there. Jackets land on pants, and underwear lands on socks and then Aaron's kneeling in front of me, his eyes locked into mine. He grabs my right hand in his, and his eyes ask all the questions he needs to.

Should I?

I frantically tug at the dark curls around his head, hoping that will be enough of an answer for him. And then he swallows every inch of my cock in one mouthful.

I've had my share of blow jobs since Rob Harris gifted me my first one when I was sixteen. I've had bad blow jobs. Good blow jobs. Mediocre blow jobs. Blow jobs in dressing rooms of clothing stores and bathrooms of clubs and blow jobs in this dorm room while a sock hung on the door, warning Jamie not to come in.

Fuck, I should probably put out the sock. Just in case.

But this blow job isn't like any of the others. Sure, my cock is hard and pulsing in Aaron's mouth, and as he licks up the side of my dick to suck and tease around the head of it, I feel that same excited burn of energy in my brain that takes over when your body is focused on the pleasure of a nearby orgasm. But there's so much more to this blow job than just an orgasm-to-come. There's the way Aaron's finger is circling the palm of my hand in time to how his tongue circles around my cock. There's the way he gently strokes up and down one of my legs with his other hand, his fingers sending sparks of electricity through me in a rhythm that matches the same one his mouth is using. There's the small humming noise he makes around me, and the way the vibrations move through my body, one small jolt at a time, over and over and over and over until—

"Aaron!" I shout as I spill down his throat. I grab his hair, holding on tight like I'm on some kind of roller coaster ride, and he grips the backs of my legs hard and holds onto me while I lose little pieces of myself inside of him over and over again. When I finally open my eyes again, I see his hand on his cock, wet with his own cum, and I shiver. There's something insanely hot about knowing another guy got himself off while his mouth was wrapped around your dick.

Eventually, we end up on the bed, with him spooning me. I'm not generally the little spoon on any bed. Then again, most blow jobs don't make me feel like I've just had every inch of my body torn apart by pure bliss.

Anyway, it's just spooning. What's the big deal? The room's cold. He's warm. I snuggle back into his arms and try not to pay too much attention to how soft and gentle and fucking amazing they feel against my torso.

"So," I say conversationally. "Turns out you're not straight."

Aaron bursts out laughing. "Nope. Turns out that way. Not ace either, like I used to wonder sometimes. I think I just had bigger priorities back when I was going to school here."

That all makes sense, actually. Jamie came out to Aaron in high school, but when we were in Moo U, Aaron confided to us both that he wasn't really sure if he was straight or gay or maybe aromantic. Relationships just didn't seem interesting to him, he said. Looking back, I can see why: he was trying to graduate college early and get into Harvard Law. Of course he didn't have time to pay attention to his dick.

I turn slightly in his arms so I can look at him. His mouth is raised in a half-smile, and his eyes look brighter than they've looked all evening. Gotta love sex endorphins. "Looks like you've been making up for lost time at law school," I tease. "That wasn't exactly a beginner blow job."

He sighs as he runs one hand up and down my stomach. "Law school is hard. Boston can be . . . lonely. Let's just say I've come around to your argument that sex is great stress relief."

"It is," I murmur. I pull his arms a little tighter around me. The bass of someone's music is thumping through the room's walls. There's a party on this floor somewhere, but I've got no desire to go find it. This is the most *right* I've felt since I first saw those three dots on my phone under the name *Aaron Morin*. I'm not sure why. I just know it is.

"Thanks, Jeremy," Aaron whispers into my ear. His breath tickles at the back of my neck, making me shudder slightly.

"For what?" I ask. "For letting you give me a killer fucking blow job? Um, you're welcome."

He nibbles at that same ear, and my dick starts to rise to attention again. "No," he says finally. "For listening to me tonight when I was going on and on about worlds and driveways and all that shit. I know you were probably just being nice when you said I was making sense, but I—"

"No." I cut him off fast by flipping over in his arms so that we're staring at each other. I pull his body a little closer to mine. "No, I mean, yes. I mean, stop, because it did make sense. I knew exactly what you meant, Aaron."

His eyebrows crease slightly until his whole face is a frown, and that look is enough to make me say the words I haven't said to anyone in years.

"My father has early-onset Alzheimer's."

His eyes widen in shock and then fall together in sadness. "Jeremy. I'm so sorry."

"Yeah." I swallow. "I'm sorry, too. I know what you mean, about the two worlds. My mom and I are like oil and water or something; we've never gotten along. But my dad? He was my whole life when I was a kid. Then he got diagnosed when I was in high school, and he started to slip away. I couldn't deal. I came to college up here, away from them, and I haven't been back home once since. Not once." Aaron tugs me closer into his body and I let myself fall into his warm, soft comfort. These are words I've never said out loud to anyone, but I know he'll understand them. And maybe that makes all the difference.

"I can't set foot in that world again," I whisper. "I just can't. You think it's bad that you can't pull into your own driveway? Well, I can't either, Aaron."

"Jeremy." The way he says my name is almost reverent; it's so quiet. He's holding me tighter than I'm pretty sure anyone has ever held me in my life, and I can't believe just how right that tightness feels. I never let Mindy hold me like this during the *very* short time when we tried to be a real-life couple. I always thought I'd feel suffocated if anyone held me like this. "Does Jamie know? Lexy?"

I shake my head into his neck. "No. Can't break the worlds," I say into his skin.

I don't see him nod back, but I feel it. Just like I knew he would.

I knew he'd understand. We lay there like that for a long time, wrapped up in blankets, while the pound of the bass echoes around us. At some point, it stops abruptly. We both start moving again, his skin flickering against mine and mine flickering against his, and then his hands are everywhere on my body, and mine are everywhere on his, and it isn't long after that before we fall asleep covered in each other's cum and sweat and stickiness, almost like it's a glue holding us together.

It's nice to remember sex can be more than just stress relief.

"Shit."

I come awake slowly to the sound of Aaron's soft swearing and a pounding on the door.

"Jeremy!" Jamie's shouting. "What the hell, man? You're supposed to be in Cabo!"

I sit up fast. Next to me, Aaron looks like he's about to pass out. "Don't worry," I whisper. "I've got this. You don't have to talk to him yet. Not if you're not ready." I grab his face in my hands and press a quick kiss to his lips. "I promise."

He just lays there, looking shell-shocked, as Jamie's voice echoes through the room.

Fuck fuck fuck. Good thing I threw that sock on the door when I got up to use the bathroom last night. Otherwise, this could have been *really* bad.

I pull on some underwear and last night's 2q1 right before I paste on a perfectly calm and serene smile. Then I pull the doorway open just an inch. "Hey, Jamie! I, uh, came back early. Can you give me a minute here?"

Jamie's eyes are narrowed into tiny slits. The ever-patient Jamie Morin has lost some of his trademark cool since Aaron left. Right now he's clearly ready to murder me. "No, I can't. I've got books to read and a paper that's way overdue to write. I don't care who's in there with you. Please just cut me a break and send them home so I can come in, okay?" He's seriously on edge, especially for someone who's supposed to be on vacation right now. Something must have happened at home, something that probably has to do with the guy lying five feet away from me right now.

"No!" I'm trying not to sound rattled, but I'm pretty sure he can hear the panic in my voice. "I'll send them home, okay? I promise. Just go away and come back. In like twenty minutes or something?"

"Can't I just come in? Please? I really don't care who's in there with you." Jamie pushes at the door, and I push back, hard. "Who's in there, anyway? Why are you being weird?"

"No one!" Jamie's eyebrows go up a little higher, which probably means I'm starting to sound desperate. Damn. Time to bring out the big guns. "Listen. Please just go away for a little bit, okay? If you do, I promise I won't put a sock on the door for the whole rest of the week. The whole week!"

That gets his attention. "You're going to go the whole rest of spring break without sex?" "Hell no. I'm just going to go the whole rest of the break without having sex in our room."

Behind me, I definitely hear the sound of someone trying not to snort.

"Fine, whatever." Jamie steps back from the door, and I breathe out a small sigh of relief. "But later on you're telling me who you've got in there that you don't want me to see."

"Never going to happen," I tell him cheerfully. "See you in a little bit." Then I slam the door on him like the asshole I am right now. I turn around to face my own music as Jamie's footsteps pad back down the hall.

Aaron's frantically dressing in bed. "I've got to go," he says. "Gotta leave. I'm just not ready to talk to them all yet, and I don't want him to find out like this that I've been back home. Does that make me an asshole? It does, doesn't it?" He's babbling, and I'd probably think it was cute if I wasn't worried that he was going to babble his way right into a panic attack. "Fuck. This . . . what happened? I . . . we shouldn't have . . . we can't . . . ."

Yup, he's freaking out. "Aaron, calm down."

"Calm down? That was Jamie! Jamie, my brother! My brother, who I haven't spoken to in months! Jamie almost caught us doing —I don't know what the hell we were doing! I don't know what we were thinking!" Aaron throws his arms wide and sends my small bedside lamp sailing across the room. I duck as it flies past my head and crashes into the floor, where it smashes into pieces.

"Oops," he whispers.

"Well." I shrug. "Could have been worse. I've got a hundred-dollar sex toy over there somewhere. That lamp was like ten bucks."

He looks at me, and we both burst out laughing.

"I'll pay to replace it," Aaron says.

"Like I said, it was cheap. Don't worry about it." I cross the room to sit on the bed next to him. "Hey. You don't need to freak out about what happened with us. You were having a rough time. And I . . . ." I don't want to think too hard about what I told Aaron last night. "Listen, you'll fix this, okay? You and your family—you'll fix this. I know you will. Someday you'll come home again. And when you do, you won't have to worry about me. It can be like this never happened. I promise."

He starts pulling on his sweater. He can't seem to look me in the eye. "I guess that's how it has to be, huh?"

I'm not sure what he means by that. Does he mean it has to be that way because Jamie's my best friend? Or because I am who I am? Either way, the statement is probably right.

I think back to kissing him in the foggy glow of Church Street, and I feel a tug of sadness, knowing nothing like that will happen ever again. I brush that feeling away fast, though. I don't do regret. I don't do relationships. I've made my peace with that choice, and there's no taking it back.

Not even for another chance at last night.

Aaron zips up his jacket. "Jeremy," he says quietly. "Thank you. Not just for last night. For the cow GIFs, too. And about what you told me, if you ever need anything—"

I cut him off with a fast, tight hug. "Thanks, Aaron. But I'm good. I don't need anything."

"Okay." He looks at the bed across the room from mine, his face suddenly crinkled with pain. "You'll take care of Jamie for me, right?"

"You know it," I promise Aaron. "And you'll take care of yourself, right?"

He lets go of me and steps toward the door. "I'll do my best. That's all any of us are doing, right?"

The door closes gently behind him, and a low, dark silence fills the room for hours after he leaves.

8

THAT TIME AARON WITNESSED HIS FIRST BIRTHDAY BOMB

I'm not sure what I expect to find in the office the Monday morning after the Fairlington Dairy Festival.

Maybe I expect to find Jeremy at my office door, demanding to speak to me, finally ready to spill his guts and admit something's wrong. Maybe I expect to find him with maple donuts and apologies for leaving me standing in the middle of the street alone when I was only trying to help him.

Only I don't find any of that. This is Jeremy Everett we're talking about here, and Jeremy's entire brand is ignoring problems. So I'm not all that surprised when he sweeps into the office fifteen minutes late, wearing sunglasses and his painted-on smile.

Honestly, I'm starting to detest that smile with every inch of my soul.

"Morning, lovelies," he calls out from his desk. It's obvious he doesn't give a shit about drawing attention to the fact that he's late. "I brought donuts for everyone!"

At least I was right about the donuts.

I could stay inside my office, keep my head down and keep proofing the contract in front of me. That's what I should do. Benson's across from me, working on the same case, and every now and then, he looks up to smirk, glare, or study me like he's cataloging every weakness I have. I've never felt so directly and personally targeted in my life. And I've just spent the last two years at Harvard Law, for crying out loud.

I need to vent, and I don't feel like venting to Jeremy—mostly because he's part of what I feel like venting about. So, I text Peter.

Me: *You won't believe this other 3L they brought into the office. I swear he's out to ruin my career. He's got some bug up his ass because I got into Harvard.*
Peter: *Want me to send you GIFs of Dwight to remind you what a real office pain in the ass is like? Or just tell Aunt Iris on him?*
Me: *Very funny. I'll figure out how to handle him.*
Peter: *Bet you're glad now that I made you read The Art of War last year.*
Me: *I've never used a single thing I learned in that book. But at least you bought my copy. Speaking of which, were you in a bookstore in Vermont last week? I swore I saw you.*

Three dots appear under my text. Then disappear. Then appear again. Then disappear.

No answer. Weird. I could swear that was Peter I saw at Vino and Veritas last week, but why wouldn't he tell me if he had decided to come back to Vermont? Now I've got another problem I don't feel like dealing with, so I stand up and do what I do best when conflict is in front of me: I try to play nice. "I'm going to grab a donut. Want one?"

"No time," Benson says clearly. "Iris has that meeting with the client at eleven. I hope you're ready, Aaron." He looks up and flashes me a nasty, shit-eating grin—the kind I used to see at Leicester all the time.

Now I really need a donut. "Suit yourself. But I bet they're from The Maple Factory. They have the best—"

"I know where the good donuts in Burlington are, Aaron," he says, sighing. "I still go to school in this podunk town, remember?"

Time to give up on trying to be friends with my nemesis this morning. Maybe I'll have better luck tomorrow. I close the door behind me as I leave our crowded, tense office and make my way toward donuts.

Jeremy's standing next to them. He pours coffee into a mug and hands it to me. "That conversation sounded fun," he says with a half-smile.

I notice he's still wearing his sunglasses. "Rough night last night?"

Jeremy sighs and lowers his glasses. His eyes are bloodshot and lined with dark circles. "I'm waiting for my eyedrops to kick in. In my defense, Vino and Veritas was having an open mic night."

"You got sloshed at an open mic night?" I grab for a donut as I try to imagine that scene.

"Well, not the open mic night itself. You remember that really good guitarist, Jon? He was playing, and his boyfriend Brent was there too, and their friend Ty came to watch. I ended up hanging out with them for a while. Ty's a horse trainer, and he knows some other horse trainers, and did you know that horse trainers are incredibly flexible? It turns out that—"

"Never mind." I hold up my hand. "I think I get the picture." I like to think I've gotten pretty good at this whole "what night fifteen months ago?" thing Jeremy and I agreed on, but that doesn't mean I want to stand around talking to him about who he got it on with last night. Especially when I spent most of yesterday catching up on work alone in my apartment and trying not to obsess over whether he was okay.

If he was lonely or still upset. If he needed me.

Four times I almost left my place to go upstairs and knock on his door. When Briar and Jamie invited me over for dinner, I waited anxiously there while they cooked, expecting him to show up. I couldn't really ask if he was going to, of course, and when Jamie casually mentioned that Jeremy was out doing "his Jeremy thing," I had to hide my flinch.

Yeah. It was a great weekend overall. It's a good fucking thing he brought donuts in this morning, or I might just be ready to choke Jeremy Everett with my bare hands.

"Well, back to the grindstone." Jeremy grabs a donut and nibbles cautiously at it. "Let's see if I can keep this puppy down. Have a good morning, Aaron."

He's wearing bright gold Converse sneakers with his khakis this morning, and I swear their sparkle mocks me with every step he takes back toward his desk.

I pour myself more coffee. Between Benson and Jeremy, this could be a long morning.

I'm feeling a little better by eleven o'clock. Benson's been growling at his laptop instead of me, and I've been able to lose myself in some more contracts Iris wanted me to review for this low-income condo project on the lake. There are a lot of moving parts to the whole deal, and I'm enjoying figuring out how to make them line up and lock together with one another.

This is the kind of work I could do for the rest of my life. The kind of work that makes me think Adam Garner at Leicester was completely wrong, and maybe I am good at what I do. Maybe I'm so much better than he realized.

And then things go wrong. Because of course they do.

The meeting with the developer for the project is at eleven. With minimal help from Benson, I've got everything set up in the room and ready to go for Iris: an updated presentation is ready on the conference room screen, copies of the contracts Jeremy printed for the meeting are lined up in neat folders for everyone, and I've even put out coffee and some leftover donuts.

"Very nice setup," Iris says as she steps in. "Excellent job preparing for the client. Charlotte does like The Maple Factory. Personally, I'd like to see them present more gluten-free offerings." She closes her eyes and places her hands in front of her in a prayer position while she does some kind of throat breathing. The first time she started doing this before an important meeting, it freaked me out a little. Now I'm just used to it. I beam while Benson glares and rolls his eyes from across the room.

Charlotte Fernandez, the developer, arrives with a flourish. I've met her once before, and she never gets less intimidating. She's almost six-foot-five with enough muscles that I'm pretty sure she could bench press my sister, and she's single-handedly making top-notch housing affordable *and* environmentally friendly in the Champlain Valley. Plus, she's *nice,* which somehow makes her even more intimidating. "Aaron, good to see you again," she says happily as she slaps her giant palm into mine. "Glad Sissy here hasn't scared you away from the firm yet."

Iris sighs. "Remember," she tells me and Benson, "she only gets to call me Sissy because she's known me since we were nine. The first time one of you tries to drop that name, I'm burying you under billing paperwork."

Good to know.

The meeting starts out fine. Iris runs through the presentation, explaining where we are with each phase of the project and going over some of the snags we've hit with permitting. Then she opens up her folder holding the contracts Jeremy printed for us, and that's when everything goes to hell.

"Charlotte, please hold off on opening up that folder in front of you just yet." She looks up at me, lips pursed. "Aaron? Will you please remove these from the room and fetch us the correct ones?"

Oh no. Something's really wrong if she's telling me to get all the contracts out of the room. *Shit shit shit.* My heart races, but somehow I manage to calmly pick up the folders from the table and step out into the hallway with them. I slip one of them open and nearly drop the entire pile.

The firm is also working on some contracts for a farm co-owned by Finn Fletcher, the husband of the guy who owns Vino and Veritas. And somehow . . . .

Jeremy printed the wrong contracts. And I didn't check his work.

Which means the firm was very nearly just in serious breach of attorney-client privilege.

Iris must have also called Jeremy over the intercom because he appears in front of me just a few seconds later. "Oops," he whispers, a sheepish grin on his face. "I'll get the right stuff printed right away. Sorry about that." He flashes me a quick wink, like he doesn't even care. And why should he? He's Jeremy. This isn't his chosen profession. This isn't his life.

And he isn't the one Iris sends a stern look at the end of the presentation.

He isn't the one who spends the next twenty minutes having flashbacks to a law firm performance review that went terribly, horribly wrong.

———

The rest of the meeting is fine. Benson says a few things, so do I, and Charlotte signs some papers while making cracks about missing the pigtails that "Sissy" used to wear.

But the mistake has been made, and the words Adam Garner said to me at Leicester won't stop running through my head on repeat.

Charlotte Fernandez nearly saw the contracts for another client. The entire meeting was held up while Jeremy reprinted documents. None of that is good.

I can't decide who I'm angrier with: Jeremy, for coming into work hungover and making that mistake, or me, for trusting him enough that I didn't bother to double-check what he printed for those folders.

Benson keeps shooting little smirks my way. The smirks definitely become something much larger when Iris asks to speak with us after Charlotte leaves.

She closes the door to the conference room and gets right into things. "The two of you were in charge of setting up the room for this meeting?"

"Actually," Benson says smoothly. "Aaron really took that on. I was working on some other things. I had nothing to do with the paperwork mix-up, ma'am."

Iris raises an eyebrow. She manages to look incredibly intimidating even though she's wearing a dress and pair of Crocs with matching sunflower patterns. "You neglected to mention that when I was saying how wonderful the room setup was earlier."

Benson has the decency to drop his eyes and look at the floor.

Iris sighs. "Well, we must all learn to live in the present, not the past, mustn't we? Aaron, mistakes happen. But Jeremy's just a receptionist. I need you to double-check things he preps for meetings, okay? That really needed to be your responsibility."

Her words are calm and kind, but all of a sudden I'm back at Leicester, being ripped apart by Adam-fucking-Garner. My chest is pounding, and I can't even open my mouth to tell my new boss, who I like and respect so much, how sorry I am.

"I apologize, Iris," Benson says smoothly. "Really, I should have double-checked Aaron's work. He's seemed a little overwhelmed by things here, and—"

Is this guy *fucking serious*? Is he really throwing me the rest of the way under the bus right now when I was already halfway under the wheel well?

"Aaron?" Iris turns to look at me again. "Is that the case? Are you feeling overwhelmed? We can adjust your workload if that would be helpful."

"No!" I blurt out. "No, that really isn't the case. I'm fine, honest. I just didn't think to . . . ."

I didn't think to double-check Jeremy's work. Because I trusted him.

"I didn't think the paperwork was an issue," I finish lamely.

She's frowning at me. "If you're sure," she finally says. "But Aaron, please do say something if we're giving you too much. Sometimes I overestimate others' abilities, and I want to make sure I'm not overloading you. It's important to me and Tom that the energy in this office is clear and strong."

She opens the door to leave, and I rush out of the room after her as fast as I can.

"Aaron," Jeremy says as I pass his desk. "I'm so sorry. I know I screwed up. Seriously, I'm so—"

"I'm taking a break," I interrupt him.

And then I'm out of the office, walking fast, hard. I focus on nothing but breathing as I try to flush the memories of Adam Garner, Leicester, and Boston out of my head.

Eventually, I get myself together enough to head back to the firm. I spend the rest of the afternoon locked in my office, working at the kind of breakneck pace I'm famous for in study groups at school. I'm determined to show Iris I really can handle the workload here.

Benson sits across the desk from me, working at the exact same breakneck pace. If there was an Olympic sprint for typing, we'd both be in the final heat. Every now and then, he looks up at me and we both glare at each other.

It's a fantastic working environment. So much for "clear and strong" energy in this office.

By four o'clock I definitely need more coffee, but that would mean going out into the office lobby. Which would mean interacting with Jeremy, and I'm not ready to do that yet. So, I keep my head down and on my to-do list. I'm just starting to wonder if I'm finally going to have to emerge from my work cave for some form of hydration, when singing suddenly starts echoing through the office.

"Happy birthday to you! Happy birthday to youuuu!"

Benson looks up. His smirk has been replaced with raised eyebrows. "What the hell is going on?"

"Must be someone's birthday," I mutter. When I first signed

my contract with the firm, Jen, who was still the receptionist then, had me put my birthday on the firm's calendar. She said Tom Gentry is obsessed with birthdays. I don't work with him much, but I've run into him a few times. He's an older guy with long, gray hair who wears flowing linen shirts and yoga pants to the office most days. Like Iris, you'd never know he's one of the top lawyers in Vermont just by looking at him. He's legendary for staring down opponents in depositions, just waiting for them to crack while he sits in a lotus position on his chair and never moves a muscle.

But he doesn't sound very calm now. That's definitely his baritone voice, echoing through the walls. And it's coming closer and closer to our office.

My curiosity gets the better of me, and I finally stand up from my desk and walk a few feet to my office door. I tug it open, and I can't believe what's in front of me.

Everyone in the firm is standing there, singing. Tom Gentry is in front of them all. He's definitely the loudest voice, and he's holding a giant cake that says HAPPY BIRTHDAY, BENSON.

"Happy birthday, dear Benson, happy birthday to you!"

Benson's face is the color of a beefsteak tomato, and he looks very, very, *very* ready to murder someone.

Jeremy's standing at the back of the group, pure innocence written all over his face.

"Uh, what's going on?" I ask after everyone's done clapping for their own performance.

"It's Benson's birthday today!" Mr. Gentry announces cheerfully. "Sorry we couldn't invite you to sing with us, Aaron," he adds. "That could have ruined the surprise, and there's nothing I hate more than a ruined surprise party. Benson, blow out the candles!" He sets the giant cake, which is covered with pink and purple swirls of icing and unicorn decorations, down on the desk. "We had to grab the cake on short notice, and this was the only one left at the bakery. Somehow, we missed your birthday on the calendar—I'm so embarrassed! We never miss a birthday here. Luckily Jeremy told us just in time!"

"Did he," Benson says in a strangled voice.

Evelyn is covering her mouth with her hand and clearly trying desperately not to laugh.

"Blow out the candles!" someone calls.

Benson stares down at the cake and the three lit candles at the top of it. The color of his face has shifted from beefsteak tomato to something like my mom's legendary marinara sauce. He's so red I'm a little worried all his capillaries have burst.

"It's not my birthday," he blurts out. "There's been a mistake."

"Really?" Tom's eyes widen. "Damn! How did that happen?"

I look over at Jeremy, whose innocent expression has not moved once since the singing party arrived at the door.

"You must have marked it down wrong on the calendar," Mr. Gentry goes on. "No worries, of course. Accidents happen, and we're always happy to eat cake around here. Next time just double-check those details when you're filling something out, okay? We need people to be detail-oriented around here, as I'm sure you know!"

Everyone in the room laughs, and Benson's expression moves to one of panic. "Sir, I know! I swear—"

"Calm down, calm down!" Tom laughs. "I was joking, son. No harm, no foul. Like I said, we all love cake. Dig in, everyone! If it's not your birthday, we'll just have to celebrate your un-birthday. Blow out those candles!" Iris passes Benson a knife as he awkwardly blows out a breath onto the cake, and then Tom starts singing the un-birthday song from *Alice in Wonderland*. Soon music's being piped over someone's Bluetooth speaker, and the next thing I know, I'm eating pink confetti cake next to my filing cabinet and listening to Lizzo while I'm talking to Bryce, another associate, about the milking machines his uncle uses on their farm.

For a Jeremy Everett birthday party, though, it's pretty low key. It's got nothing on the one he threw himself during his freshman year. That one involved a goat, a bathtub of strawberry ice cream, and a mime.

The party breaks up slowly, and soon it's just a few of us left in the office, scarfing down cake and making small talk with each other. Benson's standing next to his desk, holding a plate with a piece of cake on it that's barely been touched. He's glowering *hard* at Jeremy, who's cleaning up some used napkins and paper plates. "I know you fucking did this," he growls.

"Hey, man." Jeremy holds up his hands in surrender. "I just read the calendars. I try not to plan other people's birthday parties anymore. Not since an unfortunate incident with a chihuahua and a hot tub."

Evelyn nearly spits out her sip of soda.

"Like Tom said, accidents happen," Jeremy goes on smoothly. "Just be more detail-oriented next time, okay?"

Benson stands there, sputtering, like he can't quite figure out what to say. Jeremy stretches and steps away from him, still holding a garbage can in his hand. "How are you doing?" he asks me and Bryce as he walks by. I don't miss the way his expression lingers on me when he asks.

I can't stop the smile that's spreading across my face. All I can think about is the look Benson had when everyone started singing.

"Great," I tell him. "I've never been better."

"Excellent," Jeremy says. "That's exactly what I was hoping to hear."

9

THAT TIME JEREMY ACTUALLY CARED ABOUT SOMETHING

"You birthday bombed him? But most people would love that!" Lexy grabs another egg roll from the plate in the middle of the coffee table as she frowns at me. "What's mean about getting someone cake and singing?"

"Benson likes to bitch about the office birthday policy and how it takes away from 'valuable work time,'" I explain. "I heard him whining about how the partners at the firm like their 'hippie-dippie' crap way too much. So I figured I'd point some of that peace and love directly at him." I shrug. "Plus, nothing freaks some people out like sudden, unexpected positivity. I had a feeling Benson would be one of those people." I can't help but grin when I say that. "Seriously, though. You should have seen his face—especially when Tom Gentry made a joke about him not being detail-oriented enough to get his name right on the calendar! That was definitely worth the two hours I spent looking for a cake covered in unicorns."

Lexy arches a brow. "So that wasn't the last cake left at the bakery?"

"Hell, no. I had to go to five different places to find that thing. Worth it, though. Confetti cake's the best."

"That is accurate," agrees Briar from the kitchen, where he's pulling bottles of Shipley cider out of the fridge to distribute to the room. They serve so much of it at Vino and Veritas that we're pretty much all hooked on it at this point. "Good play, Jeremy. I mean, you better never birthday bomb me like that. But an asshole who messes with Aaron? I've got nothing but applause over here."

I look over at Aaron, who's lying across the recliner in the corner of Briar and Jamie's living room. He's been strangely quiet since he, Briar, Jamie, Lexy, and I all ended up at Briar and Jamie's place for dinner. To be honest, I was surprised he came at all after the day we both just had—even I thought about staying in tonight. But then our group chat lit up with news of the birthday bomb, and the next thing I knew, we were all ordering mediocre Chinese food together, and Lexy was demanding details about cake and whether or not there were streamers involved.

Which there were not, unfortunately. I definitely won't miss including those the next time I birthday bomb someone.

"What is this Benson shithead's problem anyway?" Jamie asks in between mouthfuls of lo mein.

"Jealousy, we think," Aaron says mildly. "Or at least that's Jeremy's theory."

I nod. "This guy screams, 'I'm an entitled asshole who didn't get into my dream Ivy, and the failure is giving me hives.' And I should know, as a fellow entitled asshole myself."

Briar hands me a cider. "My therapist would say your self-talk needs some work, Jeremy. And a little more honesty. Entitled assholes don't go to the trouble of throwing impromptu birthday parties just to help a friend."

"Agreed." Jamie holds up his cider bottle. "To Jeremy! Thank you for using confetti cake to save my brother from an entitled asshole!"

Everyone clinks their bottles together, except Aaron. He's still lying across the recliner, his eyes fixed on me as he sips at his cider. He's not smiling, but he's not really frowning, either. He looks . . . content? Thoughtful? I have a vocabulary that was good enough to get me into Yale once upon a time, but I can't quite find the word to explain his expression.

We end up playing a few rounds of some board game Briar and Jamie like, but Aaron's subdued in that same way the whole time. The look on his face is making me itchy, to be honest. Is he still mad at me? He'd have every right to be. I came into work hungover as fuck, messed up big time, and he took the fall for it. No amount of birthday bombs can make up for that.

"It's late," Briar eventually says as he looks down at his watch. "Babe, you have to open the library tomorrow."

"Yeah, I do." Jamie frowns and starts gathering up board game pieces. Lexy's already gone home. She's doing a ten-hour shift at the hospital where she works in the morning. "Aaron?" he asks tentatively.

"Yeah?" Aaron sits up in his seat.

"You're okay, right?" Jamie asks. "I know how you get down on yourself when you make a mistake, and I don't want . . . ." Jamie trails off, like he's not sure how to finish that sentence, but the silence in the room says it for him.

I don't want you to run away again.

"Aaron didn't make the mistake," I remind everyone. They've heard the story over our chat, over dinner, and a few times while we were playing the game, but it feels important that I say it again. "I did. Remember? Benson just pinned it on him."

But Aaron shakes his head. "No, it really was on me to check your work, Jeremy. Obviously, Benson was a dick about the whole thing, but he wasn't wrong about that. I should have double-checked. I just . . . ."

I trusted you. Those words go unspoken too, and I feel like curling up in a ball somewhere and hiding. Is this what shame feels like? Because I don't think I like it at all. Now I know why I usually avoid it at all costs.

"I'm fine," Aaron tells Jamie. "Really. I promise. Yeah, it was a shit day. But it was far from the shittiest I've ever had."

He and Jamie exchange a quick glance before Jamie escapes to the kitchen to throw away fried rice boxes. Briar's focused on putting away tiny green game tokens. This is definitely not a room that wants to talk about the shittiest day Jamie and Aaron have ever had.

All the feelings in the room are making me claustrophobic. "I'm taking off," I announce. And then, either because I am the screw-up my mother believes me to be or just a glutton for punishment, I add, "are you coming, Aaron?"

He takes the hand I'm holding out to him and uses it to lift himself off the recliner. "Yeah," he says steadily, and for the first time all night, he looks me in the eye. "I'll come with you, Jeremy."

———

By some unspoken agreement, we end up outside on the porch instead of inside in our separate apartments. Vermont's acing the whole "perfect summer night" thing right now. The sky is black and clear and dotted with stretching maps of stars, and the air is tilting into a warm, soft breeze. If I closed my eyes and thought hard enough, I know I could let the feeling of the night take me back to summers on the porch of my family's beach house. I haven't been back home once since I left, but last summer, I did manage to take Briar, Jamie, Lexy, and Mindy to the beach house my parents own on the Connecticut seaside. Briar had never seen the ocean before, and I could not let that stand. I crossed the Connecticut state line for him, but I still didn't go home.

Even though the beach house is over an hour away from where my parents live, it felt haunted. Every night I'd sit outside with my friends and remember the nights I used to sit there with my father, hunting for the North Star and naming constellations together. He bought me my own telescope, a miniature version of his. We spent hours charting the skies together. Right now I'm certain that all I'd have to do to go back into those memories is shut my eyes tight.

I keep them open as wide as I can.

Aaron's sitting next to me on the steps. He's looking up at the house behind us with a half-smile on his face. "How did Briar even find this place?" he asks softly.

"The Pink Monstrosity? I'm not sure." The giant Victorian building where Briar has lived since he first moved to Burlington, and where we're all staying right now, comes by its nickname honestly. The landlord painted it Easter egg pink when she bought it. The thing is so neon that I sometimes have an urge to break into a rave dance when I see it. And that's not the place's only quirk. The inside hallways are chartreuse.

I've heard other tenants complain about the paint color choices, but I like them. The Pink Monstrosity is in the Old North End of Burlington, a part of the city that doesn't have the best reputation. I like the idea that someone could buy something here and do their best to make it beautiful, even if their idea of beauty isn't everyone else's.

"I like the color," Aaron says suddenly. He's still facing the porch, and it's like he's speaking the words to the house instead of me. "I like how someone wasn't afraid to pick this color. That's sort of what makes it beautiful. The choice."

The words aren't all that far away from what I was just thinking. "Yeah?"

"Yeah. Like, I could never have the courage to paint a house this color." His face shifts into a frown.

"Why not?" I ask, and I'm honestly curious. I probably wouldn't think to paint a house to look like the Barbie aisle in a Target, but I wouldn't be afraid to do it if that's what I wanted. Aaron's brain is a mystery to me. My brain can't even relate to the way his gears wind themselves together. It's like he's wired in the completely opposite way from me.

Aaron laces his arms behind his head and drops back until he's lying across the dusty porch. He's wearing a Fairlington High School track shirt, and for a moment, my mind goes to an image of Aaron poised at the start of a race, his body tense with anticipation, every muscle on edge.

Aaron in track shorts. Fuck, that's a dangerous image, and one my dick is suddenly very interested in. *Not now,* I mentally order it.

"What if everyone hated it?" Aaron asks softly. "The house, I mean. What if the whole neighborhood started a petition to make me re-paint it? What if Insta or fucking TikTok launched a campaign making fun of it?" He's smiling as he looks up at me, but I know he's not really kidding.

I lay back next to him, feeling the grit of the old wood below my back. The T-shirt I'm wearing is Armani, and it's probably going to be ruined with how dirty this fucking porch is, but I really don't care. Lying next to Aaron on these slats of wood that have to be older than both of us, looking up at the Milky Way, I feel more myself than I have in months—since my mom cut me off, probably.

"So what?" I ask him softly. "Who cares what they think? It's your house. Your life. Right?"

Aaron sighs and turns his head slightly until he's staring directly at me. Our faces are just inches apart now, our mouths so close. I could reach out and pull his lips against mine in one motion. In one quick movement, I could repeat that night fifteen months ago. I could go back to our last kiss under the stars.

A shiver works its way through my body as I study a dimple in Aaron's chin. "Jeremy," he whispers as he shakes his head. "There are days when I would do anything to see the world the way you do." With one hand, he reaches over slightly, like he's going to pull me against him. I can practically see him thinking of the promises we've made to each other, the promises to forget that night all those months ago, as he moves his hand back. "Last summer," he says suddenly. "I was working at a law firm in Boston."

He says the words like they're being tortured out of him. I don't point out that I already knew that. I just nod.

Aaron swallows hard, and I trace the movement of his Adam's apple with my eyes. "I thought it was going well," he says hesitantly. "It was hard, but it was good hard, you know? Tons of work, and I liked the challenge."

Actually, I can't really say that I do know that feeling. Hard challenges aren't exactly something I go looking for. But I'm not about to interrupt Aaron when he's clearly on the verge of baring his soul, so I just nod again.

Aaron's blinking hard, and his voice cracks slightly as he keeps speaking. "I knew I didn't fit in. I knew that, okay? Too many people like Benson. Too much pressure to make money and rule the world. Still, I thought I was making a good impression. I thought I was . . . I thought I was good enough."

His voice breaks, and that's it. That's all it takes for me to break my *no touching him right now* rule and reach out to grab his hand. Seeing Aaron in pain like this makes my heart clench up in a way that it hasn't for a very long time, and there's no way I can let him keep sitting in that pain by himself.

"Then my final review happened," Aaron goes on. "I was working for this associate, Adam Garner. At this firm, the associates ruled over the law students. I never even saw a partner there. Anyway, he told me I didn't have the killer instinct to be a lawyer. He said I didn't dig deep enough or take enough ownership. And then . . . ." Aaron takes a deep breath. "He told me he thought I lack the intellectual capacity for a career in the field of law."

Holy fuck. All I want to do now is grab Aaron and hold onto him. I want to wrap my body around him and protect him from assholes like that and from anyone else who'd dare to tell this kind, driven, beautiful human being that he's not good enough at anything. *Lacked intellectual capacity.*

That review must have destroyed him.

Aaron worked so hard for years to get into law school. Studying law was his dream, and he excelled at every challenge

Moo U threw at him. He left his home, his family, and he gave up everything he loved for that dream.

And then this Garner guy basically told him all that sweat and determination and pain had been for nothing.

I'm still trying to figure out what the hell I could possibly say to comfort him when he starts talking again. "I was driving back to my apartment that day, the day I got the review, and you know what I kept asking myself? *What would Jeremy Everett do?* Because I knew the answer. You'd say who the fuck cares and walk away. You'd keep doing what you liked and maybe listen to someone if an ounce of what they said made sense, but you'd ignore all the rest of the noise. Because that's what you do. You ignore the noise. You don't care what people think." He squeezes his hand into mine, and his fingernails lightly burn themselves into my palm in the best way. "And that day, all I wanted to do was be like you."

"I . . . ." I open my mouth, but nothing else comes out. It's finally happened. Someone has actually managed to render me, Jeremy Never Stops Talking Everett, speechless.

Only Aaron Morin could do it. And he has.

"I . . . ." I say again.

"I've never been able to tell anyone that," he whispers. "Not my family. Not even Peter, my best friend at law school. The guy who got me the job here. Even he doesn't know."

The two of us are staring at each other, our eyes locked, and I know both of us are thinking about *that night. That kiss.*

What would happen if we did it again? Just once? What would happen, Aaron?

Would you run away again?

Aaron shakes his head. "You're kind of my hero, Jeremy Everett." He laces our fingers together, holding our hands up until they're almost pointed at the sky. "Don't forget that, okay?" And then he untangles our fingers, stopping to rub his thumb softly against my palm. He stands up slowly, his eyes still locked onto mine. "Seriously. Don't forget that. No matter what."

He starts walking away, then, and his absence begins to shift through me before he's even at the front door. He's reaching for the door handle, about to twist it, when suddenly I know—I know what I need to say to him.

"You're wrong," I blurt out.

"Huh?" He turns to look at me.

"You're wrong. I do care what people think." I pull in a long, hard breath and say the words I know he isn't expecting. "I mean, you're right. Most of the time, I really don't give a shit. Why bother? Nobody's living this life but me. But today, when I messed up that paperwork, I cared a lot. Not about what the partners or that fucking asshole Benson thought, though. I cared about what you thought."

Aaron nods, and the corner of his mouth lifts. The moonlight haloes his face, and suddenly that night from fifteen months ago is etched harder into my brain than it's ever been.

"Good to know," he whispers.

He disappears into the house, taking everything I thought I knew about the two of us with him.

10

THAT TIME AARON MET THE ICE QUEEN

"Good morning, Benson." I push open the door to our shared office and Benson, predictably, glares at me.

"Look, it's Harvard boy," he says. "Arrange to embarrass the hell out of anyone yet this morning?"

I sink down into my desk chair and drop my backpack next to my feet. "To be fair, I didn't have anything to do with that birthday party. And you know it."

"No, but your lackey did."

"You think Jeremy's my lackey?" I snort. "What gave you the idea that Jeremy does what anyone tells him to do?"

Benson drops the pen he's holding onto his desk and leans across it. "We both know," he says darkly, "that I didn't screw up that calendar. I know that for fucking sure because I didn't mark anything down on it."

"Why not?" I ask. I'm honestly curious.

"Because I hate birthdays."

I wonder if he also hates kittens and afternoon picnics. "I've gotten that impression," I say slowly. "Any reason why?"

"None of your business." He starts to turn back to his computer screen.

So much for bonding with my coworker. I sigh.

"Whatever, Benson. We both know you threw me under the bus yesterday."

He glares. I glare. For a long moment, we're trapped in the world's worst staring contest, and there's no way this one's going to break up with some laughter.

Then a miracle happens: Benson drops the glare. He leans back in his seat.

"Fine, okay," he mumbles. "But we both know it was on you to catch that mistake."

"Never said it wasn't."

Benson rolls his eyes, and I take that as my cue that I can finally sit back, too. "You want to explain what your problem with me really is? Because I've honestly tried to be a good coworker here, Benson. And I'm definitely not getting the same vibes in return."

His face shifts into something so filled with anger and tension that I almost pull my chair away from his. "You wouldn't understand," he hisses as he stands up. "Things just get handed to you, right? Harvard. This job. Everything gets handed to guys like you. There's no way you'd understand."

He shoves himself out of the chair and stalks out the door.

"Well," I mutter to myself. "That went well."

It's going to be a long day. Thank goodness it's Friday, I guess? Benson clearly isn't ready for us to kiss and make up, and on top of that, whatever the fuck happened on the porch last night with Jeremy is clinging to my brain like flies on a cow's tail. I lay in bed for hours last night trying to figure out if I really did almost make out with Jeremy Everett *again* on the front porch of our apartment complex with my brother just a few floors away.

Survey kept saying yes.

I left my apartment early and took a long walk to work instead of driving. I told myself I needed the exercise, but really, I was just trying to avoid running into Jeremy on the way into work. Because last night was exactly what I needed in so many ways. Telling Jeremy what happened at Leicester was like handing a heavy object to someone after you've been holding it for a long time and your arms are starting to give out. Lying there with him, on that porch, staring into the specks of his bright eyes . . . it was almost last March all over again. And last March can't happen again. Jeremy and I made promises about that, and they were the right promises to make.

I've got to get myself together before I see him. Nonchalance is key. I have to be able to look at him exactly the same way I did yesterday, like nothing ever happened last night, just like—

"Morning, sunshine!" Jeremy bursts through my office door without knocking. He grins widely as he surveys the room. "Oh, good, the Wicked Witch of the West is out. I did not feel like having to bring out my angry look when the donuts at The Maple Factory were so on point this morning. I left some in front of the door of Vino and Veritas for Briar and his buddies." He frowns suddenly. "I hope his boss doesn't see the note I left with them. It's not exactly PG. Anyway, can you double-check the documents I just printed for today's two o'clock meeting? I can't fuck that up again. Benson only has so many birthdays a year, you know."

He's like a hurricane circling me, and I've got no chance to keep up. But at least now I know the answer to the question that's been worrying me since I popped out of bed this morning: *will Jeremy be normal when I see him again?*

Normal? Definitely not. But normal for Jeremy? Yes. "Sure," I tell Jeremy. "I'll come look over the documents."

"Great. I brought crullers, too, even though I still can't figure out why anyone would pick a cruller over a donut. Jamie is weird."

Yup. We're definitely playing "last night never happened." And that means I get to spend the rest of the day doing my best to act like I'm not at all disappointed.

Which I'm not. I'm absolutely, definitely not.

The day goes by quickly. Benson's working on another matter with Evelyn, and he's hardly in the office. There's plenty of work to do, and I'm actually surprised when Jeremy shows up at my door holding his jacket. "Did you want a ride home?" He asks. "I didn't see your car in the parking lot."

I glance over at the clock. It's 5:35, and I have less work to bring home with me for the weekend than I thought I would. It's amazing how much I can get done when I'm using work to distract me from thinking about the office receptionist's flirty grin.

"Sure," I say as I stand and stretch. We're clearly just friends again, and friends get rides home with each other, don't they? Plus, the more normal things we do, the better the chance we can keep whatever is going on between us far in the distance. "Thanks, Jeremy." He waits while I pack up, and I follow him out of the near-empty office to the parking lot—

Where a woman is standing next to his Audi.

Jeremy stops so abruptly in front of me that I run straight into his back, like we're characters in some kind of *Three Stooges* gag. "Jeremy? What's going on?"

"Hello, Jeremy," says the woman calmly. She's about my mom's age, with the same graying brown hair. Age and hair color are where the similarities stop, though. Her hair is wrapped up in a tight bun that's styled so perfectly it almost looks fake. She's wearing a dark green suit with an ankle-length pencil skirt and shoes, which I'm guessing cost more than my mom makes in a month at her teaching job. She's standing primly and neatly, holding a phone in one hand, which she slips into her purse when she sees us. "You look well, son."

Oh shit.

I'm not sure I've ever imagined what Jeremy's mother looks like before. I always knew she worked in finance and that his family had buckets of money, but somehow, I didn't expect her to look this much like she just walked out of the Leicester firm. I remember now that she lives in Connecticut, and I suddenly find myself wondering if she ever does business in Boston.

Then I snap myself out of that random thought process because poor Jeremy is looking at her like he's looking at a ghost. "What are you doing here?" he says in a strangled voice. It's so unlike Jeremy's usual powerful, confident tone that it's almost painful to hear. I step up next to him and touch his hand gently, just to remind him I'm there.

He draws himself up slightly. "You didn't tell me you were coming," he adds.

"Yes, well." She clears her throat. "Who's your friend, Jeremy? You haven't introduced us." She crosses the parking lot and holds her hand out to me. "I'm Delia Everett. I apologize for my son's manners. I did raise him better than that, I promise you."

She even sounds like so many of the people I used to work with at Leicester—all crisp and patronizing and overly self-confident. I make sure to shake her hand hard, with authority. "I'm Aaron Morin, ma'am. I've always thought Jeremy's manners were wonderful. You've got nothing to worry about."

"I see." She studies me before turning her attention back to Jeremy. "Son, I've come to tell you this has gone on long enough. I've just visited where you're living." She shakes her head sadly. "That place is a deathtrap! And that color! It's an abomination. Why on earth would you choose to live there when you could be home right now with your family?" She gestures at the law office. "And you're working at a law office in Burlington, Vermont? I could have gotten you a spot at one of the best firms in Hartford if this is how you wanted to spend your summer!" She sighs. "Jeremy, I know things with your father have been difficult. But there's no running away from this anymore, my darling. It's that simple. Your father needs you. Your uncle needs you."

I notice she doesn't mention herself in that list.

"And," she adds, "it's time to stop being stubborn about this test. I've spoken to your doctors, and they promise me we can keep the entire process private and quick. I can get you an appointment right away. Will you continue to persist with this idea that you can simply run away from all this, Jeremy?"

Jeremy's still staring at her, speechless. It's like her diatribe pulled every last word or reaction out of him.

I've never seen Jeremy like this: frozen.

I step in front of him so I'm facing his mother. *The Ice Queen,* Lissie would call her. That's the nickname she gave to our elementary school principal, and Mrs. Everett definitely has that same *don't mess with me because I'm in charge* vibe. "Mrs. Everett," I say in the smooth, certain tone I always used with the associates at Leicester, "I happen to know Jeremy likes his apartment. And that he likes his job here. I'm curious how you knew where he was working?"

She huffs. "As if I can't find out such trivial information about my own son. Who are you, again?"

"Aaron Morin. Jeremy's friend."

Jeremy comes out of his freeze long enough to give me a pleading look, and that one small look is like a burst of fuel inside of me, spurring me on to say what I say next. "And as I was saying, Jeremy has a job and living situation he likes. He's perfectly fine. If he wants to come home this summer, he will. If not, he won't." I flash her my best *fuck you* smile—that's what Peter calls it, anyway. He says I use it whenever he takes the last eggroll, or when someone tries to tell me Boston's hockey team is better than Montreal's. "That'll be his choice. He's a grown man."

She huffs again. "He's a child. My child, in fact. But I can see this conversation will go nowhere today." She crosses her arms and looks around me. "Jeremy, please think about what I've said. You can't hide in Vermont forever. Goodbye, son."

She stalks away from us, heels clicking loudly against the pavement, and opens the door to a black BMW sedan. The car glides out of the parking lot almost silently, and I let out a long breath.

"Wow. Jeremy, are you okay?"

He's still silent as he stares down the road after the BMW.

I tug on his arm. "C'mon. Let's go home. I'll drive your car."

He follows me without a word. And I'm ninety percent sure

we can mark this down in history as the first time Jeremy Everett has ever followed anyone without a word.

"She didn't tell me she was coming."

Jeremy says the words in a choked voice in between sips of the water I just shoved into his hand. He's sitting on his couch in a blanket I wrapped him in. I'm not sure if seeing your own mother can send you into shock, but he's acting like he's in shock, so that's how I'm treating him.

"Yeah, I got that impression." I sink down next to him. "She's . . . interesting."

Jeremy snorts. "She's a fucking bully. She steamrolls over anyone who gets in her way." He tilts his head up and studies me. "You didn't let her steamroll you, though. Not even for a second."

I shrug. "I had some practice dealing with assholes at Leicester. I should probably bring out more of my moves for Benson, but I was sort of hoping the guy and I could get along."

Jeremy laughs. "You've got asshole-repellent moves for sure, Aaron. I had no idea. The way you shut her down like that? It was amazing." He shakes his head. "Especially after she brought up that test," he says softly.

Yeah. That test. He's never mentioned that before. If that's what I think it is, I definitely need to ask him about it. But not now. Not while he's still recovering from that encounter.

"It was no big deal," I tell him. "I mean, it wasn't half as hard as birthday bombing someone," I add jokingly.

Jeremy looks up at me. He puts a hand on my thigh, rubbing his thumb gently against my khakis. "It was a big deal. No one's stood up to her for me since my father," he says softly. "It was everything, Aaron."

We stare at each other for a long minute. The energy in the room is shifting, turning around us faster and faster and faster, and then—

Jeremy is on top of me with his tongue in my mouth.

He grabs at my clothes, pulling at my shirt and then my belt while I race like a madman to get his polo shirt up over his head. His skin is soft and smooth under my callused hands, his blond hair soft strands of bright summer straw under my fingers. I clutch at it with one hand while he thrusts his lips against mine in time to the same rhythm that he's using to move his torso against me. His hand shakes as he gets my belt undone and my pants pushed down. It's like my cock is wired for his touch, and the second his fingers drift against my cotton underwear, I'm as hard as a rock, arching off the couch and into him.

Both of us come up for air for a moment, panting, as Jeremy gets his own zipper undone and pushes his pants down around his ankles. "God, I love your body." He circles his hands around my belly button. My stomach isn't flat and hard like his, and there have definitely been times when I resented my inability to get actual ab muscles no matter how much work I did in the barn. But when Jeremy touches the extra skin there, I've never loved my stomach more.

I tackle his mouth with mine again and wrap my arms hard around his neck as he goes back to working frantically at our clothes. I can't get enough of the way he tastes—like the hazelnut coffee creamer we use at work and the turkey sandwiches he ordered us for lunch—or the way he smells. Every breath I take of him is like a sharp, warm sensation of sunshine and perfectly fresh air.

I shake my pants off my ankles as he throws his to the floor, and then we're skin against skin, no clothing between us except our underwear. I wrap my arms around his neck and take another breath of him as he gently pushes two fingers under the waistband of my underwear.

"Aaron," he whispers in my ear. "Can I take these off you?"

Energy is pulsing through my cock, little shocks of electricity that run through each place where his skin meets mine and head straight to the top of my dick. "I'm not going to last long," I whisper hoarsely.

"Good," he says softly. "Because I'm not either."

He dips his fingers further inside the waistband of my boxer briefs, teasing my skin with one hand while he gently slides my underwear off with the other. I can't think about anything but the way his fingers feel against my flesh, gentle and strong all at the same time, the way that electricity keeps shocking me just a little bit harder with every touch—

Then my underwear is gone, and his is too, and he wraps his hand around me to gather his own cock against mine, and everything in my vision goes dark.

"Jeremy!" I cry out as he takes both of us in his palm, pushing our flesh together so hard it almost hurts. Neither of us has bothered to find any lube, and the friction is definitely a little bit painful as he begins to jack us together with quick, forceful motions. But the pain bleeds and burns into more electricity, and my already rock-like cock is now so hard against him that I'm sure when I do finally let go, I'm going to blow apart in his hand. That's what it feels like: like he's holding me together. Like he's holding us together.

"You're so perfect," he says. His voice is distant and high; he doesn't sound like himself at all. "Every inch of you is so perfect, Aaron. You're too perfect for me." I barely register the words as he thrusts against me into his hand. A giant pulse of fast, perfect pleasure moves through me, and then I'm jutting up against him in quick, sharp motions as I come all over his hand and both of our bodies. The shocks of pure pleasure are still coursing through me as I feel Jeremy go tense in my arms. I wrap him up tightly, holding onto him hard as he jerks against me. I can feel his cum spurt against my stomach. Normally, I don't like when someone comes on me. It's messy and sticky and usually feels like more trouble than it's worth to clean it up.

But right now? All I want to do is reach down in between our bodies and rub our cum together against my skin. All I want to do is feel that sensation of me and him mixing together in one more way in time and space.

Jeremy collapses on top of me, and the two of us lay there, sweaty and boneless. The old couch we're on sinks, taking our weight until it almost feels like we're cocooned in the cushions together. "I needed that," Jeremy says softly. "You have no idea how much I needed that." He lifts his head high enough to place a soft kiss on my cheek, and his lips burn beautifully against my skin.

I want to overthink this. I want to worry and obsess about every second of what we just did. I want to dissect every moment of it, creating charts and graphs in my head full of statistics and probabilities and research questions. Will we go back to "normal" again the moment we move away from this couch? Or will things change now? What will Jamie say if he ever finds out? Shouldn't we finally tell Jamie about this? Whatever *this* is?

Will this ever be more? Should it be more?

Was this more for me than it was for Jeremy?

Was I just one more notch for him on his giant bedpost?

I can feel the rise and fall of his chest against me. His breathing is even and slow and comforting, his scent still perfect, and I fall asleep against him as all the questions in my head slow to a deep and sudden stop.

11

THAT TIME JEREMY GAVE SOME FROGS A SHOW

"Jeremy? Jeremy! Are you in there?"

The pounding on my door is only slightly louder than the low-key pounding in my head. I sit up slowly and do my usual *what the fuck happened last night* survey.

I'm on the old, plaid couch in the apartment I'm subletting for the summer. I'm wrapped in a blanket that I don't remember owning. No alcohol bottles are around, and I don't think I went out last night.

Then it all comes back to me in a flash. This isn't a hangover from too much jungle juice. My mother showed up in town last night.

This is a Delia Everett hangover.

And I slept with Aaron again.

I do another quick survey of my place, but I don't see him anywhere. I remember falling asleep with him. Did he stay the night? When did he leave?

"Jeremy! Jeremy, are you okay? You haven't been answering my texts."

And why the fuck is Briar banging on my door like he's a lumberjack instead of a bookseller?

I lurch my way off the couch, still wrapped up in the blanket, and somehow manage not to fall over my own feet on my way across the room. I pull the door open just as Briar's gearing up to attack it with his knuckles again.

"Dude," says Briar. "You look rough." He grins. "What'd you get up to last night, Jeremy?"

"Uh, nothing," I mumble. I keep my eyes firmly away from Briar's as he follows me into my apartment. *Don't think about Aaron's chest underneath yours. Don't think about his arms wrapped around you. Definitely don't think about any of that while Briar's staring at you.* I step into the kitchen area and start throwing coffee grinds into the machine. This morning requires as much coffee as I can make. "My mother came into town."

"Shit." Briar's eyes widen. I have a feeling he's remembering the night she cut me off and I went on the tequila bender. Briar was the one who ended up in the emergency room with me while I got my wrist x-rayed.

It turns out that tequila bottles and karaoke stages do not mix well.

"Are you okay?" Briar asks. "What happened?"

I open my mouth to tell him the story, and then I remember that I can't.

I decided the day I started college in Vermont that no one here could ever know the truth about my permanently fucked-up family. I've never wanted the sympathy or simpering faces, and it's a lot easier to live life on your own terms when the world doesn't know what those terms are. Briar knows that my mother and I don't get along, but he and Jamie and Lexy just assume it's because I live my life like a permanent frat boy. And I've never corrected them.

And that's not the only reason I can't say shit to Briar about what really happened last night. How would I spin the rest of that tale? *I slept with your quasi-brother-in-law after Mom finished ripping me to shreds, but no worries. It wasn't our first time! We actually fucked around last year, too, when he and Jamie weren't even speaking. Don't worry; maybe someday I'll get around to telling Jamie.*

Not a great idea. Especially when my coffee hasn't even brewed yet.

"I'm fine," I tell Briar. "She left, and I, uh, just fell asleep. By myself. Definitely and totally by myself," I add in a rush. I can't bring myself to look over at the couch. Then I might think about Aaron's cock up against mine, his chest against mine, his hands in my hair—

Shit shit shit shit shit. I've got to get it together before I see Aaron again. He's probably going to want to talk about this. Knowing Aaron, he's probably already created three different strategic plans and agendas for the conversation.

The coffee machine beeps, and I pour both of us giant cups. At least it's Saturday. I've got forty-eight hours to get my head back in the game before I have to see Aaron.

Briar looks down at the cup I'm pouring for him. "I hate to bring this up right now, but you know we're supposed to leave soon, right?"

"We are?"

"It's Saturday," Briar says gently. "Mrs. Morin's birthday is today. Jamie and Aaron already went up to Morse's Line to help with chores. You and I are supposed to drive up there and meet them around noon. Remember?"

I one hundred percent did not remember that.

"It's okay if you don't want to come," Briar says, and he's still using his super calm voice, like I'm one of the preschoolers at his story hour. "I'm sure Ellie will understand. Celebrating someone else's mom's birthday is probably the last thing you want to do right now."

Actually, there's nothing I'd rather do today than celebrate the life of the woman who became my second mom after my own mother and I stopped being able to stand in the same room together. That's not the problem with going to Morse's Line.

Nope. The problem is a tall, dark, farmer-turned-lawyer. One whose cum is still drying on my stomach.

The problem is that thinking about his cum is making my dick chub up again.

Fuucccckkkkk.

I can't miss this party. Everyone will have questions, and Ellie will be upset, even if she says she isn't. Aaron might think he did something wrong. Not to mention that I have *never* let one of my hookups stop me from doing exactly what I want the next day. That's just not me.

So I do the only thing I can think of: I chug the entire mug of coffee in one go. And then I slam the mug down on the counter like I'm in some kind of B-level action movie.

"I'm taking a shower," I announce to Briar. "And then we're leaving."

I disappear into the bathroom with Briar still staring after me. I don't even realize until I get out of the shower that I broke the stupid mug.

Briar and I get to the party a little after noon. The Morins' farm is up by the Canadian border. It comes complete with rolling green hills, a giant barn with red steel siding, an old farmhouse, apple trees, and an actual, real-life frog pond. Sometimes I try to imagine what it was like for Jamie and Aaron growing up here, but I can't wrap my head around it. The whole scene is about as far as you can get from my parents' contemporary mini-mansion in Wellsford, with its state-of-the-art kitchen, in-ground pool, and tennis court in the backyard.

"You're here!" Lissie calls from one of the rocking chairs on the wraparound porch the moment we step out of the car. "Uh, what's that?" Her eyes widen.

"Duh. Clearly, it's a bouquet of fourteen Mylar balloons spelling out the words *Happy Birthday* with Mrs. M's face super-imposed on the balloon where the space would be," I answer cheerfully as I finally manage to wedge the *Y* balloon out of the backseat. "Happy birthday, Fake Mom!" I yell out when the balloons all pop up together in my hand.

Ellie Morin, who I like to call Fake Mom because it makes her smile, jumps up from her seat on the porch and starts clapping. "I love them, Fake Son!" she yells back.

Thank goodness she likes them. It was a little touch-and-go driving here with BIRTH and HAP making my rear visibility near zero. Briar was convinced we were going to die somewhere between Winooski and Fairlington, and I spent a few miles wishing I'd gone for a nice fruit bouquet instead.

I take stock of the scene while I get my balloons to behave. The usual crowd of people that appear at Morin events are all here. Ellie, Lexy, and Lissie are on one end of the porch sipping lemonade with some other people I don't recognize, probably people Ellie teaches with. On the other side of the porch, Jamie's having an intense conversation with his dad, Frank, and a few others I vaguely know. Mindy—Lexy's twin and my ex-girlfriend —is here too. "Jeremy, hi!" she says. "Haven't seen you in forever."

"That's because he's an actual responsible adult now!" Lexy calls back. "I bet he finally even knows what a W2 is."

I don't respond to that. I'm pretty sure I know what a W2 is . . . but I'd rather not open up my mouth and be wrong.

Everyone I expected to see is here. Minus one very conspicuously missing person: Aaron.

"I'm so glad you're here!" Ellie says. "Come on up here and say hello."

Briar makes a beeline to her, and I'm not far behind. Ellie Morin is sunshine and pure love. After my encounter with Delia last night, she's exactly the Mom Energy I need right now.

"Hi, sweeties," she says as she pulls us in for hugs. I find a space to tie up the balloons on a porch post near her chair. "How's life in the big city?"

"Burlington's not that big," Lissie grumbles. She sighs. "I can't wait until I'm old enough to go to New York City. Is it amazing, Jeremy?"

I think of the nights I spent visiting New York right after my father was officially diagnosed. I'd take the train there and wander around for hours, dancing with strangers in clubs where no one cared how underage or mentally fucked-up I was. I used that city like a drug, injecting myself with the lights and the sounds and the music until I couldn't feel anything anymore. I haven't been back once since I came to Vermont. I just shrug. "It's an experience, that's for sure. Hey, uh, where's Aaron?"

Briar sends me a raised eyebrow. I ignore it.

"He's inside checking on the lasagna," Ellie says. "I should probably go in and help him, though. When we were getting them into the oven earlier, that poor lasagna nearly ended up as my new kitchen floor pattern." She glances at me. "Nothing's wrong at work, is it? Usually, Aaron only starts dropping everything in sight when he's worried about something."

"Everything's great," I tell her. "We've just been working a lot. He's probably tired."

"You've both been working a lot, J-Bear." Lexy pokes me in the stomach. "I was telling Mindy that she wouldn't recognize you these days."

Mindy sends me a soft smile from across the porch and doesn't make one single comment about what a giant mess I was during the month we spent dating my freshman year. Mindy is great like that. I know I'm lucky she stayed friends with me after everything that happened. "Maybe I'll just go help Aaron," I say as casually as I possibly can. Briar gives me some mini side-eye, but no one else seems to think this suggestion is strange.

"That would be great, hon," Ellie says. "Tell him Jamie left a salad in the fridge, okay?"

I ignore Briar as I open up the screen door of the house.

What the fuck are you doing? my Inner Voice of Reason—if I even have one of those—calls out. And honestly, I have no answer for my IVR. Talking to Aaron right now, less than twelve hours after his hand was on my dick, is probably a terrible idea. But there's no way I can just hang out on the porch, making small talk with Ellie and my ex, until I've seen Aaron. I need to know for sure that we're going to make it through this party without me dying of blue balls or Aaron falling into the stove.

I kick off my shoes in the mudroom and make my way into the giant open kitchen, where Aaron's poking around in the refrigerator. "Uh, hi?"

"Jeremy? Jeremy!" Aaron stands up so fast he smacks his head into the freezer door. "Ow," he mutters.

"Sorry. I didn't mean to startle you," I say. Then I do my best not to stare at him.

And I fail.

He's holding a giant salad bowl with one hand and rubbing his forehead with the other. His brown curls are a dark mess across his forehead, and the faded Fairlington Cooperative Dairy T-shirt he's wearing is riding up just slightly above his arm muscles and the top of his stomach. The centimeter of soft skin there jogs my brain into instant memories of last night.

"Jeremy," Aaron whispers.

And just like that, I tackle him against the fridge.

I've got no idea where the salad ends up. I can only hope it makes it to the table as I run my hand up under his shirt and bury my tongue in his mouth. He's got his hands wrapped up in my hair, and he's pulling me up against him like he needs his skin against mine. I can feel his cock hardening against my leg, and I swear, just the image of fucking him against his family refrigerator has me nearly coming in my pants.

There's probably something messed up and Freudian about that, but I'm not taking the time to explore it right now.

"Aaron," I say, and the words come out more like a moan. "Holy fuck, Aaron." My hand drifts down his back, toward the waistband of his pants, and I nudge a finger into it. "Fucking want you," I mutter.

"Jeremy?" The voice that leaps into the kitchen is young and bright and high. Definitely Lissie. Aaron and I instantly separate. He leans back against the fridge, breathing heavily, while I retreat to the other side of the kitchen. "Mom wants to know if you can bring out some more lemonade," Lissie asks from the mudroom.

"Sure thing, Lis," I answer. She doesn't say anything else, and soon the door closes behind her.

Aaron runs his hands through his hair. "Jeremy," he says in a strangled voice. "We need to talk. I think we need a new action plan."

Even I can't disagree with that. I wonder if he's made an agenda for our conversation yet.

Somehow the two of us manage to keep our hands off each other during dinner. I eat three helpings of lasagna, and we all sing to Ellie when Frank brings out her cake. She gets teary as she blows out the candles. "I'm just so happy to have all my babies in one place again," she says with her eyes on Jamie and Aaron.

I can't even imagine what things were like for her when Aaron was gone. Ellie Morin is the quintessential mom—the kind I always wished my mom was more like. It must have been hell for her to have her family split up like that. I glance over quickly at Aaron and see he's got his eyes on me. When our vision locks for a minute, I know we're both thinking the same thing.

Whatever's going on between us, we have to be careful.

Most people leave pretty quickly after the cake, and Aaron and I make our escape when Briar and Jamie offer to help Frank fix something on one of the tractors. I follow him behind the barn and across the bright green pasture of the Morin land. I keep myself busy watching out for cow pies and trying not to think too hard about the fact that Aaron is the first person I legit feel like I can't keep my hands off of. Despite my reputation, I have pretty decent self-control. I know what I want, and I go for it, but I also usually know when to stay away from something—or someone.

We end up sitting on rocks next to the small frog pond by the trees at the back of the Morin property. A few cows are drifting around us, grazing, and the noise the frogs make—I've always thought they sounded like they were burping—fills the air.

"This is my favorite spot on the farm," Aaron says.

I get why. This place feels like Aaron: quiet and comfortable in its complex simplicity. There's a whole ecosystem happening underneath us, but the surface of it all is one of the most relaxing places I could ever imagine. "Jamie brought me here once," I tell him. "I couldn't believe your family had a legit frog pond. I'd only ever seen those things in movies or whatever." I smile at him. "Your life is some wild shit, dude."

Aaron laughs. Then he straightens himself on the rock he's sitting on, and I can see him pulling himself together. He's making himself Serious and In-Charge Aaron. I wonder what Serious and In-Charge Aaron is going to say to me.

"I think we should sleep together as much as we want," he blurts out.

Wow. I did not have that on my "things Aaron Morin says" bingo card. "Say the fuck what?" I ask.

He runs his hands through his hair and sighs. "Listen. I know you don't want a relationship, and it's pretty obvious we'd be terrible together anyway." That comment feels like a tiny gut punch, though I can't deny he's right. "But I can't get you out of my head, okay? Last night . . . ." He shakes his head and stares out at the pond. "That was the best sex I ever had. And I got the impression from what just happened in the kitchen that you liked it too. So why bother to fight it? I'm going back to Boston at the end of the summer. Can't we just do what we want for a few months? Like a summer fling?"

A summer fling. It sounds like something out of one of Jamie and Briar's romance novels, but I can't deny that it's an interesting idea. I've never had one before. Maybe it's time to cross that item off my bucket list. "A summer fling, huh?"

"Why not? Like I said, you're in my head. I'm guessing I'm in yours, too. So let's stop fighting this and do whatever we want for the summer. We end the whole thing when I go back to school. . And in the meantime, don't hold back on the rest of your summer plans. Do whatever else you want with whoever else you want. I know you're careful."

It's like Aaron is handing me every single one of my favorite foods on a platter and telling me I get to eat it while I watch porn. "Seriously? You'd be okay with that?"

Aaron shrugs. "I remember that one time you tried to be monogamous, Jeremy. It didn't go so well."

I think back to the short time Mindy and I were together and wince. I was fresh out of Connecticut then, and not dealing well with the regular updates from my uncle telling me that my dad was going downhill. I impulsively—shocker, I know—decided that I needed the life experience of a real relationship. And there was Mindy. A sweet, cute maple syrup maker (there's probably a fancier term for that, but I don't know it), with a great sense of humor and an easy ability to ignore me when I got out of hand. Like the time I tried to take her out for dinner in a helicopter.

Our relationship should have been perfect. But it wasn't.

For one thing, our chemistry was never quite right, and I think we both knew that early on. But the bigger problem came when my mom started sending me regular texts asking me to please get the test to see if I had the same gene as my dad, and I realized something: there couldn't be any long-term relationships in my future. Ever. I was a potential ticking timebomb, and it would never be fair of me to saddle myself to someone else.

Especially since I wasn't ready then to take that test. I'm still not, and I don't think I ever will be. That test might give me a vision of my future, but it won't change that future. The doctors don't have treatments yet to correct the problem if they do discover I have the same gene as my dad. We'll all know what's coming, but we won't be able to stop it.

Still, on the days when my mother isn't blowing up my phone with texts about how reckless and difficult I am, I can almost understand her obsession with me taking that test. It could change so many things for me. It's hard to even imagine how different my life would be if I took that test and it came back negative.

But what if it came back positive? That's a vision for the future I'm not ready to live with. That's why I broke things off with Mindy and declared myself the playboy of Burlington. I've never looked back, and I've never regretted that choice.

"Monogamy and I don't get along," I tell Aaron. That's the best way I can explain it.

"Right. And you don't have to try it out again," Aaron says softly. "This will just be a summer fling. We get to do whatever we want, no strings attached."

I still can't quite believe Aaron's handing me more sex with him on a beautiful, free, silver platter. Sure, there might be consequences down the line. But since when the fuck have I ever cared about consequences? "Let's try it," I tell him eagerly. "At least this means I won't have to find a new job. I was starting to worry Benson was going to end up seeing me do really inappropriate things to you over his computer station."

Aaron bursts out laughing. "Let's avoid that," he says. "We'll try this instead. Because the Vegas idea definitely didn't work."

"It did not," I agree. My mind drifts back to the night before. I shiver as I remember exploding all over Aaron's stomach. "It very much did not."

"Okay. Then it's a plan." Aaron claps his hands together. "Can we tell everyone, or do you still want to keep this a secret? I know you've got concerns about Jamie finding out."

Aaron always seems to know what's in my head before I even think it. "Would you be okay with that? With keeping this a secret from Jamie?"

"I don't love it, honestly. I don't like keeping things from him. We both know it didn't end well when I kept my secret about getting into law school early. But I understand where you're coming from. I get why you don't want to say anything." He hesitates for a moment. "Can I ask you a favor, though?"

"Sure. Of course." Right now, next to this frog pond, I'd probably give him anything he asked for. Especially now that I know the conversation could end with blow jobs.

"I've got no problem with you sleeping with other people, Jeremy. Really. That's why I suggested this plan. But could you maybe not tell me about it when it happens?"

He's twisting more grass in his hand like he's not sure he should have asked. "Of course," I tell him. I don't even have to think twice about my answer. Aaron Morin's a guy who was wired for comfortable, long-term monogamy. If he's willing to try out a short-term non-monogamous fling, the least I can do is not throw my other hook-ups in his face.

"Okay." He takes a deep breath. "So. We're doing this, then?" He holds out his hand for me to shake, like we're back at the law firm.

I grin and grab his hand. "Let's do it. The summer fling is officially fucking *on*."

And then the frogs see a whole lot more than just a handshake.

12

THAT TIME AARON HAD PLENTY OF INTELLECTUAL CAPACITY

Jeremy: *Have I sent you this one yet?*

The GIF of a large bullfrog, glaring at a much smaller frog while it hops excitedly around him, appears on my phone as I'm parsing through what has got to be one of the world's longest contracts. Business mergers are no joke, even when they involve the merging of a honey producer with a maple candy company.

> **Me:** *No, Jeremy. Somehow, I have not seen that one yet, even though it's the fifty-second frog GIF you've sent me this week.*

I smile as I let my eyes drift across my office to the open door. He's less than fifty feet away from me right now, at the front desk. Lately, he seems to spend most of his time there sending me GIFs of frogs.

> **Jeremy:** *Wait until you see what I've got planned for tomorrow. Animation may be involved.*

I snort-laugh as I lock my phone and go back to reading. It's been a good few days. A good week, actually. The random decision I made next to that frog pond to ask Jeremy for more of whatever it is we have together seems to be working. He's snuck into my apartment one night this week, I snuck into his another, he texts me weird frog GIFs at random moments throughout the day, and we're a whole lot more normal around each other the rest of the time. Evelyn even made a comment about how I must be getting more comfortable here at the office because I hardly ever walk into the furniture anymore.

I guess I have to call that a win.

"What are you smiling about?" Benson says from the desk across from me, with all the intonation of a man who is not getting nearly as much good sex as I am. "And did you finish up the research for that business merger yet? Iris and Tom need it like yesterday. Get your ass in gear."

This guy is permanently in asshole mode. At least he's a constant reminder of why I'm glad to be in Vermont and not back at Leicester this summer. There were so many versions of Benson running around that office. At least here, I only have to deal with one of him. "I'm working on it," I tell him neutrally. That's my newest tactic for dealing with Benson: exhibit zero anger or frustration around him. Jeremy suggested it, and I appreciate how much this approach seems to drive Benson nuts.

Speaking of law firm coworkers, I still haven't heard from Peter. He never texted me back after I asked about seeing him in Vermont. I pull out my phone and send him another message.

Me: *Hey. How's studying for the bar going? Hope everything's okay.*

Three dots appear right away.

Peter: *Sorry I've been MIA. Studying's a lot. I'll call you soon, okay?*
Me: *Sure. Good luck.*

I'm more confused than ever, but I'm not the type to push people into sharing things with me. If Peter wants to tell me what's going on with him, he will. Eventually.

Benson growls under his breath just as someone knocks on the doorframe of our open door. *Jeremy?* My heart hopes for his face just a little more than it probably should, given that I see him constantly lately. But Jeremy Everett brings light into every part of my day. Now that I know I can have that light as much as I want, I crave it.

"Yoo-hoo, friends!" Tom Gentry is in the doorway. Benson and I both straighten up in our chairs fast. I'm still not quite used to the culture of Sprysky and Gentry, where the two partners randomly show up in office doorways to chat. I never once even met any of the partners at Leicester. "Just wanted to have a quick check-in with you both." His graying ponytail swings behind his head, and I notice he's wearing a shirt patterned like a black and white Holstein cow under his suit jacket. "Listen, Benny, excellent work on that research for the wildlife refuge case. Very nice job."

Benny? Did Tom Gentry just call Benson *Benny?*

"I was impressed," Tom adds. "And your energy level's been much better, too! Aren't you glad I suggested that meditation practice? Did you try it with the incense burner I told you about?"

From somewhere outside the door, I can hear Jeremy coughing like he's trying not to laugh.

Benson—*Benny*—has gone as red in the face as he was the day of his birthday party. "Uh, yesIdidthankyou," he says to his desk. He clears his throat and looks back up. "And I'm glad you appreciate the work I've been doing."

"Absolutely!" Tom beams at him and then turns to me. He frowns. "Aaron, unfortunately, I come bearing bad news. The clients for that business merger project you're researching have asked to move up the timeline on the deal. I'm afraid I need all the due diligence completed by tomorrow, and as you know, the rest of us here in the office are knee-deep in that development project or other things." He sighs. "I'm wondering if you could get it all done by tomorrow? I was thinking Benny could pitch in and help you."

Tomorrow? Is he kidding? Even with Benson/Benny's help, that barely seems humanly possible. There are at least thirty hours' more research that needs to be done for this case. But Tom's giving me such a hopeful, confident expression that I already know I'm going to say yes. Especially after he made that speech about what a wonderful job Benson's doing. I haven't had a speech like that from him yet. "Um, yes, sir. I can certainly try."

"Good man!" He claps his hands together. "Shoot for noon tomorrow, then. Ben-o, help your office partner out. I'm off to a meeting with some soul-sucking city officials. Talk about people who need a meditation practice." And then he disappears from the office, the scent of something that smells distinctly like patchouli following not far behind.

"Going to finish that project by tomorrow, huh?" Benson's voice has so much sneer in it he may as well be a cartoon villain. "Like fucking hell you are. I've seen what's involved in that deal."

My head begins to pound as I think of everything I need to do before tomorrow. "We can do it. I know we can. Listen, if you can take the—"

"Sorry, pal, no can help." Benson shrugs and starts packing up his desk. "I've got an appointment this afternoon. Already cleared it with Iris. I guess you're on your own." He stands up and checks his watch. "And it's already four o'clock. Looks like you're in for a long night."

I barely hear his words over the sound of my heart beating in my chest. "Why didn't you say something to Tom?" I hiss.

"Why should I? It's your project. If you can't handle it on your own, you shouldn't have told him you could. Gotta go." He grabs his jacket from the back of his chair and stalks out of the room.

And I try to stave off a panic attack. Holy fuck, it's happening again. I may as well be back at Leicester, where no matter how hard I worked, no matter what I did, it was never good enough.

I'm never going to finish this project for Tom by tomorrow. He's going to be so disappointed.

Maybe even angry.

He might give me that look he's famous for using in depositions and courtrooms.

You lack intellectual capacity, Aaron.

You might not be cut out for this.

Some people just aren't meant to be lawyers.

You lack intellectual capacity.

"Aaron!"

I snap my head up as I realize Jeremy's been calling my name. "That fucker," he growls. "Can you even believe him? He makes me so angry. It's too bad people only have one birthday a year or he'd be getting a desk of bright yellow cake tomorrow. But don't worry. We'll get him back. Aaron? Aaron, are you okay?"

"No," I mutter as I bury my face in my hands. "I can't do this by myself in one night. There's no way, Jeremy. It's not possible."

"Good thing I'm here, then," he answers cheerfully. "I just made more coffee, and most of the office is empty now, so we can spread out paperwork at my desk if we need to. What do you need me to do first?"

I can barely compute the words. "Why are you staying here? Don't you have plans?"

Jeremy shrugs. "Yeah, I do. Helping you." Then he sits down in the chair across from my desk. "Tell me what you need help with. I'll start right after I make some phone calls, okay?"

Is Jeremy giving up a night out with his friends to do legal research with me? I'm still trying to process that when my computer dings with an email message. The stacks of paper around me feel like they're mocking me as I try to put the words together to answer.

I lose time for a few hours after that. I read things and take notes and Jeremy finds files for me and reads other things. Both of our hands are covered in highlighter, but with every task we complete, I feel a little better. Jeremy's a fast reader, and he's incredibly analytical. It's not at all surprising he got into Yale with a brain like his. This isn't a side of him I see very much—this highly academically focused side—and I'd be lying if I said it wasn't turning me on. At one point, when he starts talking about management integrations, I actually have to adjust myself in my pants.

We've been working for hours when Jeremy murmurs something about getting us dinner. I haven't even noticed if I'm hungry, but I'll probably need some food if I'm going to keep working at this pace, so I just nod in agreement and go back to reading. Everyone else left the office a long time ago, and it's quiet and dark now. The lamps at Jeremy's desk and mine are casting soft orange glows in the space. A speaker is playing quiet music from Jeremy's desk. It's something ambient but with a little more beat to it, and lyrics that feel calm and sweet. The person is singing about sunrises, I think, and how those sunrises exist in the other person's eyes.

"Aaron?" Jeremy appears back in my office doorway. "You ready to stop for a break?"

I blink back my exhaustion and look past him, into the main office, to see the strangest scene.

There's a blanket laid out in the middle of the office floor—a soft fleece one, the kind my sister likes. Four fat battery-operated candles are lined up around the outside of it, blinking into the shadows of the room. The blanket is set with paper plates and cups, and there's a large bag lined up next to it.

"Jeremy," I whisper. "What did you do?"

He shrugs. "Jamie and Lexy are always saying I'm extra, right? I thought today was a good time to bring some of that extra here. So I called Joss and Tanner at V and V, and I asked Tanner to throw in some candles." He holds out a hand to me. "Care to join me for dinner, Mr. Morin?"

I take his hand and follow him to the blanket.

Jeremy sets out containers filled with the same delicious fried chicken sandwiches we had the last time we ate together at V and

V. They're sitting next to crisp French fries and coleslaw that smells like apple orchards in the fall. He produces a bottle of wine that he opens and pours into paper cups. "Do you do this for all your flings?" I joke.

Jeremy laughs. "Nope. Just the ones who give me hand jobs next to frog ponds." He shrugs. "And maybe the ones who stand up to my mom in parking lots. And the ones who are really hard workers who try fucking hard at their jobs." He hands me a cup.

I take a sip. "This is Brody's maple wine," I mutter. "How did you know?"

"That it's your favorite? I sometimes pay attention when Briar goes all maple nerdy. I heard the two of you talking about it, and I asked Tanner for a bottle. So, you wanna discuss how tonight is giving you flashbacks to your last job?"

"You figured that out, huh?" I take the fork he hands me and spin it into the pile of coleslaw he's just placed on my plate. "Jeremy, do you ever feel like you're doing everything wrong? Like nothing you do will ever be good enough?"

A new song has come on the speaker at Jeremy's desk. It's haunting and sweet, a mixture of swirling string instruments against guitars. The singer is repeating the words *no time* over and over in a chorus. Jeremy takes a bite of a salad and studies me, smiling. "You mean like I'm going to run out of time before I accomplish what I'm supposed to?" he asks me quietly.

My body goes cold as I think about what he's saying. "Shit, I didn't mean . . . ."

"It's okay, Aaron." He sets down his plate and leans forward across the blanket. One of the candles is lighting his face perfectly, and his eyes seem to take up the entire room. "I'm saying I do know what you mean. I know exactly what you mean. You and me? We're not that different. We're just out to accomplish different things."

I guess he's right. I know he's right, even. I'm out to prove myself to the world, and Jeremy? I think he may be out to make the world prove itself to him. And I think both of us feel the rush of a clock ticking somewhere above our heads. But right now, sitting on a blanket in the middle of my boss's office, drinking wine and listening to music on a night when Jeremy has saved me in a way I never imagined he would, our goals feel perfectly aligned.

We fall across the blanket in a heap together, pushing paper plates and to-go containers out of the way. Jeremy's mouth finds my neck as he lays down over me. He nips at it with his tongue and teeth, slowly making his way up to my mouth while his hands push my tucked shirt out of my pants and begin to explore my belly.

"Should we include this in the billable hours for tonight?" he whispers.

I laugh out loud as I push my own hands under his shirt and start undoing buttons. "Absolutely," I mutter. "There's very important research to be done here."

I should be panicking about how much we have to do. I should be worried that this little break is going to keep us from finishing the project. I should be worried someone—one of our coworkers or bosses—will come back to the office for something and walk in on us. But Jeremy's body is on top of mine right now, his breath against my skin. And he's just spent hours making me feel like I can finish this project. Like we can.

Like maybe we can do anything together.

And this? What we're doing on this blanket? *This* we can definitely do together.

Our pants and underwear disappear somewhere in between kisses. Then our shirts go while Jeremy's exploring my earlobes with his tongue. Next, he tackles my nipples. I gasp as he teases gently at each one, his tongue making slow circles all around the outer edges of my areolas. "You like that," he says. His hand's on my cock now, and mine is on his. He starts to sink slowly down my body, and I know what he's about to do. But I don't want him to do it alone. I grab at his arm.

"Wait," I tell him. "Let me." He stops, one eyebrow raised,

while I circle my body under his. I somehow manage to avoid the food containers and the wine bottle as I come to a stop with my mouth directly under his cock. He's thick and hard, and the purpling at the end of it shows just how ready he is for more. I take him in my mouth to make sure he doesn't have to wait one second longer.

Jeremy lets out a long moan and then buries my cock down his throat.

I've never liked 69 positions much before. They tend to be awkward. The last time I tried to pull one off, it felt like me and the other guy were two puzzle pieces who couldn't make ourselves fit together. But this time, the puzzle pieces click like they were always meant to be by each other's sides. Jeremy holds himself up at just the right height above my body as he teases and tugs at my dick with his perfect mouth. I can feel him pulsing harder and harder every time I move my mouth up and down his length, and every movement—his and mine—feels natural. Choreographed.

Like we were always meant to do this on a picnic blanket in the middle of a law office.

"Fuck, Aaron," Jeremy says around my cock at one point, and the vibrations are almost enough to send me over the edge. "I'm going to . . . ."

That's all the hint I need. I take him as deep as I can, hard and fast, and he explodes into my mouth. The sensation of his cum against my tongue sends fiery sparks into the tip of my own dick, and it isn't long before I'm thrusting hard into his mouth, exploding into him over and over.

Jeremy rolls off of me and over onto the blanket. "Best work break ever," he mutters. "At least I think so. I mean, this is my first job, but I'm guessing that doesn't happen at all of them?"

"It definitely does not," I agree.

Somehow, we finish all the research by 3 a.m.

13

THAT TIME JEREMY WAS DEFINITELY NOT A RAKE

Man, work sex is *awesome*. I'm starting to think I should have gotten a job years ago.

Not that Aaron and I have messed around in the office since the night last week when we got busy next to the copying machine. And for the record, I didn't plan for that to happen. When I ordered dinner for us that night, I was just trying to give Aaron a break. He looked so fucking stressed out. His forehead was creased into about a zillion lines, the dark circles under his eyes were starting to go ash black, and he kept talking to his computer like some kind of mad scientist trying to invent time travel.

I really wish someone would get around to inventing time travel. But that's not the point. The point is that Aaron was a hot mess, and I wanted to help, and if there's one thing I know will perk a Morin up, it's food.

So I called in the cavalry at V and V, and *wow*, did that work out for me. I got to have screaming hot sex with Aaron, *and* Tom Gentry ended up giving us both a bonus in our paychecks for getting the research work done so quickly. I made sure he found out the next day that Benson had nothing to do with the project, and Aaron made sure he found out that I'd helped.

The whole night ended up being a winner all around. Not to mention that Benson's been even crankier than usual since he got left out of Tom's kudos, *and* Aaron can't walk by the spot where we did it without blushing. Which is super hot.

Work life is good.

"Jeremy!" Iris Sprysky appears at my desk wearing a flowy pink pants suit with bright orange Crocs. I didn't know Crocs came in so many colors until I started working with Iris. "Tom and I missed you for morning meditation today."

Considering that she and Tom meditate when the sun rises—which was somewhere around 5:10 this morning—I have a feeling they're going to keep missing me at morning meditation sessions. But I'm sure she'll keep inviting me. "Sorry about that, Iris. What's up?" It's four o'clock, and as good as work has been lately, I'm looking forward to getting out of here. I set a pile of paperwork that needs to be filed aside and try not to grin as my eyes pass over *the spot* in the main office area. And yeah, I'm definitely calling it *the spot* from now on.

"I've heard from Jen. She's decided to extend her maternity leave this fall."

"Oh." Good for her, but I'm not sure what that has to do with me. I'm filling in for Jen this summer, but the position was always supposed to be just a temporary one. Maybe they want me to help train a new front desk person to replace Jen?

Iris clears her throat when I don't say anything else. "Jeremy, Tom and I have been speaking. We know you'll be heading back to school in the fall, but we're wondering if you might want to stay on here part-time through the next year. You run the office quite efficiently, and we'd rather hire someone to support you than have to teach someone our systems again from the ground up. Is that something you'd be interested in?"

Now I'm pretty sure I know what the phrase *my jaw dropped* actually means because I swear my mouth legit falls open as she's talking. They're offering me a job? Because they want to?

Because they think I'm good at what I do?

"I . . . ." Words have failed me. I'm suddenly more silent than Jamie Morin with a romance novel in his hands.

"You don't have to decide right now. We still have a few weeks before we need to post any positions." Iris stands up. "Jeremy, I'm curious. Have you ever thought of applying to law school?"

If I had a glass of water in front of me, I swear I'd be doing a spit take right now. "Me? Law school?"

"Yes, you. Tom and I were both very impressed with the work you did on that research project with Aaron last week. You're very good with clients, and you seem to enjoy the work we do here. Why not consider it?"

Because I'm a party boy who doesn't care about the future. That's the answer, and I know it. But I'm starting to realize something: Iris doesn't see me that way at all. Tom either, apparently. They think I'm good at what I do. Tom even called me "highly competent" the other day. To them, I'm not that guy who hangs out at frats and pulls Bs and Cs when I bother to show up to class.

They think I could *fucking go to law school.*

"I guess I'll think about it," I finally tell Iris, because what else am I supposed to say? I'm still picking my jaw up off the floor. Metaphorically speaking, of course.

"Good. And whether you decide on that path or not, I hope you choose to stay with us in the fall. We'd love to keep you here, Jeremy." Iris nods at me quickly before she heads into the conference room.

I go back to work, filing papers and answering phones, but her words stay in my head for a long time.

We'd love to keep you.

No one in a position of authority over me has wanted to keep me for anything for a long time. Not my professors. Definitely not my mother.

No one since my father, really.

Iris's words are still ringing in my ears while I help the friend group set up the most complicated board game in human history that night. We've just finished pushing together some tables at the back of V and V so Autumn and Briar can teach us this game the bookstore ordered that the two of them have gotten obsessed with. Apparently, it involves magic and taking over other peoples' land? I was only half-listening.

"It's going to take me like four hours to learn the rules to this," I complain as I try to figure out which of the eighteen stacks of cards go on which spot on the board. "Couldn't we just play a nice round of Trivial Pursuit or something?"

"Really, Jeremy. I would think you, of all people, would be open to learning new things," Autumn tells me with a sly smile.

"Oh, I'm *very* open to learning new things. I've been considering taking up connect-the-dots. I can use your twelve bazillion freckles for practice, right?" Autumn's got strawberry blonde hair and freckles that basically cover her body. It's a pretty hot look, actually, and I spend a lot of time alternating between telling her that and making fun of her for it. She doesn't seem to mind. Like Lexy, she gives as good as she gets.

"It's amazing what a person can do with edible body paint, some connect-the-dots skills, and freckles as impressive as mine," she tells me seriously. "You'll likely need to improve your speed and stamina at connect-the-dots before I'll consider a session with you." Then she runs off to help Briar get more cider from the bar, leaving me with some interesting mental images and the question of whether she was serious about the edible body paint.

Jamie's studying the directions of the game intently. "This game gets really good reviews," he tells me. "And Briar said it isn't that bad once you learn it. Lexy? You've played this before, right? Do you know what the hell they mean when they say 'turn the square peg'?"

Lexy and Jamie circle up around the boardgame box, and I retreat back toward the stage area of the bar, where Mindy and Aaron are talking about Mindy's plans for the new sugarhouse her family just built. Mindy's a farmer for life: she took over the Barnsby dairy farm and maple operation straight out of high school, and she's never looked back. I've always admired how sure she is about the path in front of her. She and Aaron are a lot alike that way.

"The startup cost for doing cheese products is a little extreme," Mindy's telling Aaron as I sidle up next to them. "But I'm projecting a profit within three years."

"Interesting," Aaron answers. "I've been proofing some contracts for a dairy co-op, and I . . . ."

I half-listen to them as I study the room around me, and something strange occurs to me: all of my friends have become adults. Full-on adults.

When Lexy and Jamie and I first met our freshman year, Jamie still had peach fuzz. Lexy and Mindy were both living at home. Briar wasn't even in our lives yet, and Aaron was the only one of us who was old enough to drink. Now Jamie and Briar live together and have a five-year plan for buying a house. We're all taking bets on when they'll get engaged. Lexy's about to apply to medical school. Mindy owns her own damn business, and she's talking about expanding it. And Aaron's going to be an actual real-life lawyer in a year if he can get those Leicester assholes out of his head.

And me? What am I going to be doing in a year? Technically I'm a business and marketing major, but only because my mom won't pay for my tuition if I'm not. I'm supposed to work for her in the Everett family business at some point, but the idea of ever setting foot in that office, where my father used to take me and let me play under his desk while he worked when I was a kid, makes my stomach ache. I've always known I'll probably never be able to walk in there again.

A dude I slept with once told me he thought I had Peter Pan syndrome. At the time, I thought that insult was kind of awesome —that it meant that I was achieving my goal of always living for the moment. But now? Now I'm starting to wonder what my life is going to look like if everyone I care about grows up around me and I stay still. Frozen.

"Jeremy?" Jamie's snapping his fingers in my face. "We finally got the game set up. You ready to play?"

"Yeah. Sorry." I pull on my best smile and try to shake that melancholy shit out of my head, but Aaron's looking at me like he knows something's up. I hope that means a cheer-up blow job is coming later. That's what I was hoping for in the first place when I gave up a Friday night out to play board games with the crew. I'm usually the first to bolt when Briar pulls out board games that have more than one page of directions.

The game doesn't turn out to be as bad as I thought it would. We all get the hang of it pretty quickly, and then everyone starts talking about other stuff between turns. No one's performing at V and V tonight, and the bar is quieter than usual, so it feels like we've got the whole back section of it to ourselves: just me and some of my favorite people teasing each other and trying to steal each other's "land" while music plays around us and Murph, the bartender on duty, keeps us in cider. Autumn asks what book Jamie and Briar are reading for their romance book club right now. "It's a regency romance," Jamie says. "Victorian era. All about a rake who sleeps with everything that moves. Pretty typical tropes, but the writing's good."

"Great characters, too," Briar agrees.

"What's a rake?" I ask.

"A Victorian character who's usually rich—in this case, a duke —who's known for having sex with every scullery maid who crosses his path until he meets the love of his life, and she tames him. Or he tames him," Briar adds.

"A rich dude who sleeps with everything that moves? Jeremy, I didn't know you were a romance novel!" Lexy says.

"Do I sell well?" I ask Briar, trying to ignore the weird knot that Lexy's words are creating in my stomach. Since when do I care if Lexy makes comments about my sex life? That's basically our everyday existence together. It's never bothered me before.

"The rake is a very popular character archetype," Briar confirms. "But I'm not sure we can call you a rake since you started this new job. You're playing board games with us on a regular basis lately."

"It's weird," Autumn adds. "I ran into some guys from the hockey house last week, and they asked me if you'd died or something. They're not used to going this long without seeing you at a party."

"It is weird," Lexy agrees. "And you haven't tried to talk any of us into cliff diving or going to an orgy lately. Is there a word for that character? For a rake who stops going to orgies?" Lexy asks jokingly.

"Reformed rake," Jamie and Briar say at the same time. They both laugh, and Jamie leans over to kiss Briar. "Jinx, babe."

I'm letting their words swirl around me, mixing them in my head against everything Iris said earlier and all the shit I was thinking about before we started playing, when Aaron speaks up for the first time in a while. "Jeremy's crushing it at work," he says. "They even asked him to stay on this fall."

How the fuck did he know that? The table goes quiet for a moment as everyone stares at me. "I'm probably not going to, though," I blurt out. "I don't do commitments, remember?"

Mindy shoots me one of her quiet smiles—those soft, knowing looks were how I ended up in the most ill-fated relationship of all time with her. "It's great that they offered, Jeremy," she says. "I'm glad they appreciate you."

"Maybe you really are reforming, J-Bear," Lexy adds cheerfully. "Going to finally join the rest of us in adult land?"

They're all still staring at me—even Aaron, who's looking at me like I'm one of his research projects at work. And suddenly, I can't figure out what the fuck I'm doing here. I'm playing board games when I could be out dancing and meeting people and getting laid. That's not me. I swore when I left Connecticut that I wouldn't miss out on a single life experience. What am I missing out on right now, by sitting at this table? And why am I trying to adult with everyone else when my adulthood is the only one at this table that's probably locked to a ticking clock?

Respectable adulthoods are for reformed rakes who don't have potential time bombs in their DNA. I've got to get out of here. I know that now.

But because I do love my friends, even if sometimes Lexy fucks with me just a little too much, I wait until the game is over. And then I announce that I have to leave. "Time to go be a rake," I joke. I wince even as I say it, wondering if that's too close to Aaron's line of not knowing when I'm sleeping with other people. But he doesn't look angry. Instead, he looks worried. Maybe even a little sad. His eyes follow me to the door of the bar and stay on me as I open it. They stay on me as I close it behind me.

That look on his face, the strange sadness in his eyes, stays with me on my drive to the Moo U hockey house, where the music is loud and the keg is flowing.

It stays with me the entire time I'm there, talking to a girl from my art history class who's definitely hitting on me.

And it stays with me when she invites me back to her place, and it *very* definitely stays with me when I finally tell her I'm tired and need to head home.

It stays with me when I stand in the hallway next to Aaron's apartment. I'm just a few steps away from the stairs that will lead up to my door—but I can't bring myself to go in that direction. Instead, I take three steps to my right and knock softly on Aaron's door.

It opens so fast I almost wonder if he's been standing there, waiting for me. "Can I come in?" I whisper, just in case Jamie and Briar are still awake.

He doesn't even hesitate. "Of course," he answers.

14

THAT TIME AARON SAILED WITHOUT SAILING

"Okay, team." Tom claps his hands together and then holds them for a moment in prayer position while he takes a long breath in. "We've got a big pro bono case we need to get to work on. A farmstand in the community is on the verge of bankruptcy. Their landlords are pulling a fast one with rent hikes. We suspect the farmstand is being forced out, and we've got limited time to step in before they're evicted from their land." He turns on the screen in the conference room, and I can't believe it when I see the name of the website that comes up.

"Tursky Farms?" I blurt out. "They're about to go bankrupt?" Tursky Farms is in Morse's Line. My family has shopped there for years. I'm pretty sure the first pumpkin I ever carved came from Tursky Farms.

"Unfortunately, yes." Iris shakes her head. "This case is going to require significant hours. We're thinking we'd like one of you two to take a lead role on the project." She nods at me and Benson. "Do either of you feel ready for that?"

Do I feel ready to take a lead role on the case of one of my favorite businesses when their entire livelihood is at stake? Uh, no. Do I want to? Hell, yes. "I do," I say at the exact same time Benson says, "Of course I'm ready for that."

Benson narrows his eyes. "With all due respect to Aaron," he says smoothly, "I have more knowledge of proprietorship and rental laws in Vermont. Since I actually go to school here."

Geez, I hate this guy. "With all due respect to Benson," I say, "I've been visiting that farmstand since I was a little kid. It's in my hometown. And I've actually set foot on a farm before."

Benson swings around to send me a cool look. "I'm sure I can find a pair of boots once I'm made the lead on the project," he says smoothly.

"Hey, team." Tom holds up his hand. "There's no need to mess up our office chi here. It's good to know you're both interested. We'll chat and get back to you. Now, Miguel," he says, addressing one of the associates at the other end of the table. "Can you give us an update on the Rogers case?"

The meeting goes on, but I can't focus on much except the Turskys. Our family has been in dire financial straits a few times, and that's terrifying enough when you at least own your land and your own fate. I can't imagine how scary it must be to know that you're about to lose years and years of hard work because of something you can't even control, like who your landlords are. I'm still thinking about that when Tom dismisses the meeting and sends us all home for the day.

"I can't wait to see the look on your face when I get the farmstand case," Benson says to me quietly as we pass Jeremy's desk.

"You don't even care about that farmstand."

"I definitely do not care about some stupid fucking vegetables," Benson agrees. "I just care about showing your ass to everyone else in this firm." He flounces off into our tiny office and shuts the door behind him.

"Deep breaths, Aaron," Jeremy says. "Deep breaths. Try to imagine him standing next to the manure pit at Tiny Acres. Maybe I walk by and accidentally nudge him. He slips. Next thing you know, he's falling right into all that shit."

I burst out laughing. "That's terrible," I tell him. "And actually, we shouldn't joke about that. People can die in manure pits."

"Really?" He wrinkles his nose. "That *is* terrible. Well, if anyone deserves an outro from the world as smelly as that one, I suppose it would be Benson Lewis. What's he talking about, anyway?"

I give Jeremy the quick rundown of the Tursky case and the stakes involved while the rest of the firm is packing up around us. It's late, past closing time, and I'm surprised Jeremy is even still here.

I can't help but wonder if he's been waiting for me to get out of the staff meeting.

"Fuck," Jeremy says when I finally finish the story. "Benson's really nailed exactly how to piss you off."

"I think I'm too tired right now to be pissed." I rub the corners of my eyes with my fingers. Work's been good this week, but busy as hell. A dick-measuring contest with Benson is the last thing I want to add to my to-do list right now.

"You need a break," Jeremy says softly. He looks thoughtful. "You have anything you need to do after work?"

"I should probably do more work on the research for the—"

"Nope." Jeremy cuts me off mid-sentence. "Pack up your stuff. Then meet me at my car. We officially have plans."

I'm too tired to argue—not to mention that the last time I let Jeremy take the lead on making plans for us, I ended up having some of the best sex of my life in the middle of our office floor. I'm not going to risk missing out on something that good again. "Where are we going?" I ask.

Jeremy grins at me as he picks up his backpack. "We're going to The Fuck Boat," he says.

"The Fuck Boat," as Lexy calls it, is Jeremy's family's sailboat. It's docked on Lake Champlain, though I've never understood why. As far as I know, Jeremy's family hardly leaves Connecticut, and there's plenty of water there. But the boat's been docked here since we were freshmen, and it's become a legendary part of the Jeremy Everett ethos. I'm pretty sure Jeremy's wooed half of Burlington there. Hence: The Fuck Boat.

I've never been to it before, and I'm not confused about why we're going there now. Or upset about it either. Sex with Jeremy on a sailboat sounds like exactly the stress reliever I need at the moment.

I'll admit, there was a minute there when I was starting to think of this fling Jeremy and I have going as more than just a fling. It's hard not to see the potential for a relationship with someone when they're setting up candles on picnic blankets for you. But then game night happened, and Jeremy disappeared out into Burlington's nightlife, and I quickly remembered that this is all just temporary. The candles, the great sex, the way Jeremy makes me feel like the most important person in the world—none of it was designed or built to last. By the time he appeared on my doorstep later that night, I'd gotten the reality of our situation back into my head. I'm not going to let myself forget it again.

Nope. I'm going to take a page out of Jeremy's book, live in the moment, and enjoy some sex on The Fuck Boat.

Summer days are long in northern Vermont, and even though it's already evening, the sun is still bright overhead when Jeremy parks the car in the marina parking lot. The sky and the water are matching shades of perfect blue, and white clouds drift overhead, casting shadows on the sparkling lake below. I follow Jeremy past a large building with a huge sign that says SHOWERS in the window and onto a wooden dock with a series of smaller docks sticking off from it like appendages. The air is clear and smells of salt and sweetgrass, and I let the scene around me pull all the thoughts of Benson and work and bankrupt farmstands from my head as I follow Jeremy across creaking wooden planks.

The sailboat's smaller than I expected, honestly. Given the wealth Jeremy's family has, I sort of expected the thing to be yacht-like. But it's just a basic sailboat. I don't know much about the lengths or sizes of sailboats, but it looks like it wouldn't fit all that many people. At one end is a small seating area and a steering wheel—I'm guessing the captain sits there—and there's a cabin area jutting up slightly in the center. The boat's also a lot older than I expected it to be. Still, you can tell it's taken care of. The paint on it looks fresh, and the name of it shines brightly on one side: DELIA'S DREAM. Jeremy disappears inside the lower cabin for a minute and reappears with a giant bottle of wine, two water bottles, and a huge bag of potato chips. "Classy, right?" he says, grinning at me as he hands over the wine.

"I dunno, man." I send him a sly smile. "After all the tales I've heard of The Fuck Boat, I sort of expected you to come out with a bottle of Dom Perignon and jars of caviar. Isn't that why Lexy's always calling you *extra*?"

He stops for a moment, studying me while he pulls a corkscrew out of his pocket. "You never make me feel like I have to be extra Jeremy around you," he finally says.

I'm not sure I fully understand what those words mean to him —but I know they leave me feeling as warm and comforted as if I've just taken a sip of my dad's famous chicken soup.

Then he sets to work pulling cushions and bean bags out from the cabin below. Soon the two of us are cuddled together in a giant nest of softness in the seating area, drinking cheap chardonnay out of paper cups and eating cheddar and sour cream chips while The Lumineers play in the background. Jeremy's boat is on the very end of one of the marina docks, and there's no one around to hear or see us. The back of this boat is our own little world.

I settle into the cushions and don't ask any of the obvious questions, like why we're not actually sailing anywhere, or why this boat is even in Vermont in the first place. Instead, I sink back into a bean bag, take a sip of wine, and lean over to press my lips against Jeremy's.

He tastes like vanilla and potato chips, and for one perfect moment, he feels like the only thing in the world. Even if it is just a temporarily perfect moment.

Some very excellent blow jobs happen under a blanket Jeremy produces from somewhere, and then he curls up into my arms in one of the giant beanbags. He's just slightly shorter and smaller than me, and he fits almost perfectly against my body. The song on the speaker now is something about a person being someone else's bright side of life, and I'm not paying much attention to the lyrics until Jeremy says, "This boat was my dad's favorite place. His bright side, I think. He used to get so excited every summer when it was finally warm enough to take it out on the water. We'd spend hours together on this lake. He taught me to swim. Fish. Sometimes we'd just sit around, letting the boat rock below us, talking and doing nothing at all. He loved sailing."

I close my eyes and imagine a young Jeremy: eyes sparkling with life and real smiles, not manufactured ones. "You going to take me sailing today, Jeremy?"

Jeremy traces a hand against the bottom hem of the undershirt I've stripped down to. "Actually, I don't know how to sail."

"What?" My eyes fly open. "But this is The Fuck Boat. Isn't that what you do on it? Sail and woo people?"

Jeremy laughs. "Second part, yes. The first part, no. Once in a while, I'll hire someone to captain the boat if I want to take it out with other people. They always assume I hire someone so I can drink. But most of the time, I just hang out on it like you and I are now." He shrugs. "No one's ever even bothered to ask if I actually know how to sail. Not even Lexy or Jamie. They all just assumed."

Now I have more questions than ever. "Why is your boat in Vermont, anyway?" I ask. "I thought you grew up in Connecticut."

"My granddad grew up in Vermont," he says. "Not far from here, actually, in a little town near Stowe. His family didn't have much money, but he put himself through college and went to Connecticut for work, and he met my grandmother there. He loved Vermont. As soon as he had enough money, he bought a ski condo in Stowe and a boat to put on Lake Champlain. I've always lived in Connecticut, but my dad used to take me back here for most of our vacations. He replaced the first boat eventually and bought this one when I was a little kid." He snorts. "My mom used to hate it. She always talked about how 'uncivilized' Vermont is compared to Connecticut. That's where the boat's name came from. It was my dad's idea of a joke. Didn't go over very well."

"Uncivilized? It's not like we don't have indoor plumbing or something."

"Yeah, she's a total snob. Mostly, though, I think she just resented how much my dad and I liked spending time here together. He'd sail the boat, and I'd help him—he always called me his co-captain. I was supposed to learn to sail on my own, but I never did. It's a long story." Jeremy's face goes hard in the falling light of the late Vermont evening.

"I'm sorry," I whisper. I don't know what else to say.

Jeremy sighs. "I was always a lot closer to him than her. My dad was a giant teddy bear, and my mom's more like a porcupine. Somehow it worked for their marriage, but when it came to parenting . . . ."

Sometimes I think Jeremy is the most complicated puzzle I'll ever try to put together, but right now, it almost feels like he's just handed me the corner pieces I've been searching for. "Is that why you picked Moo U for school? For your dad?"

"Yes and no." Jeremy turns over slightly in my arms. "When he first got word from his docs that he might have—well, you know—he brought me here to tell me. To this boat." He peers around us at the water and sky. "To this exact spot on this boat, actually."

"Jeremy," I whisper. "That's . . . ."

"It was awful," he finishes. "But he made it clear he didn't want me spending one moment I had mourning or missing him. He made me promise that I'd never forget how little time we get on this planet. He told me to make sure I treated every single moment I got like it was the most important one I'd ever lived." Jeremy's eyes are filling with tears now, and I squeeze him tighter into my arms. "You know the tattoo on my ass?"

Of course I do: it's legendary on the Moo U campus. Jeremy is the guy with YOLO tattooed right across his left butt cheek. Videos of Jeremy Everett's buttocks have gone viral more than once. "Yeah."

"I got that the day he was officially diagnosed. And then I chose Moo U for my college the next day." He flips further into my arms until he's staring at me, his eyes boring into mine. "I know people make jokes about this boat. I know they make jokes about my tattoo. But for me, they're both reminders, you know? Important ones."

"Jeremy," I whisper again.

He takes my face in his hands and leans his forehead into mine. "Please don't say anything else, Aaron. I just wanted you to know all that. And now I want you to make me forget it." He stands up and holds out his hand for mine. "C'mon. Let's go down into the cabin. What I want to do with you next isn't going to be quiet."

It's like time swirls slowly around us as I follow him down into the small cabin of the boat. There's a tiny kitchen, which isn't much more than a sink, an eating area, and an alcove with a giant bed that takes up almost every single inch of space. Jeremy strips his shirt off over his head and drops his pants and underwear to the floor. He's standing there, naked, his golden skin shining in the sunlight that's peeking through the windows of the boat. "Fuck me, Aaron," he whispers. "I want you to fuck me until I forget."

His skin is hot against my hands as I press my palms against his cheeks and hold him still while I kiss him long and hard. I drop one hand down his body, feeling him shiver as I move it across one nipple and then the other, and I bring it to a stop to circle it over the head of his dick. He moans into my mouth as he undoes the button on my pants. "Need you inside of me," he whispers.

"I should probably warn you," I tell him, "that I don't have a lot of experience. Still kind of a newbie, remember? I've only done anal a few times."

Jeremy shoves my pants down my body and takes my hand in his. He drags it back and forth across his cock and licks at his lips. "Good thing you're such a perfectionist, then," he whispers. "I have no doubt you're going to put your best effort in and take all my feedback very seriously."

I laugh out loud. "You're such a brat." I step away long enough to pull my shirt over my head, and then I tackle him into the bed.

For a long time, we just lay there, grinding into each other and kissing so hard that Jeremy's lips start to feel swollen against mine. At some point, he puts a container of something into my hand. "Get me ready," he says huskily, and then he pops the container open.

I pour the lube into one hand while I start nibbling at his nipples with my teeth. Jeremy gaps and thrusts up, and I take the opportunity to sink one finger gently, slightly, into his hole.

"A+ so far," he says. "How the fuck do you always know exactly how to turn me on?"

The truth is that it isn't difficult. Jeremy's body is so responsive, so reactive, that I've already mapped every single part of it I can touch. His nipples are two of my favorite areas to play with. I take a swipe at the other one with my tongue while I tease at his hole.

Jeremy writhes under me while I slowly prep him. He isn't kidding about the feedback; every few minutes, he manages to stop moaning long enough to give me positive reinforcement ("fuck, you're so hot when you do that") or suggestions for improvement ("a little deeper, a little deeper now"). Just watching him thrust and pump upward as I prep him has my cock so hard I'm sure I'm going to explode at any moment. I'm more than a little relieved when Jeremy grabs my wrist with his hand and whispers, "Want you in me now."

He looks so perfect like this—all splayed out on the bed, with one of my fingers still inside his body. I don't want to ever take it out. I love the way it feels when he pushes back and forth, up and down, on it. But my cock wants to be where that finger is, and it's not waiting any longer. I nearly come when Jeremy pulls a condom out of a drawer and slowly rolls it over me, but I somehow manage to keep myself together.

I lean over him, his legs up around my neck. I trace my other hand over his cheek, his forehead, and then back down his neck, while he pulls my face down so he can kiss me, hard.

He's so fucking perfect exactly the way he is, and I just want to hide him in this cabin forever. Far away from the pain the world has inflicted on him.

I thrust inside him in one movement, and Jeremy cries out and wraps his arms around my neck. "Aaron!"

I'm ready to explode inside of him at any moment, so I go slowly at first, easing in and out and then moving hard at the end of each push. I know I'm hitting his prostate perfectly because of the way he calls out and clutches at my hair every time. Our movements alternate between slow and soft and hard and desperate, and then they get more and more desperate. Every time I push back inside of him something lights up inside of me, and I don't want this feeling to ever end—I want to live on Jeremy Everett endorphins forever. But my dick is practically shaking inside of him now. "Jeremy," I whisper urgently.

He grabs for one of my hands and places it over the top of his cock with his own. "Come with me!" he shouts.

I do. I come hard and fast, yelling into the space of the alcove as I explode into the condom. My brain can't help but wonder what it would be like to cum inside of him, my skin against his, every inch of us melding together. I feel him lose himself in our hands, liquid suddenly covering both of them. We fall onto our sides together, me spooning him.

"Definite A+," Jeremy says quietly as he nuzzles into my arms. "Effort and execution were both very solid. For someone who claims you haven't done this a lot . . . ." He traces a hand up my arm. "I never would have known you aren't an expert."

I laugh as he snuggles into me more deeply. I can feel him drifting off in my arms, and I'm tired too, but my mind is suddenly buzzing with a thought I can't let go of.

It's true that I haven't had a lot of sex, so I'm not sure I know exactly what it's always supposed to feel like. But I do know one thing.

That felt a lot more like making love than it did like sex.

"Sorry I couldn't take you sailing," Jeremy whispers. He closes his eyes, and his lashes brush softly against my skin.

But you did, I think. *You did.*

I fall asleep imagining a world where Jeremy and I are more than a summer fling: where we're the kind of couple Jamie and Briar are. Together forever, the two of us against the world.

Then I wake up. Jeremy has already left the bed, and I can hear his footsteps on the deck above me. The empty cabin rocks gently on the water, and I'm instantly reminded that there's no world where the dream I just had is possible. Jeremy's committed to living in the present, and that means the two of us have no future.

I have to spend the summer enjoying this fling while I have it. YOLO.

15

THAT TIME JEREMY SAW FIREWORKS

"I still can't believe you're spending the Fourth of July with us." Jamie holds out his beer to me, and I tip mine back against it. "Who would've thought? Jeremy Everett at a family-friendly fireworks celebration in Morse's Line."

I'm a little surprised, too, if I'm being honest. I spent last Fourth of July at a huge sorority party, where I managed to end up in what conventional wisdom would definitely call an orgy. Several Moo U hockey players of various genders were involved, but I never kiss and tell. "I thought it was time for something different this year," I reply. I *do not* let myself look over at Aaron, who's sitting on a camping chair on the other side of me, catching potato chips Lissie is throwing at him.

We're sitting on a hill overlooking fields of farmland, surrounded by blankets and chairs and picnic baskets. The sun is just starting to set, and soon Morse's Line will start their annual fireworks show. I'm not expecting much, to be honest. Aaron already warned me that the Morse's Line fireworks budget this year sustained some cuts when they decided to restore an old railroad bridge.

Why I said I'd come here tonight, instead of heading to one of the hundreds of parties happening in Burlington right now, is still a mystery to me—except that every single time Aaron glances over at me and smiles, my dick twitches, and then my choice isn't much of a mystery at all.

I shift in my chair and mentally order my cock to stand down. I may let it take over for me with decision-making fairly often, but it's not going to get its way while we're in the middle of a field surrounded by every single member of Aaron's family.

"How's work going, Aaron?" Frank, Aaron's dad, sips at a soda and relaxes back into his chair. During moments like this with the Morins, it's sometimes hard for me to believe that Frank and Aaron ever had the problems they did. He looks every bit the perfect father right now, studying Aaron with concern and pride.

Maybe there's hope for my mother after all.

Then I remember the email she sent me last week and wince. It was one line. *I will not tolerate this lack of communication. Email me immediately, Jeremy.*

Then again, maybe not.

"It's great," Aaron says. "Well, I mean, it mostly is. Lots of tough cases right now."

Ellie sighs from her seat next to Frank. "I heard your firm is working with the Turskys."

"You heard about that?" Aaron asks anxiously.

"I saw Fran Tursky in the Quick Stop last week. She said if the legal route doesn't work, they're closing down at the end of this year. Such a shame. That family's worked so hard their whole lives. They at least deserve to be able to make choices on their own terms." She frowns and then brightens suddenly. "Are you going to be part of their case?"

Aaron looks uncomfortable. "I, uh, can't say. Client confidentiality and all that." But both of his parents nod knowingly.

Frank leans over to pat Aaron on the shoulder, and the smile on his face is bigger than I've ever seen on him before. In fact, this might actually be considered *beaming* by Frank Morin standards.

"Well, son, look at you. Using all that knowledge of yours to help the people around here who really need it." He raises his soda can into the air. "If you win that case, I'll be awfully proud, Aaron."

Ellie grins broadly as she passes Aaron a cookie. Jamie and Briar are deep in a game of War with Lissie, and I'm sure I'm the only one who sees the look that crosses Aaron's face at this father's words: "If you win that case, I'll be awfully proud."

I've been around Frank Morin long enough at this point to know he didn't mean that *if* the way it sounded. He's always been proud of Aaron, and he always will be—he's made that clear since Aaron and the Morins made up last year. But Frank's never been great with the whole "using words" thing, and I'm pretty sure sentences like that are exactly how Aaron ended up disappearing to Boston without a word when he got into law school.

Right now, Aaron's trying to smile back at his dad, but he looks like he's clenching every single muscle in his face. There's a definite tension headache in his future if he doesn't let go of his jaw soon. There's also a glint in his eyes, like his mind is racing at a million miles an hour, trying to solve the entire case from a camping chair in the middle of a cow pasture.

"Aaron, let's go get a hot dog." I stand up fast and hold out my hand. Aaron looks up at me, blinking as if he's forgotten I'm there. "Hot dog?" he asks. I might as well be speaking a foreign language.

"Hot dog. You know, the things high schoolers are selling over there." They're raising money for a trip to Washington, D.C., and right now their stand seems like the perfect excuse to get Aaron a few steps away from the twelve tons of pressure I know he just heaped on top of himself.

"Sure, okay. Hot dog." Aaron takes my hand and lets me drag him up from his chair.

"Grab me a brownie! The maple kind!" Briar calls after us as we walk away.

"How does he not have cavities in every single one of his teeth?" I mutter under my breath as I lead Aaron away from the

Morins' spot in the field. I don't bring us in the direction of the hot dog stand, though. Instead, I start walking toward the creek Lissie was showing me earlier on the other side of the field. We're near the elementary school where she and Jamie and Aaron all used to go, and she told me that the kids from her school sneak over to the creek to "make out with each other," as she put it, giggling.

Seems like the perfect place to bring Aaron right now. If I can't get that tension out of his face by kissing it away, nothing's going to work.

"Where are we going?" Aaron asks when he finally wakes up to the fact that we're nowhere near the food stand. The sun has almost set now, but there's still just enough light in the sky to see that we've arrived at a gently rushing creek nestled at the entrance of some woods. The crowd of people waiting for the fireworks are up the hill from us about a hundred yards away, and we may as well have walked into our own little world. No wonder the kids of Morse's Line use this place as their own private make-out spot.

"I thought you needed a break." I grab the blanket I picked up when we left the Morins and stretch it across the ground. "What your father said really freaked you out, huh?"

"What? No." Aaron falls down onto the blanket next to me while he worries his lips with his teeth. "Why would it? He said he's proud of me."

"You sure what he said isn't bothering you?" I ask. If Aaron's not ready to talk about that conversation, I'm not going to force him.

Aaron sighs. "Okay, it bothered me. Why'd he have to say 'if' like that?"

"But you do know he didn't mean it the way it sounded?" I ask gently. As someone who grew up with a mother who did make a lot of her love and pride conditional, I understand what that kind of parenting looks like. And it doesn't look like Frank.

"I know. I mean, I think I know that." Aaron lays back on the blanket, staring up at the sky. It's not a perfectly clear night.

Clouds circle the edge of the horizon, adding to the darkening quality of the night that's settling over us. "Sometimes it's just hard not to feel like I have everything to prove, you know? Like I have to show this was all worth it—leaving them. Disappearing the way I did. Going to law school."

"Getting into Harvard wasn't enough proof for you that you're a fucking badass?" I tease as I lay down next to him. "Benson would shit bricks to have what you have, you know."

"I've gotten that impression," Aaron answers dryly. The moon's rising in the sky now as the sun disappears underneath it, and I can feel Aaron's hand tracing gently in my palm. "That's why part of me wants to call Dad on it when he says stuff like that, you know? Tell him how it feels. Because I know you're right —he didn't mean that the way it came out."

"Why don't you? Say something, I mean?"

Aaron frowns. "I'm not sure. Maybe because we're still finding our way around each other after everything that happened. It's like there are still all these landmines sitting in the middle of our conversations. I think we're both doing everything we can not to set the other off." He sighs. "I really don't want to be the first one to blow us up."

I can understand that. Still . . . . "Well, if there's one thing I've learned from being the town rake—isn't that what Jamie and Briar called me?—it's that life doesn't get lived without a little conflict."

Aaron laughs as he rolls over to face me. The sky is almost completely dark now, and I can hardly see the hill where we left the Morins behind. The fireworks should be starting soon. "Look at you, being all Dear Abby. When did you get so wise?"

"Must be around the same time I started working at one of the best law firms in Burlington," I tell him, deadpan. But Aaron just shakes his head.

"Seriously, Jeremy. I don't think I tell you enough how glad I am you ended up working with me at Sprysky and Gentry this summer. The work's been hard in ways I never imagined. I'm not sure how I'd have made it this far if you weren't there."

His words are so weirdly reminiscent of what Iris said about me staying at the firm that I almost jolt back in surprise. But Aaron leans over to kiss me, and I quickly forget to lean away because all my mouth wants is to stay attached to his for as long as humanly possible.

There's a loud crack somewhere above us, and then lights begin sparkling in the sky. I have no idea, though, if the Morse's Line bridge rebuild made their fireworks display subpar or not. I'm too busy paying attention to all the fireworks happening on the blanket.

"Where were you guys tonight?" Jamie asks as he, Briar, Aaron, and I trudge up the steps of The Pink Monstrosity, holding the coolers and bags of food that Ellie and Frank loaded up with us before we left the farm. "You missed the whole fireworks show."

"We didn't miss it," Aaron tells him. "We just found another spot to watch while we were looking for hot dogs."

"Where?"

"The creek," Aaron says, and I immediately wince at the look on Jamie's face. Aw, shit. Has Aaron just blown our cover?

"The creek?" Jamie asks incredulously as he unlocks the door to his and Briar's apartment. "You mean where all the kids used to go to make out? What the hell were you two doing down there?"

Briar's staring at us with a look on his face I can't read—not like that's unusual for Briar—and Aaron starts sputtering. "Make out? What do you mean *make out*? People go there to do other things, too! It's just a pretty little creek, okay? It's not like—"

Oh, for fuck's sake. If I don't dive in and save him soon, he really is going to blow our entire cover. "Aaron was just showing me around, and we ended up there by accident," I say calmly. "We did see some people fooling around in the dark. Not a bad spot to do it. I'll have to remember that place if I ever take any of my dates up to Morse's Line."

Jamie snorts. "I'm not sure I can imagine you hooking up with anyone by a creek."

Aaron coughs loudly.

"Well, I'm going to bed," I announce. "See you all tomorrow!" Jamie and Briar disappear into their apartment while they wave good night, and I collapse dramatically against the wall next to Aaron's door. "You," I tell him, "would make a terrible secret agent."

Aaron grimaces. "I know, right? My friend Peter always says I'd be a terrible criminal lawyer because I've got no poker face. You think they suspected anything?"

"Jamie? Definitely not." I shake my head. My best friend's as oblivious as he always is, thank goodness. "Briar? Well, Briar, I'm never too sure about. But I think he would have said something by now if he knew what was going on." I shrug. "We're just going to have to get you a better poker face. Want to start practicing now?" I whisper in his ear. "In my bed?"

He practically chases me up the stairs to my apartment. We don't get much practice with schooling Aaron's expressions when he's lying, but we do get some other very important practice in. I fall asleep hard and fast, and I have the strangest dream.

Aaron and I are living in The Pink Monstrosity in Briar and Jamie's apartment. Aaron's getting ready for work and I'm making him coffee. He's asking me when I have work that day and then he tells me what he's cooking for dinner.

He kisses me goodbye and tells me he loves me, and as he leaves, I notice a ring on the third finger of his left hand. I look down at my own hand and see one there too.

And then I wake up.

Light is just starting to seep into the windows of my studio apartment. Aaron's fast asleep next to me, one arm wrapped around me and his head resting on my stomach. He's snoring softly.

Did I just dream about . . . *the future?* A future with Aaron?

I don't dream a lot, and when I do, those dreams are always vague and distant. They're never clear and distinct like this one was.

And they're definitely never of my future.

How can you dream of something that will never exist?

16

THAT TIME AARON CONSORTED WITH THE ENEMY

"Where have you been?" Benson snarls the minute I push open the door to our office.

I glance down at my watch. "At my house? It's eight o'clock in the morning."

"I meant yesterday," Benson says impatiently. "You didn't come into work."

I had a feeling this conversation was going to come up today. The firm was closed yesterday because it was the day after the Fourth of July. I had planned to go in anyway to finish up paperwork, but then . . . .

Well, let's just say Jeremy can be very convincing when he's got a bottle of maple syrup in one hand and a pack of condoms in the other.

Wait a minute. Is that why Briar's so obsessed with maple syrup? Now I can't get the image of my brother, Briar, and a bottle of maple syrup out of my head. I'm still trying to shake *that* mental picture out of my skull when Benson starts snapping at me again.

"And here I thought you were serious about wanting this farmstand project," he says. "But you were off with your fucktoy all day, weren't you?"

"Excuse me?" Sometimes the shit Benson says is so over-the-top obnoxious that I wonder if he walked out of the pages of one of Jamie's novels. If my summer at Leicester hadn't taught me that people do, in fact, have the ability to act like cartoon villains, I wouldn't believe he was real. "Who the hell are you talking about? And what's your problem, anyway?" My heart pounds slightly in my chest, and I will it to slow down. There's no way Benson could have figured out what's going on with me and Jeremy. And even if he did, who cares?

Except—I haven't looked into the HR policies on inter-office relationships. Shit shit shit. How could I have been so careless? I need to double-check the workplace handbook and possibly file some paperwork, and of course I'll need to talk to—

"Are you even listening to me?" Benson crosses his arms as he glares at me. "You and Mr. Secretary over there. It's pretty fucking obvious something's going on." He shakes his head. "Man, you really are just another entitled Harvard asshole. Too busy screwing around with your secretary to do your job right." He storms out of the office before I can even respond.

Jeremy appears at the office doorway while I'm still staring at it, my mouth open wide. "Thought I should drop by before you sent yourself into a shame spiral," he says cheerfully.

"He—I—knows—entitled?" I can't seem to form sentences properly. Too many of Benson's words are at war in my head. What if he's right? Am I shirking my job duties to mess around with Jeremy? There's no way I would have taken the full holiday off when I worked at Leicester. And I haven't looked into that HR paperwork, and I—

"Stop." Jeremy walks over and sets his hands on my shoulders. "Whatever your brain is doing right now, tell it to stop."

I snort. "Like it's that easy. The off-switch doesn't seem to be all that accessible for me. A few different therapists in Boston tried to help me find it. No luck so far."

"I think I might have it. Check your email." Jeremy gestures over to my computer. "I was CCed on something that should have just come to you—and Benson, unfortunately." Jeremy sighs. "He definitely hadn't seen it yet when he went off on you there. Or he had and he's even more of an asshole than we thought."

"Doesn't really seem possible," I mutter as I sign into my account. Right away I see the email Jeremy must be talking about: it's from Tom, and most of the firm is CCed.

I almost drop my coffee as I start reading. Tom wants Benson —Benny, as Tom calls him in the email—and I to take lead roles on the Tursky case. Evelyn will be overseeing us, but we'll be in charge of all the main research.

My first *real* case. My first one that feels like it really belongs to me—and it's for a family in the town where I grew up. A family I've known my whole life. I don't care whether lawyers are supposed to cry or not; tears start welling up in my eyes. "Holy shit," I whisper to the monitor. Then I spot another email from Iris directly to me and only me.

Keep up the great work—you deserve this case. You've been impressing everyone here! And it's nice to see you smiling more lately. I hope this means you're finding a balance between this work and your own life. —Iris

"Huh," says Jeremy as he reads over my shoulder. "Want me to call Benson back in here? I'm thinking we could do a musical number for him. The working title is 'Fuck You, I'm Awesome and You're Always Wrong.' You'll sing lead, of course. I'll see if I can work out the harmonies."

I burst out laughing. I swear, if the office wasn't filling up with people right now, I'd kiss him right here. But it is, so I settle for telling him that instead.

"Not a bad way to celebrate," he agrees. "But since we can't do that—at least not right now—I've got a better idea." He pulls his phone out of his pocket. "Jon's singing tonight at V and V. Briar texted the group asking if we all wanted to go. Let's do it. We'll toast your new case."

"Yeah, sound good. This is . . . it's so exciting. Except . . . ." Now that the news is settling in, I'm realizing something.

This means I have to work with Benson. A *lot*. A lot a lot.

A lot more than I already do. And that already feels like a lot.

"Except this means you have to work with Benson," Jeremy mutters. I'm not sure how he always manages to read my mind like that. I guess it's all just part of the Jeremy Everett experience. Jeremy sighs.

"Don't throw things at me," he mutters. "But what if . . . we invited him to come to V and V with us tonight?"

My stomach sinks. Spending entire workdays with Benson is bad enough. The last thing I want to do is spend my evenings with him too. But I also know it's not a bad idea. If Benson and I are going to work together, I'm going to have to convince him I'm not this pretentious dick he decided I was before he even met me. "Fine," I grumble. "I'll invite him. But can you have that musical number ready just in case he actually decides to come?"

"I'll work on my high kicks now," Jeremy says. He's so deadpan that for a minute I wonder if he's serious.

If anyone has a surprise high kick in their back pocket, it would be Jeremy Everett.

"Do you think Benson will actually show up?" I mutter to Jamie as we take turns sipping off the Shipley cider sampler in front of us. The bar side of Vino and Veritas is quiet and calm tonight, probably because it's the day after a long weekend. The lighting is low, setting off the rich, dark colors in the mahogany wood and leather that make up most of the décor. Jon's tuning up on stage, and the chords of his guitar echo through the room. Briar, Autumn, and Lexy are over at the bar, talking to Joss and Tanner. Joss is waving an egg around in one hand excitedly—and why he's standing around the bar area holding eggs is a question I'm not sure I want the answer to. Just before the egg looks like it's about to fly out of his hand, Tanner snags it from his fingers.

Maybe I won't order the scotch egg tonight.

Jeremy left the table a few minutes ago to say hi to one of the waitresses. I haven't seen him since.

Not that this bothers me. It definitely does not bother me at all.

"Do you want him to show up?" Jamie asks. He passes me the plate of cheddar-ale dip and bread we've been snacking on.

I frown. "I mean, he's an asshole. Of course I don't want him to come if he's going to act like an asshole. But we are running this case together. I feel like we need to bury the hatchet if we're going to do that well. Plus, he acted very strangely when I invited him. I expected him to get all high and mighty and tell me he doesn't have time for bars or something, but instead he looked . . . not unhappy. It was weird, honestly. So now I don't know what I want."

"Well, I have a feeling you're about to find out." Jamie gestures at the door. "That sure looks like a law student who's uncomfortable in new social situations to me."

I glance up to find he's right: Benson Lewis is standing in the doorway of Vino and Veritas, staring at his surroundings like he's landed on an alien planet. I quickly wave him over. I've been that person standing in the doorway of a strange bar before, and it's no fun.

Benson's still got on the suit he was wearing all day at work. He looks at Jamie and me warily as he slouches over to us and drops into a seat across from us. He nods at me. "Aaron," he says as he tugs his jacket off.

"Hi, Benson. Or do you prefer Benny?"

"I definitely do *not*," he practically growls. He looks over at Jamie. "You two have got to be related."

Jamie grins. "I'm the little brother. Nice to meet you." He and Benson shake hands. So far this whole invitation is going better than I expected. Benson hasn't made one snarky comment, and most people find Jamie's charming kindness irresistible. Maybe Jamie can convince Benson I'm not some evil tyrant out to ruin his life.

"Mmm hmmm," Benson mutters. "You're in law school too, I assume? Or pre-law?"

Jamie bursts out laughing. "Oh, hell no. I want to get my master's in library science."

Benson's eyes widen. "You're going to be a librarian?"

"Yup. And my boyfriend's a bookseller." He shrugs. "Aaron's the only wannabe lawyer in the family. The rest of us are all teachers and dairy farmers and musicians and book people." He wrinkles his nose. "Actually, when I say it like that, we sound like a pretty eclectic group." Briar starts gesturing to him from the bar. "I'll be right back. Let me grab you a beer, Benson. What would you like?"

Benson asks for some kind of IPA I've never heard of. Jamie leaves, and then it's just the two of us.

I take a sip of cider while Benson stares at me. "Why are you looking at me like that?" I finally ask.

"No one—I mean, none—." He's stuttering now. "No one in your family is a lawyer? None of you?"

"You knew I grew up on a farm," I remind him. That's come up more than once since the Tursky case came to the firm.

"Yeah, but I thought that was like a hobby farm. My uncle, he owns an investment firm down in Bennington and also has some land he leases and raises a few animals on—but he's no farmer. You mean you grew up on an actual farm? An actual dairy farm? That your family runs yourselves?"

I can practically see Benson's perspective of me switching angles in his head, but I'm not entirely sure why. "Yeah. My dad still runs it. He couldn't believe it when I told him I wanted to go to law school." That's an understatement, but I'm not about to get into all my family drama with my nemesis.

"But . . . ." Benson frowns. "Your family owns a farm? And you went to Moo U? How the hell did you get into Harvard Law?"

I shrug and lean forward. "Honestly? It's kind of a mystery to me, too. I never expected to get in. But I worked my ass off in undergrad and graduated early, and I did well on the LSATs. Maybe they liked my essay? Who knows. You know how admissions committees are. It's all a crapshoot."

Benson's face clouds over. "It's not supposed to be," he mutters. "Some things are supposed to be guaranteed."

I sip at my cider while I wait for him to say more, but he doesn't elaborate. Finally, he says, "I need to impress the partners with this case we're leading."

"Me too," I agree. And for me, it's even more than that—I need to save that farm for my community. My family. But I have a feeling Benson's not going to understand that kind of motivation. "You willing to work together with me on it, or are you going to keep throwing me under the bus every chance you get?"

Benson rolls his eyes. "Whatever. Get a fucking thicker skin, will you? You're going to need it to finish Harvard."

He's probably right about that. I just nod and shrug. "I'm working on it."

Benson frowns. "Look. We both need this win. So yeah, we work together. And I won't say anything about you and the secretary getting it on."

I blush. "I was looking at the HR paperwork, and we're not actually required to say anything because under policy 7b—"

"Whatever," Benson interrupts. "The point is, I won't get in your way, you don't get in mine, we run this ship together, we get it done. Deal?"

It's not exactly a declaration that we should exchange friendship bracelets, but it's a start. I hold up my glass and gesture toward him. "Here's to the Tursky farm."

Benson nods begrudgingly.

"Wow, I had no idea Benson could even talk to other human beings successfully. You're like the asshole whisperer, Aaron." Jeremy finishes wiping his hands on a paper towel and throws it away as he studies his face in the mirror of the Vino and Veritas bathroom. "Did you see that he and Ty, that friend of Jon's, talked for like half an hour about Morgan horses?"

"Ty raises them. I think Benson said something about his younger brother and sister riding." I lean onto the row of sinks next to Jeremy. "And he's been friendly with Jamie and Lexy. He even said he liked Jon's music. Plus, he hasn't made any snarky comments to anyone about you and I getting it on."

Jeremy whirls around to look at me, something like panic in his eyes. "Benson knows?"

"Yeah." I sigh. "Somehow, he figured it out. Don't worry, though. I looked it up in the employee handbook, and because we're both temporary employees, we don't have to report it or say anything. And Benson promised he's not going to say anything to the partners."

"Who the fuck cares about them?" Jeremy heads for the door. "What if he slips and says something to Jamie? Or Briar? Fucking hell, Aaron, I can't believe he figured it out and you just left him out there with them!" Jeremy lunges for the door handle, but I quickly grab his arm.

"It really bothers you that much?" I ask him quietly. "Jamie finding out?"

Jeremy runs his hands through his hair. The lines on his forehead are scrunched together. I'm not used to seeing him like this: stressed. Anxious. I don't like it.

"I'm not ready for that," he finally says quietly. "I'm not ready for Jamie to look at me . . . differently." He shakes his head. "Especially because our maybe-or-maybe-not still an asshole coworker couldn't keep his mouth shut."

It stings to see exactly how much Jeremy doesn't want Jamie and the rest of my family to know we're together. Looking at him now, in this dimly lit bathroom, I'm reminded yet again that no matter how good Jeremy and I are together, and no matter how good what we have gets before the end of the summer, our relationship is always going to have an expiration date on it.

This is over the day I go back to Boston. I have to make sure I keep remembering that.

I pull in a deep breath. "Benson won't say anything. And if you're really worried, let's leave separately tonight. I'll take off soon, and you can come home with Jamie and Briar later. Okay?"

"Yeah, that sounds good. Yeah." Jeremy nods and smiles slightly as he thinks through that plan. "That's a great idea . . . especially after all those questions Jamie asked when we disappeared during the fireworks show. It's a really good idea. I'll see you out there, okay?" He quickly pecks his lips against mine and disappears out of the bathroom door.

I tell myself it's a good thing he left so quickly, without turning around or saying goodbye or acknowledging that we're probably not going to be able to spend the night together.

Yeah. It's a good thing.

I need a lot more practice letting Jeremy Everett walk away from me.

17

THAT TIME JEREMY TRIED TO BE GOOD

"I still can't believe you know how to make your own spaghetti sauce." Lexy frowns at the pot I'm stirring, like she doesn't totally trust it. "Are you sure that's not just weed oil mixed with oregano and tomatoes or something?"

"I'd eat that sauce," Mindy answers from where she's curled up on my couch scrolling through her phone.

"Of course you would, you're the hippie farmer in the family," Lexy replies. "Seriously, though, J-Bear. When the hell did you learn to cook?"

"I learned in high school," I explain as I quickly taste the sauce and start to add salt. "I have some skills and talents beyond knocking boots and doing keg stands, you know."

Lexy stares at me blankly. "I mean, I really didn't. In my defense, though, your keg stands are very impressive. That one you do in handstand form especially."

"He's pretty good at the whole knocking boots thing, too," Mindy calls from the couch.

"Thanks," I call back.

"Ewww, gross." Lexy pretends to cover her ears with her hands. "I do not need the mental image of you two boning. It took me all of sophomore year to cleanse that from my skull. And who calls having sex *knocking boots* anyway?"

"You're just jealous you don't have my way with language," I tell her as I breathe a slow sigh of mental relief. I do not feel like telling Lexy where I really learned to make marinara sauce: from my father, who learned it from his Italian mother.

Mindy stands up and stretches. "I'm getting borderline hangry. When's everyone else getting here?"

I glance at my phone, looking for new texts. "Jamie said he and Briar should be back from their club meeting in about ten minutes. Autumn's coming with them. We can bring the food down to their apartment since they have more space. Aaron . . . ." I scroll up through my messages. "Nothing yet. He must still be at the office."

"It's Saturday." Mindy comes over to smell the pot. "Yummm. This looks awesome, Jeremy."

"Thanks," I say proudly. I may not need other people's compliments, but that doesn't mean I don't enjoy them. "Aaron's been working overtime since he got assigned to this super important case. Really late hours. I don't think he'd eat if I didn't bring him dinner every night."

"You've been staying late with him, too, haven't you?" Lexy asks. "Neither of you have been around much this week."

I shrug. "I've been helping with some of the research. Like I said, it's an important case. Lots of implications for small farms in Vermont." It really sucks, what's happened to the Turskys. They put their life into that farm, and a ridiculous rent hike from some money-hungry land developers may destroy it. Not cool. "I'm trying to do my part to fight for the common man. Or common human. Why's language always gotta be so sexist?"

"Doesn't your family own a wealth management firm?" Mindy arches an eyebrow at me.

"They do. And they don't have shitty practices and morals or treat human beings like nothing more than dollar signs." As much as my mother and I manage to disagree on basically everything in the world, I've never disagreed with her business practices.

Lexy surprises me by hugging me suddenly around the waist. Lexy isn't exactly a hugger—in fact, one Christmas Jamie got her a shirt that said HUG ME AND DIE, BITCH. "Where the hell is this coming from?" I ask. I manage to pull the spoon from the pot before marinara ends up all over both of us.

Lexy shrugs and blows some hair off her forehead. "J, I know I give you a lot of shit, but I've always thought you were pretty fucking awesome. And you're next-level awesome this summer. You've been working so hard, and Aaron keeps saying how supportive you are at the office."

"I know, you barely recognize me," I joke.

Lexy and Mindy do that *twin* thing they sometimes do where they make the exact same movement at the same time: they both frown and shake their heads slightly, and it's like I'm seeing double.

"Nope," says Mindy quietly. "We recognize you just fine, Jeremy." She hugs me from the other side and tickles my ribs. The next thing I know, the three of us are on the floor wrestling and laughing like some kind of bizarre puppy pile full of red hair.

Lexy pops up out of the melee first. "I always knew more of the real Jeremy was buried underneath all that swagger," she says. I'm still trying to figure out what the hell I'm supposed to say in response to that when she yells out, "I fucking need fooood! Let's go bang on Jamie and Briar's door. They should be back by now."

She and Mindy start packing up wine and covering the sauce and debating whether they need to text Autumn to ask her to hurry Jamie and Briar up—and I sit there, trying to parse Lexy's words.

Is it weird that I'm not even sure who the real Jeremy is anymore? Aren't you supposed to just know things like that about yourself?

I'm still trying to figure out the answer to that question two days later. Aaron and Benson are buried under case research, and I'm looking at some tax forms for them when my phone lights up with a new message.

DANGER! MOM! reads the name on the screen.

I'm definitely ready to lock my phone back up and slide it into my backpack, where I won't hear it vibrate, but then I see the first few words of the message.

And I open it. Because I'm a dumbass like that.

Danger! Mom!: *Jeremy, I've been patient. You're nearly a college graduate, and your immature behavior has gone on long enough. You are expected in Wellsford by August for at least a weekend. Otherwise, I will not be paying for your senior year of college. Please call me with questions.*

It's like I'm one of her clients who forgot to remit payment on a bill. I'm still processing her message when another text comes through—this one from my uncle.

Uncle J: *Jeremy, your mom just called. You really need to get home soon. I want to support you, but you're making it tough. You can't keep ignoring us like this.*

Actually, I've got about three years of college experience that proves otherwise. I stand up from my desk and pace around. When family shit stresses me out, my usual reaction is to disappear: into a bar, into a frat house, into a really hot human being's bed. I could take any of those options right now. The office closed an hour ago, and it's not like I'm getting paid overtime for any of this extra work I'm doing with Aaron.

So yeah. Option #1: go be a rake all over Burlington. That option's sounding pretty good right now.

But maybe there's an Option #2.

I glance over at Aaron and Benson's office. They have the door half-closed and their heads down. Maybe I could blow off some steam with Aaron. He's been talking about wanting to take me to this ice cream stand. He and a bunch of the people around here call soft ice cream "creemees," a super weird term that I can't hear without snickering. Aaron claims I will happily call ice cream "creemees" with him once I have the peanut butter cone from this place, which is apparently life-changing. He keeps talking about how good it is with extra nuts on top.

Yeah. Making fun of a dessert with the word "creemee" in the title and extra nuts on top sounds like exactly what I need in my life right now. And maybe I'll even mention these texts to Aaron. He keeps telling me I can talk to him about all this stuff, right? And it's not like I'm any closer to solving my problems on my own. There's no way my mom's backing down here, and there's no way I'm dropping out of Moo U in my final year.

The more I think about it, the more ice cream—and maybe even some discussion of feelings—sounds better and better. I clean up my desk and knock on Aaron and Benson's office door.

Aaron and Benson are deep in conversation about something involving the Tursky's land rental contract, but Aaron looks up as soon as I walk in. "Hey, Jeremy. What's up?"

They're surrounded by stacks of papers and file folders, and Aaron's eyes are lined with dark circles. His tie is loose around his neck, his shirt pushed up at the sleeves, and now all I want to do is take him to bed and let him fuck me until we both fall asleep. And then I'm definitely making him sleep for like nine hours straight. "How much longer do you think you need to work today?" I ask him.

Benson looks up at me and snorts. "Are you kidding? We've got at least four more hours here. Maybe five. We need to get this brief done by tomorrow." The dude's not using the same "fuck-you" tone he used to use with Aaron and me constantly, but he still doesn't exactly sound friendly.

"Yeah, we're pretty in the weeds right now." Aaron sends me a tired smile. "I think Jamie and Briar wanted to do game night at

The Pink Monstrosity, but I'm probably going to have to tell them I'm out. You don't have to stay, though. You've already been such a huge help." The edge of his smile creeps up slightly, and if Benson wasn't here, I'd probably have at least a make-out session in my future.

But Benson is here, and Aaron clearly can't leave the office. Maybe for a real-life boyfriend, he could. Maybe. But for a friend-slash-summer-fling who can't figure out how to talk to his own damn mother?

Nah. I can't ask Aaron to give up on his overachiever values for that.

And now I'm back to Option #1, I guess. Time to hit the bars.

"You sure it's cool if I leave?" I ask. Now I know I've got to get out of here fast. If I stay too much longer, I'm going to break down and say something about those text messages. Aaron doesn't need to deal with any of my drama right now.

"I think we'll manage without our secretary fetching us coffee," Benson says coolly.

"Don't be an asshole," Aaron tells him sharply, and Benson at least has the decency to blush.

"We'll be fine," Aaron says. "Benny here can make the coffee." He winks over at me when Benson wrinkles up his nose, but I'm not in the mood for office jokes or dealing with Benson's temper right now.

"Cool, thanks," I tell Aaron. And then I'm out of there. Fast. And I don't look back.

"What do you think the meaning of life is?" Holding my head up is hard. I'm tired. Very, very tired. I wonder if the bar would be a good place to sleep. I won't know unless I try, so I lay my head down across it.

"Hmmm, the meaning of life." My brand-new drinking buddy raises his glass to his lips and frowns at it. Has he had as many as

I've had? I can't remember how many he's had. Maybe it was six? Or four? Does six go after four? "We-ell," he slurs, "Robert Herrick said we should all gather rosebuds while we may."

I squint at him. "I dunno what that means."

"It means we should use our time the right way!" He throws his arms wide, and liquid splashes out of the glass. "That's the name of the poem he wrote: 'To the Virgins, to Make Much of Time.'"

"Oh, that won't help me. I'm definitely not a virgin. Sometimes I wish I was, though." Life would be easier if I were a virgin, wouldn't it? Then I probably wouldn't be all hung up on Aaron right now.

"Hey, it's okay." My drinking buddy pats my arm. He's nice. I wish I could remember his name. He's also cute. I wish I wanted to sleep with him right now instead of Aaron.

"I kinda wish I wanted to sleep with you too," the guy mutters. Oops. I must have said that out loud. "But I always wanna sleep with allll the wrong people. You're not wrong enough for me, Jeremy."

I'm not sure what that means, but I don't have time to figure it out before Auden, the bartender on duty at Vino and Veritas tonight, sighs. "That would be a recipe for disaster, it would. You are both very definitely cut off."

"What? Why?" I try to sit up as fast as I can, but then I get dizzy. And dizzy is not good. Now my stomach's big mad that I ate all that cheddar-ale dip earlier. It tasted good. Very Vermont-y. "My new friend and I are discussing the meaning of *life*, Auden. Don't you think that's important?" I frown over at my drinking buddy. "I forgot your name, though. Can you tell me again?"

"Scott," he says as he downs the rest of his glass and sets it on the counter. He frowns. "You know what? I'm outta money anyway. We're going to have to do what Auden says." He shakes his head. "Too bad. You're fun, Jeremy. I can already tell. Even if you've got problems like me."

"Problems?" I don't remember telling him about any problems. What did I say? "What problems?"

Scott squints up at the ceiling. "I think you're in love with a guy."

"No way. I'm not allowed to be in love. It's against the *rules.*"

"Oh. Huh." Scott frowns. "Well, that's better than me, anyway. I don't have any rules about falling in love. But no one wants to fall in love with me anyway."

"Why not?" Scott is cute. I would probably sleep with him if he wanted to, except I'd rather sleep with Aaron.

But Aaron's too busy with *Benson.*

"No idea," Scott says. His eyes are crossing a little as he leans toward me. "I'm not sure. Cause I'm awesome! And super fun!" He shakes his head. "I need to find someone who thinks I'm as super fun as I know I'm super fun. Because I am! Super fun!"

Auden sighs again and starts wiping at the area of the bar I think I had my head on earlier. "We're closing soon, mates. You both going to be okay? Got someone to bring you home?"

"Home?" I frown at him. "Home like Connecticut? No, I'm not going there." I shake my head. "I can't go there. Bad things are there. The baddest things, Auden. No." I sip at the glass of water he's just put in front of me. It's good—cold and sharp, and now the fog in my head is clearing just a little.

Now Auden's face looks very strange—sad, maybe? I'm not sure, because it's also swimming a little. "I mean home like here in Burlington, Jeremy," he says gently.

"Home?" The first place that comes to mind when I think of homes in Burlington is The Pink Monstrosity. My bed, with Aaron in it. His arms wrapped around me, his breath against the back of my neck. "I can't have home tonight," I tell Auden. "Nope. Home is busy."

"That sucks. You need a hug." Scott reaches over to grab me and nearly falls off his bar stool. Auden catches him by the shirt just in time.

"Stay where you are, okay? Just sit tight. I'm going to call some people for both of you."

"How do I sit tight on a stool?" I ask him, only the words don't sound quite right on my tongue. It's like they're half on my tongue and half not. I try to tell Scott that, but I can't find him. And then Auden is gone and back again. He says something, but it's all muffled, and I don't really understand it.

Then Briar's there.

"Thanks for coming down, man," Auden says. I really love Auden's voice. He's from someplace where they have great accents. Scotland, I think. "Is Scotland its own country?" I ask Briar and Auden.

"That depends on who you ask," Auden says. "Briar, your little group may have a new member who wants to join. Scott and Jeremy were fast friends tonight."

I think Briar and Scott shake hands, and maybe Briar talks to Scott? I'm not sure. Then Briar starts talking to me.

"Ready to head home?" Briar asks me gently.

I shake my head. "Can't go home. It's not there. It's in Connecticut, but it's not. Or it's pink, but it's not there." Now Briar and Scott are looking at me like I'm not making any sense. But everything I'm saying is right, and I know it is.

Briar holds out a hand to me, and I take it because I like Briar. I decide to tell him that. "Really glad Jamie found you," I tell him. "So glad. You're great, Briar. You and Jamie are great. Most of us don't get to be great with other people, you know? Scott says that too. But you do. I'm really happy for you." Now Briar looks sad, and it makes me sad that I made him sad, but I can't focus on too much because the minute I stand up, my stomach decides it hates me. A whole, whole lot.

Things get blurry again after that. I throw up somewhere—maybe an alleyway, I'm not sure—and I think I'm in Jamie's truck for a little bit.

Somehow, I end up in my bed. Briar and Jamie are both standing next to it, and Briar's holding a glass of water.

"Think he's okay?" I hear Jamie ask.

"No." Briar sighs. "He keeps talking about Connecticut and The Pink Monstrosity and home. Something's wrong for sure."

"Think he's ever going to tell us what's going on with him? Really?" Jamie asks.

"I hope so," says Briar.

"We've been friends for years." Now Jamie sounds frustrated. I don't like that. Jamie's been my best friend for a long time. I don't want to be the reason Jamie's unhappy. Not ever. "You think there's some reason he won't tell us? Something we're doing wrong? Something I'm doing wrong?"

It's quiet for a little bit. I'm drifting in and out, and my head's beginning to pound now. But I still manage to hear Briar's answer.

"No, Jamie. I don't think you're doing anything wrong. Some things just feel impossible to say out loud."

Briar's a genius. A definite, definite genius. Some things are so hard to say out loud. Especially when the person you finally want to say them out loud to has contracts to read that are more important.

18

THAT TIME AARON DID NOT GIVE A BLOW JOB TO A NE'ER-DO-WELL

"Good morning, sunshine," I say, intentionally stealing Jeremy's favorite morning greeting as I walk into the firm's main office.

"Ummmm," Jeremy replies into the giant mug of coffee he's holding. He looks like he's been dragged under a truck. His hair hasn't seen a comb anytime recently, he's got shiny, dark circles under his eyes, and the sweater he's wearing looks like it's on backward. "Morning." He doesn't even look up at me—instead, he goes back to looking at the computer screen on his desk, his eyes almost crossing as the light from it hits him.

"Geez, what happened to you?" I ask.

"My guess is alcohol." Benson appears next to us with a file folder in his hand and a grin the size of Montpelier on his face. "Lots and lots of alcohol. Did someone forget how to hold their liquor last night?"

Jeremy glares at him through lidded eyes. "Did you need something, *Benny*?"

"Nope. I'm just enjoying the view. Always nice to watch a ne'er-do-well reap the rewards of his own poor choices."

"Ne'er-do-well?" Jeremy and I both ask incredulously at the same time. "The only person I've ever heard use that word is my brother, and he only uses it when he's talking about a romance novel," I add.

Benson shrugs. "What? I liked *Bridgerton*. Opened my eyes to some new things. Enjoy your day, Jeremy," he almost yells. "I'll try not to make excessive noises around you every time I get the chance." Then he slaps the file folder onto Jeremy's desk as loudly as possible, calls out, "File that please," and walks away while Jeremy's still wincing.

"Just when I think we're making progress," I mutter. I turn my attention back to Jeremy. "Are you okay? What the hell happened last night?"

"What do you think happened?" Jeremy sighs. "I went to Vino and Veritas, I got a little too friendly with Auden's pours, and you don't want to know the rest anyway. Remember?"

Ouch. And also: fuck. Did Jeremy hook up last night? Not that he doesn't have the right to hook up with anyone he wants—we've established that. But now all I can think about is Jeremy in someone else's bed, his skin rubbing into someone else's skin, and . . . .

I'm not usually one for rage, but right now I could probably rip apart this office Hulk-style if I really wanted to.

"I have work to do," Jeremy mumbles to his desk. "Have a good morning, okay?"

That brush-off stings more than the thought of Jeremy finding another person to spend the night with at Vino and Veritas. I'm licking my wounds as I walk into my office, where Benson is happily waiting to make me feel like shit.

"Trouble in paradise?"

"Do you ever stop trying to make people miserable?"

"Once, about three years ago. Wasn't fun, so I gave it up."

"I vote for a silent workspace this morning," I tell him.

"Fine by me. For what it's worth, though, I hope you're not beating the shit out of yourself over what you did yesterday. It was about damn time, in my opinion."

What I did yesterday? What the fuck did I do yesterday? "Excuse me?"

"The way you blew off Fake Lawyer Ken out there when he was all upset. It was good to see you put work first like that. You get distracted by him way too often. Nice to see you keep your priorities in order."

Wait—Jeremy was upset yesterday? I run a quick playback of the day through my head, and I'm not far into the rewind process when I find it: when he came in while Benson and I were working late.

As much as I hate to even say the words inside my own head, Benson's right: something was wrong yesterday, and I didn't see it. I was too focused on paperwork, and I blew Jeremy off.

And then, apparently, he went on a bender.

Fuck.

I need to deal with this. And I will, I promise myself. Right after I answer the sixteen e-mails currently screaming HIGH IMPORTANCE from my inbox.

It's lunchtime before I finally get a chance to talk to Jeremy. At least he's looking a little more human when I approach his desk. The firm's busy today, but I know Jeremy's got his lunch hour coming soon. "I want to take you somewhere," I tell him.

He looks wary for a moment, and that stings. But I understand. Or at least I think maybe I do.

At least he gets into my car with me. He's very quiet as I drive —doesn't even ask where we're going. This silence is definitely not his usual style, and I'm getting more and more worried by the second. Did I break Jeremy? Can you break a relationship that's not even a real relationship?

But then I pull into our lunch destination, and Jeremy's face lights up.

I've taken him to my favorite snack bar/creemee stand in Burlington. It sits on a park next to Lake Champlain, surrounded by trees and water and dappling sunlight that stretches and beams through and across both. The stand itself is nothing fancy. It's just a big box-like structure that looks like a cross between a food truck and a shed, with picnic tables surrounding it.

"Best creemees in Burlington," I tell Jeremy softly. "And they make damn good hamburgers too."

Jeremy sends me a wry smile. "I still think the word creemee sounds like something from a porno."

"I know you do." I grab his hand and gently squeeze it, sending out a mental cheer when he lets me. "You want to tell me what happened yesterday? You were upset. I'm sorry I missed it then."

Jeremy squeezes my hand once and then lets go. His absence stretches through the nerves at the ends of my fingertips.

"Let's get some ice cream," he says.

For now, I'll take it.

We're halfway through our second burgers, a shared bag of perfectly greasy fries, and a story involving some traumatizing text messages before I fully realize just how much I fucked up the day before. "I'm so sorry," I tell Jeremy again. "I told you that you could talk to me about your family. Then you tried, and I completely blew you off." I know I've seriously fucked up here. Jeremy Everett was finally ready to open up—at least a little—and instead, I left him hanging in the proverbial wind. No wonder he headed right for Vino and Veritas.

"Stop apologizing." Jeremy dips a French fry into his ice cream. Personally, I think that combination's disgusting, but to each their own. I've noticed Lexy eats fries the same way. "You didn't do anything wrong, Aaron. You were busy. It's okay."

"Well, I'm not now. Let's talk. Do you need me to go to

Connecticut with you? Are you ready for that?"

Jeremy stares off into the distance. His eyes drop to a seagull picking up leftover fries on the ground nearby. Usually, if you see one of those things hunting down food, it's surrounded by others, but this one's alone right now. All on its own. Jeremy keeps his eyes on the bird as he says, "No. I don't know. I don't think so. Maybe for like three minutes yesterday I was ready for that? But . . . ." He sighs. "Not now." He turns on the seat of the picnic bench to look at me. "But thank you. For offering, I mean."

I'm not sure exactly when Jeremy became this formalized, stiff version of himself, but I don't like it. I miss teasing, sarcastic, charming Jeremy. I miss the fully realized and joyous smiles that live under those fake ones he wears for the world.

I'm starting to worry I may never see one of those smiles again. But I've got an idea for bringing them back. It's not a foolproof plan, but it's based on important knowledge I've gained about Jeremy in the last few months: nothing takes him out of his own head like a good blow job. "C'mon," I say, standing up. "Let's get some ice cream to go. I'm texting Benson that we're having a long lunch, and he's going to need to cover the front desk a little longer."

Jeremy's eyes widen. "Where are we going?"

"You'll see."

We both lick at peanut butter creemee cones with extra nuts—and now I'm starting to see what Jeremy means about all the sexual innuendo involved with eating ice cream in northern Vermont—while I wind the Jeep around some back roads. Soon we're in an empty parking lot surrounded by trees and the nearby sound of rushing water. No one's in sight. Just like I'd hoped.

"I used to go hiking here sometimes," I tell Jeremy.

"We're going hiking? Like this?" He gestures at my suit pants.

"Nope. And we're going to lose the pants." I drop down over his seat and start undoing his belt buckle.

He runs his hands through my hair, tugging gently at my curls as I slip his pants down past his hips and take him in my mouth.

At first, he's still soft, the skin there thick but malleable against my tongue. It only takes a few rotations of my lips around his dick, though, for it to harden. Soon I've got one hand stroking the base, gently teasing at his balls, and Jeremy groans as I move my tongue around the tip to lap at the pre-cum there. It's salty and sweet at the same time. I never liked the taste of cum before I met Jeremy Everett, but there's something about his. Sometimes I feel like I crave it.

"Aaron . . . ." He's almost begging now, his voice a soft, beautiful whine in my eardrums. The sound sits there, echoing musically. I know I can't make up for what happened yesterday, but at least I can give him this. At least I can make him feel good.

"Tell me what you need," I whisper to his cock, knowing the vibrations are going to wind him up even more.

"Need to cum," he says urgently. "Need you," he adds in the same voice, and I don't hesitate. I thrust my mouth deep over his cock, deepthroating him as far as I can, while I pump at his base with my hand. It's only a few seconds before he's jutting up off the bench seat of my Jeep, rocking and vibrating into my hand and spurting into my mouth.

We end up with my head in his lap and him stroking my hair. "I'm sorry," I whisper again into the heavy, humid summer air that's sitting like gravel in the truck. "I really am, J. And in case I didn't already say it, you're not a ne'er-do-well. I would never give a blow job to a ne'er-do-well. I'm not even one hundred percent sure what a ne'er-do-well is."

"Aaron." Jeremy lets out a small laugh. "You don't need to apologize, okay? I know how much pressure you put on yourself. I get it. You never need to put that kind of pressure on yourself for me." He sighs contentedly. "All's forgiven. Not that there was anything to forgive."

We drive back to the firm with his hand in mine. It makes using the stick shift on the Jeep tough at times, but the trouble's all worth it.

I can't let go of Jeremy's words, though, and they stay with me for hours, through a long afternoon and evening of work, through a quick dinner and some dumb TV with Briar and Jamie in their apartment. They stay with me until I'm lying in bed that night.

Is Jeremy right? Is the pressure I feel really pressure from myself? Because I always thought it came from other people.

19

THAT TIME JEREMY DID NOT READ THE ALLEYWAY

I'm not normally one to rate my blow jobs. But as blow jobs go, the apology blow job Aaron gave me in the woods by Lake Champlain definitely rates as one of the top three of my life.

If I'm being honest, all top three blow jobs of my life so far have come from Aaron. But I'm trying not to think about that as we buy donuts at The Maple Factory with Briar the morning after said epic blow job by the lake.

"The research we did stands solid," Aaron's telling me and Briar as he tackles a croissant like it's done him some kind of harm in a past life. "We're hoping to show that, according to the contract, the landlords cannot increase the rent in these circumstances, and I—"

"Uh, Aaron?" I tug at his sleeve. "We're blocking the line. Did you want something else?"

Aaron looks around at where we're standing, at the checkout counter next to the pastries, as if he's surprised to find himself there. Which he probably is. He's been in a daze since I picked him up at his apartment this morning; I doubt he even remembers me driving the three of us to Church Street. His mind is already in the meeting with the partners that's happening in a few hours.

This is the meeting where Aaron and Benson-Hole will present all the research they've done so far on the Tursky case to Iris and Tom. From there, I guess they decide what to tell the clients. I don't really understand all the details of the process, but I'm starting to. Every day I understand more and more. Every day I like the work we do more and more.

Yesterday I caught myself looking up LSAT practice tests. I swear, Aaron and the firm are a bad influence on me.

Briar pays the cashier, and I gently guide Aaron away from the counter and sit him down at a high-top table. "You're going to kick ass today," I tell him as I hand him a coffee cup. "I didn't double the espresso in your order, though."

"I think one shot will be plenty this morning," Briar says wryly as he appears next to us. Then he adds, more quietly, "Jamie and I are cheering you on today, Aaron. You know that, right?"

Aaron squares his shoulders and nods. He's going into high-power Aaron mode: the mode that always makes my dick stiffen slightly. Right now, he's drawn up to his full height in the chair, his blue suit jacket cresting perfectly over his wide shoulders.

Damn. Why does Briar have to be here? Why do we have to be standing in the middle of a bakery? Aaron could use some serious stress relief, and I'd really like to help him out with that.

"Okay." Aaron stands up suddenly, fiercely, his brow high and his mouth set in a firm line. "I'm ready to do this." He picks up his coffee cup and marches toward the door.

"You've got this, man!" Briar calls after him. He turns to me. "You think we should tell him he's wearing two different colored socks?"

We managed to find another set of socks for Aaron in my car, and when he heads into the conference room at ten o'clock, he looks ready to take on the world. But I'm still a giant-ass ball of nerves as I sit at my desk. I can't concentrate on the billing software on the screen in front of me, or the LSAT prep guide I downloaded on my phone.

I wanted to buy a paperback copy from Vino, but there's no way I could do that without Briar finding out. And there's no way I'm ready to talk to the friend group yet about my potential law school plans.

Tick . . . tock . . . tick . . . tock. Has the clock on the wall next to my desk always been this loud? Because I don't think I've ever even noticed the noise it makes before, but today I'm ready to rip it off the wall.

It's been two hours, and I just want to know how things in that meeting are going. Not exactly because I care that much about the Turskys. I mean, I do care—I don't want their farmstand to go under. But I care more because I know how much work Aaron's put into the research for this case. I know how much saving the farmstand means to him.

I just want him to be happy. I'm honestly not sure I've ever cared about another human's happiness this much. Not even Jamie or Briar's.

The only person I think I've ever cared this much about is in a nursing home in Connecticut right now.

The clock keeps ticking, very little billing gets done, and I'm ready to crawl out of my skin when the door of the conference room opens. Aaron steps out of the door, and right away, I know that things have gone badly.

His face is overcast, and a set of clouds cross his forehead as they move down over the set of his mouth. The shoulders that were risen in power and purpose earlier have slumped. He looks as fucking defeated as he did the day he tried to see his family and couldn't—the last day I really saw him fail at something.

Iris is behind him. She pats him gently on the shoulder. "I know this is hard, but there are still other paths. Evelyn will speak to the clients. They still have other options."

He mumbles something to her I can't hear. Benson comes out behind the two of them, looking almost blank. I'm so used to seeing him in a permanent state of anger that I don't even know how to process his expression.

Iris comes over to the desk. "Why don't you take lunch, Jeremy?" she says. "Maybe you can take a walk with Aaron and Benny. It might be good for the two of them to have a break."

It's a testament to how worried I am about Aaron that I don't even inwardly snicker when she refers to Benson as *Benny*.

Aaron heads out of the office on some kind of autopilot. He doesn't even take a second glance at me as he walks by. What the fuck? I follow him, and Benson brings up the rear.

Aaron's already charging up the street so fast I can barely keep up with him. "Uh, Aaron?" I call. "What happened? Want to slow down?" I haven't exactly been doing my cardio lately, and all that side farm work keeps Aaron in shape. I'm puffing just trying to stay within a few steps of him.

"Hey," Benson calls. "Would you slow down, man? Where are you even going?"

We've ended up in the alleyway behind Vino and Veritas. I'm not sure how, exactly. I doubt Aaron was even paying attention to where he was walking, but we go to V and V so often that at this point we're like homing pigeons where this place is concerned.

Aaron slumps up against the brick wall of the bookstore. "It's over," he whispers into his hands. "It's over, Jeremy. The Tursky farmstand is over. We failed."

Benson shifts on his feet and sighs. "Yeah. We did." He kicks at a rock lying on the ground. It doesn't go far.

"It's over?" I ask. "I mean, it's not really over, right? There must be more you can do. She said Evelyn's going to—"

"Nah." Benson shakes his head. "She was just trying to make us feel better. The cases we found, the legal precedents we looked at, they just won't work." He shrugs. "Whatever. I'll just have to find another case to blow their minds with. Anyway, you . . . did good work, Aaron." It sounds like the words are being pulled out of him. "I mean, we both did," he quickly adds. "But, yeah. Just wanted to say that." He leaves the alleyway, kicking at more rocks as he goes.

"Holy shit," I say to the rocks. "Is Benson Lewis an actual human being?"

Aaron shrugs. "Too soon to tell. But he wasn't his usual dickish self in that meeting. Maybe it's all this work we've been doing together." He rubs his hands through his hair. "Fuck. Fuck fuck fuck. My family's going to find out, Jeremy. Everyone in Morse's Line knows my firm is working on that case. I can't believe that a place everyone in Morse's Line loves so much is just going to . . . disappear. All because I couldn't save it."

"Hey." I grab his hands and hold onto them. "Don't put that on yourself. There are other people at that firm too, remember? People who've been practicing law a lot longer than you. If they couldn't fix this, maybe it's just not fixable."

Aaron pulls his hands out of mine and steps away from me. He moves back into a slow, circular pace. "Maybe. But they were relying on research from me and Benson. Maybe we needed to do more. Maybe there's more we could still do?" He grabs at his hair again. "I should have worked harder yesterday. I should have prepped better for this meeting. I shouldn't have . . . ."

The rest of his words hang in the air, unspoken, but I hear them loud and clear: *I shouldn't have fucked off to the woods with you for hours.*

Ouch.

The not-spoken-but-definitely-there words sting, and suddenly all I want is to erase them permanently from the air. Aaron's got to see that this isn't the end of the world. It's just a case. A failed one, sure, but he's going to have a lot of those in his life. "Hey, c'mon, Aaron," I say softly. "It's going to be okay. It's just a farmstand. Does Vermont really need another one of those anyway?" I joke.

My words crash to the alleyway floor like a brick sinking in water, and I know right away what I just did wrong: I did not read the room.

Or, in this case, the alleyway.

Aaron wasn't ready for that joke yet. Fuck, Aaron may never be ready for that joke.

His face has gone bright red, and he's standing there, staring like he's never seen me before. I lunge into words, trying to fix what I just broke. "Aaron, I didn't mean it that way. I was just kidding! I just meant that—"

"You said what you meant," Aaron says quietly. His voice is ice cold, distant in a way I've never heard. It's like he's channeling Delia Everett as he speaks. He shakes his head. "Of course, you wouldn't get it," he says softly to the ground below us. "Jeremy Everett doesn't care about anything but having a good time. I knew that the very first night we ever got together—that night last March," he adds. He tightens his hands into fists and balls them up as he crosses his arms over his chest. "I can't believe I let myself forget that. I can't believe I slept with someone who has YOLO tattooed on their ass."

The words are a knife plunging right into my chest. Aaron, of all people, knows exactly what that tattoo means and why I have it. And now I'm pissed. "For real? That's what you want to say to me right now?" I reply. I can hear my voice echoing off the brick walls of the alleyway, and I'm sure anyone nearby can hear me loud and clear, but I don't care. "At least I'm not obsessed with pleasing everyone else in the damn world. At least I'm not afraid to live life on my own terms. You're so afraid of what everyone else thinks that you can't stop tripping over their opinions of you!"

"Oh yeah?" Now Aaron's yelling too, and it occurs to me for a split second that I'm not sure if I've ever heard him yell before. I don't have much time to think about that, though, because his next words use up all the mental space I have. "You think you're not afraid to live life on your own terms? Because it sure looks to me like you're afraid of everything, Jeremy. Especially reality." He shakes his head. "What we've been doing this summer? Us hooking up last March? This is all just both of us avoiding the truth."

There's a strangled noise from the side of the alleyway. A strangled noise that, unfortunately, I know. I've heard it before: usually, when I've had a sock on my dorm room door and the person making that exact noise was annoyed and wanted to come inside.

My heart clenches in my chest as I turn slowly. Standing there, eyes wide open and jaw fallen, is Jamie.

"You two?" he asks incredulously. "Back when we weren't talking, Aaron? All summer? Why didn't you say something?"

Aaron steps forward, and I see something like panic in his eyes. "Jamie, it's really not a big deal. We can explain. I promise—"

Jamie doesn't give him a chance to finish. "Why are you keeping secrets again?" he asks, his voice shaking slightly.

Oh shit. This is what Aaron was always worried would happen if Jamie found out we were keeping secrets from him: Jamie's flashing back to when Aaron kept his acceptance to law school hidden from the Morins. He's reliving all the hours of pain and heartache that secret led to. Fuck fuck fuck. And this is my fault. I'm the one who didn't want to tell Jamie about the two of us. "Listen, Jamie." I step up next to Aaron. "This is on me, okay? I didn't want to tell you because . . . ."

Because you're one of the only people who think I'm worth anything. And I didn't want to screw that up.

But the way Jamie's looking at me now suggests that I have, absolutely and without a doubt, screwed this up.

And he wasn't the only one who thought I was worth something. Aaron thought I was worth something, too. I know he did. And the way he's looking back and forth between me and Jamie right now?

There's zero doubt that I've screwed that up too.

"I need to think about this," Jamie whispers. Then he disappears out of the alleyway. Aaron and I both take off after him, but that little shit is fast. Chasing cows is good for sprinting speed, I guess. Out on the pedestrian area of Church Street, Jamie quickly gets swallowed into the afternoon lunch crowd. Aaron, meanwhile, looks angry enough to take out the bench we're standing next to. And possibly the lamppost beside it.

"Shit," he hisses. "And I have another meeting with Iris soon that I can't miss. Fuck fuck fuck." He shakes his head. "We're both supposed to be back at the office in like five minutes. We're going to have to track Jamie down from there. Or find him later." Aaron stalks off down the street, moving almost as fast as Jamie was— and just like that, they're both gone.

I stand in the middle of one of the most crowded streets in Burlington, surrounded by people, and I am the absolute loneliest I've ever felt in my entire life.

20

THAT TIME AARON BURIED SOME MORE HATCHETS

"You going to stop staring at that desk and do some work anytime soon?"

Benson's voice is less of a snarl than usual, but it still grates into my skin. "I'm just wondering if Jeremy's back from lunch," I mutter as I flip another page of the contract in front of me. He should have been back about thirty minutes ago. Instead, Evelyn has been covering the desk.

"Evelyn said he called out for the rest of the day," Benson says. "She asked if I could cover the desk later." He snorts. "Now I've got phone duty because your booty call can't be bothered to do his job."

What the hell? Jeremy called out? Is he okay? I mean, of course he's not okay. He can't be after what just happened. Is he with Jamie? I wouldn't know because Jamie's ignoring my texts and calls. Briar's not picking up his phone either, and Lexy's on a shift at the hospital right now. I've got nothing but radio silence from all of them in my tiny office, and I have no idea if Jamie's ever going to speak to me again.

I'm pretty sure Jeremy never will. I wouldn't blame him. That comment I made about his tattoo was probably one of the worst things I've ever said to another person. I know exactly what that tattoo means to Jeremy . . . and I still used it against him like a bullet in a cocked gun.

"Hey," says Benson, "I don't know what happened with you and the booty call in that alleyway, but can you snap out of it and get your head in the game here? We have work to do."

Maybe it's the guilt I feel over what I said to Jeremy, or the guilt I feel about keeping secrets from Jamie all summer when I knew that wasn't the right choice. Maybe it's the fact that I thought Benson and I were finally making some progress in our working relationship, and now he's right back to his insipid asshole self. But suddenly, I have no problem taking all my anger out on him.

"What's your problem, anyway?" I snap. "Why are you always out to make everyone else feel like shit?"

Benson looks at me coolly. "Hey, man, I just call things like I see them."

"You think this is just 'calling things like you see them'? Seriously? Open up your eyes. See what the rest of the world does. You're a dick. And maybe I'd be fine letting you go on being your dickish self, but I've seen enough of you to know that you can be a decent human when you want to be. So why the hell do you act the way you do?"

Benson stares at me for a long, chilling moment. Then he drops the papers he's holding and leans across his desk.

"I get now that you're not some legacy admission to Harvard like I thought you were. But I *was* supposed to be a legacy admission. My grandfather was a Harvard alum. My dad, too. Guess who was the first person in multiple generations not to get an acceptance letter?"

Interesting. That does explain some things.

Benson isn't done yet, though. "You got in, somehow. And I sure as shit know you're not smarter than me." He shrugs. "I've got nothing against you personally, Aaron. I think you're a pretty good guy. But I've got things to prove to my family, and the only way to do that is to build the future they expect me to have. And if that means I have to take down some people in the process, then so be it."

And just like that, it's as if I'm looking in a mirror.

Not an exact mirror, of course. More like a funhouse mirror, where everything in the image is shifted slightly. Benson's out to prove to his family that he belongs. I'm out to prove to mine that leaving their business was the right thing to do. Benson believes that building his future at any cost to anyone else is worth it. And I . . . .

I tell myself I'm not like that. But right now, my brother's out in the world wondering why his best friend and I kept a massively important secret from him. And Jeremy's out there somewhere living with those terrible words I said to him. And I'm here. In a law office. Prepping for a meeting.

You're no different than Benson—the work, the goal, impressing people, the future. That's what matters. All that over everything else. Even the people you claim to care the most about. Right?

It's not a realization that comes to me easily. But once it's there, I can't let go of it. Because I know it's true.

And then a question appears right next to that realization: *What would Jeremy do right now?*

I know the answer to that question. I stand up from my desk.

"Where are you going?" Benson asks.

"I'm leaving. Please tell Iris I had an emergency. I need to take the rest of the day off."

"What the hell?" Benson sputters out the words. "We have a meeting! You've got research to finish! I'm not doing your job for you too, you know!"

He's still talking as I walk out of the room, but I barely hear him.

"Dad? Have you seen Jamie?"

The barn is dappled in sunlight this time of day. It streams through the large doors at either end of the cement floors, dancing its way over water bowls and half-filled gutters and sweet-smelling hay. The cows are outside right now, enjoying the balmy but cooler temperature of a perfect summer afternoon in Vermont.

"Aaron?" Dad emerges from the sawdust room. "Jamie's not here, son. I think he's at work. Isn't that where you should be right now?"

I sink down onto a haybale. "I should be. But I'm not."

Dad studies me as he sits down next to me. "Kiddo? You okay?" I know the voice he's using. It's the same voice he used to use when I'd fallen down on the hard cement of the barn floor, or when I was trying too hard to do a chore the perfect way and couldn't seem to get it right.

I end up back in a place I haven't been in a very long time: leaning into my father's arms. "I did it again," I whisper. "I screwed everything up, Dad. Just like I did last time, when I got into law school. I messed up at work. And then I left for the day without even talking to my boss, so maybe I'll get fired. But it doesn't matter, because I'm not even sure I'm cut out to be a lawyer, so I guess I almost destroyed our family for nothing, huh? And that's not even the worst part. The worst part is that Jamie probably hates me because Jeremy and I didn't tell him that we've been sort of together all summer, and I said some really terrible things to Jeremy and I'm sure he hates me now too. I'm trying so hard to do everything right, Dad. But somehow, I just keep getting it all wrong."

I expect Dad to pull away, to look at me in shock and horror every single time I add a new sentence to my diatribe. But he just sits there, holding me and patting my back while I spill out all the words that kept running through my head on the drive here.

"Oh, Aaron," he finally says. "What did I do to you, son?"

"Huh?" I pull away. "You? You didn't do any of this."

He sits deeper into the haybale, shaking his head. "You know," Dad says, "you were always obsessed with being perfect. You used to get upset if you got a 98 on a test. You'd count the number of squares in a haybale to make sure every cow got the same amount. You used to drive your mom and me wild, the way you'd obsess over putting a milk machine on a cow exactly the right way." He smiles at me fondly. "Son, I've always loved that you want to be the best man you can be. But I promised myself I'd never put that kind of pressure on you—I'd never make you think you had to be perfect for us to love you. Then you got into law school like you did, and we had that fight."

The fight that changed everything.

"I broke every promise I ever made to myself about you that day," he whispers. "I told you I needed you here. I made you think you had to choose. I made you think you had to be the perfect son for me or leave—I made you think you had no other options."

"Dad, no. I wasn't . . . ." Except I can't finish the sentence. Because he's right: that's exactly what happened. *Between two worlds,* I'd told Jeremy once. That's where I used to feel trapped. I didn't think I could have both of those worlds because I knew I couldn't be perfect in both of them.

"Aaron." Dad takes my face in his hands. His eyes are soft and sad, and they look so much like Jamie's. Like mine. The three of us have always been variant copies of each other in looks. It's strange how three people can have genes that are so close and yet be so different from one other. "I know I've apologized for what happened back then, but I need to say this now, as clearly as I can: you don't need to be perfect for us. Whatever happens with farmstands or law offices or boyfriends or your brother—this will always be your home. We will always be your home. I'm so sorry I ever made you feel differently than that. And I'm so sorry you're still carrying that around with you."

I've needed to hear those words from him for so long. I hug him hard around the shoulders, holding on tight, relishing this moment. This is the conversation I've needed to have with my father for a very, very long time, and I'm not surprised by the tears I feel falling down my cheeks as he holds me—or the tears I see in the corners of his eyes.

I think this might be the first time my father and I have ever cried together. I know I didn't cry when I left the farm all those months ago. And when I came back? There were definitely tears. But they weren't like this.

They didn't feel cleansing the way these tears do. These tears feel like they're wiping a slate clean: months and maybe even years of pain and pressure. Almost like when Dad washes the cement floor of this barn completely clear of dirt and dust and manure.

Eventually, we both pull ourselves back together. Dad gets the travel mug of iced tea that he keeps in the milkhouse, and we sit there, sipping silently, passing the mug back and forth.

"You and Jeremy, huh?" he finally asks.

I shrug. "Probably not anymore. We had a fight. We should've told Jamie, and the rest of you. I don't know why we didn't." Except I do: we kept that secret for Jeremy. And even knowing what I know now, I don't think I'd do things any differently. Keeping that secret meant something to Jeremy. And honestly? I'd probably walk off a cliff for Jeremy Everett if he asked me to.

"I'm sure you had your reasons," Dad said. "And if it helps, it wasn't much of a secret. Your mother and I figured it out months ago. Lissie, too. We were taking bets on when you'd tell us."

"What?" I almost spit out my tea. "Are you kidding me? How come Jamie didn't know, then?"

Dad laughs. "Your brother's stubborn. We all tried to say something about it a few times. Even Briar. But he insisted there was no way you or Jeremy would keep a secret from him like that." He sighs. "Not again, at least."

I flinch. "Yeah. I think I understand why he's so upset."

"Well." Dad looks thoughtful. "This isn't the same, though, is it? This secret isn't going to end like the last one did. You're not going anywhere this time." He swallows hard. "Right?"

"I'm definitely not," I promise. "Never again, Dad."

And I know I mean it this time. The two worlds I've always crossed between won't ever fully merge, I don't think. But there's a bridge between them now.

Dad pats me on the leg. "For what it's worth," he says, "I hope you two work it out. I've always liked Jeremy. Little devil, that one. And he's good for you. Brings out a side of you I'm not used to seeing."

I shake my head. I may be bridging worlds today, but I also know that some worlds just don't exist together and never can. "I think he's good for me too," I tell Dad. "But we can't have anything real together. Jeremy . . . well, I think he'll always have his reasons not to be with me."

Dad nods. "Shame, then. He'd make a good Morin, that boy. Hell, he already does."

My heart clenches again in my chest so hard I have to breathe through the pain. He's right: Jeremy's always been a Morin. I hope it stays that way even after the summer's over. He needs our family. And we need him, I think. All of us.

But you don't always get what you want. Or what you need. Speaking of which . . . .

"I need to find Jamie," I mumble.

"That shouldn't be hard." Dad grins. "What's Jamie go looking for whenever he's sad or madder than a hornet about something?"

We look at each other, and I smile as we both say the same word at the exact same time.

"Books."

21

THAT TIME JEREMY WAS A TROPE

"Is Jamie here?"

It's pretty clear he's not, unfortunately. The Vino and Veritas bookstore isn't that big, and I did a lap around it when I first walked in. No Jamie.

Just like there was no Jamie at The Pink Monstrosity.

And no Jamie eating crullers at The Maple Factory.

And no Jamie answering his phone.

Briar looks up from the computer at the V and V checkout counter, where he's staring at the screen with Kolby, another friend of ours who goes to Moo U and also works at the store. "Hey, Jeremy. What are you doing here? And no, I haven't seen Jamie. He was supposed to meet me here for a lunchtime donut, but then he messaged that something came up. Said he'd see me tonight."

"Lunchtime donut?" I ask.

Briar shrugs. "It's one of our things."

Of course it is. Because Jamie and Briar have endless *things*. Book clubs and lunchtime donuts and morning breakfast routines and family firework traditions, and all I have is a missing best friend who probably hates me and an obsession with a guy I can never be with because my future probably doesn't exist.

I drop my head down onto the counter and moan.

"What's wrong?" Kolby asks.

"I'm having an existential crisis," I mumble.

"That sucks," Kolby says. "You want some chocolate? I always like chocolate when I'm having an existential crisis."

Someone hands me a square of something sweet and wrapped in foil. It doesn't really help, but the thought behind it is nice. Kolby and Briar start whispering, and the next thing I know Briar is tugging gently at my arm. I follow him across the bookstore and through a door I've never even seen before. Inside are stacks and stacks of books.

"Storeroom?" I ask. Briar nods.

"This place is like your and Jamie's wet dream," I mutter. If there's any fantasy I can imagine my two friends having, it's something involving a stack of books.

Briar smirks. Widely.

"Ah." I'm going to be very careful about where I sit if Briar and I spend a lot of time in here.

Briar pulls out two folding chairs that are leaning up against the wall and gestures for me to sit in one. I sink into it like some fainting silent film star in the old movies my dad used to watch. Actually, I do feel a little faint. Now that I think about it, I can't remember the last time I ate. I never had lunch. Neither did Aaron. I hope he ate something. He has a tendency to forget to eat, and then he gets all hangry.

"Jeremy?" Briar says gently. "You want to tell me what's going on?"

I swallow hard. I do and I don't. There are words you can never take back once you say them out loud, and the words I'm about to tell Briar are some of those. What if I really have lost both Jamie and Aaron forever? What if I lose Briar too? And Lexy?

But I also know that I can't keep all my secrets to myself anymore. Some words find their way into the world no matter how much you don't want them to.

"I fucked up," I start with.

And then I tell him everything—well, not everything. I'm still not ready to talk about my messed-up family or my mother's plot to torture me via text message.

But I tell him about last March. I tell him how I convinced Aaron to come home but ended up messing around with him. I tell him how we tried to forget that ever happened when we started working together, but that didn't work, so then we decided to fling together or whatever, but I asked him not to tell Jamie. And then I tell him about the alleyway and the look on Jamie's face when he ran away from us.

The thing about Briar is that he's a very, very good listener. He's quiet through my entire story—never says a word. And he's still quiet when I stop and look up at him. "Like I said," I add dully, "I fucked up. Jamie's probably never going to speak to me again. Maybe not Lexy either. Do you hate me too?"

Briar sighs and crosses his arms. "Jeremy," he says, "You and Aaron are basically the worst kept secret *ever*. Lexy and I decided weeks ago that something was probably going on."

"Excuse me?" I sit up fast.

Briar nods. "Even Ellie and Frank thought something was up. You two aren't exactly subtle. You kept looking at him like you wanted to take a bite out of his neck in front of the rest of us. And you haven't been going out or hooking up all summer. It was pretty obvious there was something between the two of you."

"Then . . . what? Why? What?" I can't seem to finish a full sentence. "Then why did Jamie look so surprised?"

Briar frowns. "Jamie didn't want to hear it when we tried to tell him. Not because he didn't like the idea of the two of you together," he adds quickly. "But because he didn't like the idea that Aaron could be keeping a secret from him again." He shakes his head. "You remember what happened the last time Aaron kept secrets from Jamie?"

I sure do. And Aaron tried to tell me that was why we shouldn't keep this to ourselves. But I wouldn't listen.

"Jamie kept telling us there was no way Aaron would keep a

secret that big from him. Not after what happened last time," Briar adds.

"What about me?" I ask quietly. "Did he think I'd keep a secret like that from him?"

Briar frowns again. "That's not even the biggest secret you keep from us, is it?" he finally asks quietly.

I don't know how to answer that, and I don't know how to look at Briar right now. I drop my head into my arms.

"Hey." Briar places a soft hand on my shoulder. "Listen, J. It's okay—I know what it feels like to need to keep some things to yourself. I really do. And Jamie and Lexy have always known there were things you held back. It doesn't make them feel any differently about you. But I have to ask." He pauses for a moment. "Why didn't you want Aaron to tell us? Why did you want to keep this a secret?"

"Because," I whisper as I look up at him, and I don't even try to hide the tears falling from the corners of my eyes. "I know what most people think about me. That I'm just a playboy. A fuckup. And maybe I am sometimes. I know I don't make the same choices most people make. But you and Jamie and Lexy have never seen me that way. I didn't want you to start."

Briar looks incredulous. "Why'd you think sleeping with Aaron would make us think less of you?"

I shrug. "I dunno. Maybe because last March I tried to bring Aaron back and fix everything and I couldn't. I hooked up with him instead. And what if hooking up with Aaron was the line? What if that was one hookup too far for Jamie?" I drop my head again. "So, I thought it was better if we just didn't say anything. But I screwed that up too, didn't I? Now Jamie's mad *because* we didn't say anything."

"Jamie isn't going to be mad about this for long," Briar says. "You trying to bring Aaron back last March? Jeremy, that's real friendship. That's the kind of friendship people write books about."

I give Briar a weak smile as I wipe tears off my face with my sleeve.

"And what Jamie's feeling now—well, I know him enough to know that this is fear, not anger. Jamie's afraid of losing his brother again like he did the last time Aaron kept secrets. And he might just be afraid of losing his best friend."

"What?" I look up, shocked that Briar could even think that. "Jamie's always going to be my best friend—as long as he wants me to be, anyway. He's stuck with me for life."

"Yeah, I know that." Briar leans over and wraps his arms around me. "And Jamie does too, I promise. Just give him some time to remember it." He stands up and rubs at my hair like I'm a little kid. "Do you want me to take you home? Harrison won't mind if I need to leave early. I only have like an hour left in my shift anyway."

The Pink Monstrosity, filled with memories of all the times Aaron and I have spent together this summer, is the last place I want to be right now. "Can I stay here and hang out with you?" I ask him. "Maybe Jamie will come back. Eventually."

"Of course."

And that's how I end up curled up on one of the Vino and Veritas couches, sipping coffee and reading a book called *The Reformed Rake*. It's pretty good. The rake has nothing on me, though.

"Jeremy Everett!"

The rake's just about to get caught with his pants down—literally—when a vaguely familiar voice interrupts my reading flow. I look up and see . . . well, I can't remember his name, honestly. I think it was Sam? Sandy?

Something with an S. Maybe. Whatever his name is, it's the guy I latched onto at the bar the night Aaron blew me off. "Hey there!" I pat the seat next to me. "Pretty impressed you remember my name. Sorry to say this, but I kind of can't remember yours."

The guy laughs out loud as he sits down next to me on the couch. "Understandable. It's Scott. I was hoping I'd run into you again. I wanted to thank you for keeping me company that night. I was having a rough day. I'm not usually that . . . maudlin."

"Me neither, actually."

"So I've heard. I mentioned that I met you to a friend of mine, and all he could talk about was the time the two of you danced until 4 a.m., and then did more than dance." He grins. "I got the impression I saw an unusual side of you the other night."

"I guess you could say that."

Scott tilts his head. "He also mentioned he hasn't seen you around much this summer. He wanted me to give you his number if I saw you again. Tell you he's available if you're ever looking for another fun night."

I'm all set to reply that I've been busy working—that's the truth—and then take his friend's number. But when I open my mouth, those aren't the words I say. "I've just been seeing one guy this summer," I blurt out.

Scott nods. "I figured. I tried to tell my friend that, but he didn't believe me." He stretches out on the couch, arms wide above his long frame. "You're lucky, you know," he says quietly. "Finding one guy who wants me the way I want him . . . ." he shakes his head. "That sounds really fucking good right now."

Scott's lonely. Lonely AF, actually. I vaguely remember realizing that the night we got drunk together, but then the information got lost somewhere in my hangover.

Lonely is an emotion I know all too well, and I'm not about leaving other people to sit in it. "You know what?" I tell him. "We should hang out. That guy doing check-out at the counter is my friend Briar. You'd like him. He's suddenly all into board games, which I honestly don't get, but sometimes they're fun. And his boyfriend Jamie is my ride or die—at least I hope he still is—and he'll love you. Lexy'll tell you what to do all the time, but that's kind of great once you get used to it. And then there's Autumn and Mindy and—"

"Jeremy, stop." Scott holds up his hand, laughing. "I mean, don't stop. This friend group of yours sounds really great. But

Briar already invited me to your group's next game night when he picked you up that night. I wasn't sure if I'd be crashing, but . . . yeah. I'd love to go if you think that's a good idea."

"It's a great idea," I tell him.

"Excellent. Guess I have to tell my buddy that Jeremy Everett left the party scene. I have a feeling he isn't going to believe me." He frowns slightly. "I hope I get to meet the guy you were talking about the other night. The one you've been spending this summer with."

I glance back at the cover of the book I've been reading. Maybe reformed rakes aren't just a thing in Briar and Jamie's favorite novels. Because I know I was a real-life rake, and I was a damn a good one. I was never ashamed of it, and I'm still not. There's nothing wrong with pleasure or sex as long as everyone is safe and consensual. I'll never be ashamed of the fun I had when I was one of Moo U's best playboys.

But I don't think I'm that guy anymore. The more I talk to Scott, the more I realize that. This summer will come to an end, and Aaron will leave, but I've figured out something during the time we've spent together: being a rake isn't going to make me happy anymore. This summer is the happiest I've been in a long time, and I want more of it.

I want cuddling.

I want dates in front of fireworks.

I want romantic picnics by candlelight.

I want those things with a person who'll listen to my shit and call me on it, and be there for me day after day, even when I don't deserve it.

And despite all the things we said to each other earlier, I know I want those things with Aaron. Except I also know I can't have them. My future will always be filled with blank spaces, and Aaron deserves more than that.

But I also know I'm not the same person I was at the beginning of this summer. So, where does that leave me?

That question is doing laps in my brain when my phone

buzzes. Naturally, it's my uncle. Because this day wasn't already shitty enough.

My blood runs cold as I read the words on the screen.

Uncle J: *Your father's in the hospital. We don't think it's anything serious. Would be great if you'd come see him, though.*

I know what Jeremy-the-rake would do. Panic. Ditch the phone. Go out drinking and smile and laugh and hide under endorphins and fun. And if I'm being honest, that's still what Jeremy-the-reformed-rake wants to do.

I'm not ready to see my father again. I don't think I'll ever be ready.

But if I'm not the same person that I was in the beginning of the summer, don't I need to act like it? I may not have much choice about my future, but at least I have choices I can make about my present and my past. It's time I acted like the guy Aaron seems to think I am. Or can be.

I stand up. "Scott," I announce loudly, "I'm going to Connecticut. Make sure Briar has your number. I'll text you when I get back."

"Excuse me?" I hear Scott ask as I head for the door of Vino and Veritas. "Why the hell are you going to Connecticut?"

"Because I'm a fucking reformed rake!" I close the door of the bookstore hard behind me, and I don't look back as I walk away.

22

THAT TIME AARON DID NOT SHUSH

"I had a feeling I'd find you here."

Jamie curls up more tightly into the neon green beanbag he's sitting in and flips a page on the book in his hand. He doesn't look up at me.

"You know you're too big for that thing now, right?" I mumble as I sink into the Barbie-pink beanbag next to him. My back barely squeezes into one side, so I end up wedged into a corner of it with my legs hanging out. There was a time when Jamie and I could situate ourselves perfectly into these beanbags. We'd sit here for hours, laughing at comic book pages and silently visiting faraway worlds together. Now we look like two overgrown cows trying to squeeze into a calf shed.

"You don't fit either," Jamie mumbles.

"Yeah, well, I had a growth spurt sometime since I was nine." That's probably the last time I sat here with Jamie in these beanbags in the Children's Corner of the Morse's Line Public Library. The beanbags aren't the only things about this library that are small. The entire library is the size of a small studio apartment. It doesn't even have its own building; it's one-half of the town hall. Right now, Jamie and I are only a few feet away from the town clerk's office. She sometimes does book check-outs over her lunch hour if Mr. Moseley, the part-time librarian, gets too busy with his goat farm to remember to come in for work.

This library has always been one of Jamie's favorite places, even though there may be fewer books here than in our own house. Once, when he got really angry at all of us because we wouldn't stop interrupting him while he was reading some series he loved, he tried walking all the way from the farm to the library. It's three miles, and he barely made it up the road before Mom found him. Still, I'm not surprised he pulled the adult version of running away today and drove here.

"So. You're just hanging out, reading romance novels in a beanbag?" I ask him as I try to adjust my hip into the floor. "Want to talk about anything? Like what happened in the alleyway at Vino and Veritas today?"

Jamie flips a page, even though I doubt he's read a single word on it. He doesn't look up as he says, "I'm not sure, actually. You want to tell me what secrets you've been keeping from me this year?"

"Yeah, I do." I do my best to sit up, but the beanbag isn't having it. I end up leaning across the side until I'm nearly falling into the kid-size play table. It's a miracle I don't end up with a mouthful of dried-up play dough. "Look. I get why you're angry. You have every right to be pissed. Jeremy and I should have told you something was going on with us."

Jamie finally glances up from his book. "When did it start?" he asks quietly.

I fidget uncomfortably again, and this time it's not the bean-bag's fault. "Last March, when I wasn't talking to you all, over spring break. Jeremy reached out and tried to convince me to come home. I chickened out once I got here, but . . . ."

Jamie's eyes widen. "That was you! The person Jeremy was with when he wouldn't let me into our room! Holy shit, Aaron, that was *you*!"

I nod. "Yeah. It was just a one-time thing, though. I went back to being all mopey in Boston, and Jeremy and I agreed to forget it happened. Or we tried to. But then he and I ended up working together at the law firm this summer."

"And you've been fucking around this whole time? And you didn't tell me." Jamie's voice is miserable and angry, and that alone makes me feel small enough to fit into this stupid bean bag.

"Jamie, it was a mistake," I say, as clearly as I can. "We should have told you. But we agreed from the start that it would only be a summer thing."

"So why not tell me about this summer *thing*?" He looks up, his eyes dagger-like now. "Aaron, you never used to keep secrets from me. It was always the two of us against the world. But the next thing I know, you've gotten into law school and you're graduating early, and I never even knew you applied! Then you disappear and don't talk to me for almost a year. You finally come back, and I think we're back to normal again—and you hide *this* from me? Sleeping with my best friend? What now, Aaron? Are you going to fucking leave again without even saying goodbye? Will you block me this time? Maybe extradite yourself to a different country?"

"Jamie, none of that even makes sense. I just—"

"Oh, now I don't make sense!" Jamie's voice goes a little higher, and I glance around for Mr. Moseley. He doesn't seem to be anywhere nearby, though, and he should be easy to spot—you can see the entire library from anywhere in it. "Is that what you think about me, Aaron? That I don't make sense? That I don't deserve to know things? That I don't deserve to know when my brother is sleeping with my best friend?" Jamie's full-on yelling now, his voice echoing across the bookshelves as he sits up in the beanbag. "What is wrong with you? Why can't you just be honest with me about *anything*?"

"Jamie, please calm down. If you'll just let me tell you—"

"Don't tell me to calm down!" He roars. And then, out of nowhere, he tackles me out of the beanbag, wrestling me onto the floor and shoving me down against it. "You're the one who needs to calm down!" he yells.

"Jamie, get off of me!" I try to roll him back over, but he's got me pinned in place. "Listen, I screwed up, okay? I shouldn't have kept law school from you, and I should have told you about Jeremy this summer. I'm a screwup! I screwed up! Is that what you want to hear?"

"No, that's not what I want to hear! I want to hear that you're not going anywhere this time!" Jamie roars at me.

"Boys!" Mr. Moseley shuffles out from behind a shelf. "If the two of you can't get along, I'm going to have to call your father and ask him to come down here and fetch you."

Jamie rolls off of me and we both sit up, our faces red. We turn to look at each other and then back at Mr. Moseley. He's a tall man with a long beard, and right now, with his hands crossed over his flannel shirt, he looks like a grayer version of the Mr. Moseley who used to tell us to shush when we were in elementary school.

Jamie and I both burst out laughing.

"I'm so sorry, Mr. Moseley," I finally manage to say.

"Me too," Jamie tells him. Tears are practically running out of his eyes now. "We forgot where we were for a moment. We'll leave now. I promise."

"No need to leave," says Mr. Moseley easily. "Just quiet down. And don't dog-ear any pages in that book, please. I remember how you used to leave all my page corners turned over."

Jamie looks horrified. "I would never do that, Mr. Moseley! You must be thinking of my sister."

"Good. Then tell her not to dog-ear my books, either." Mr. Moseley turns around to leave, and Jamie and I both start laughing again.

"As if I would ever dog-ear a book," Jamie mumbles.

We're sitting together at a picnic table outside the creemee stand down the road from the library, licking at giant maple swirl ice cream cones.

"Most insulting thing anyone's ever said to you," I agree. "Listen, Jamie. The reason Jeremy and I didn't tell you about us—he asked me not to. He was afraid you'd think less of him or something if you knew."

Jamie scrunches up his nose. "Why the hell would he think that?"

"He said that you, Lexy, and Briar are the only ones who've never judged him for how he lives his life. He thought that might change, I guess."

Jamie scoffs. "What a dumbass. I'll have to kick his butt in a different beanbag later, I guess." He licks at his ice cream and grins. "I would have won that wrestling match if Mr. Moseley hadn't interrupted us, you know."

"Doubtful." He might be right, though. Jamie put on some muscle during the year I was gone and he was working the farm with Dad. Speaking of which . . . . "It really freaked you out today, huh? Me keeping another secret from you?"

Jamie takes a deep breath as he studies his ice cream. When he looks up at me, there's a shine in his eyes that I know I won't unsee for a long time. "Aaron, the months that you were gone? Those were some of the worst of my life. Not just because I was working my ass off, but because I missed you so damn much. Every single day. I can't do that again, Aaron. I just know I can't."

"Jamie." I sigh out all the pain and guilt I feel for what I did to him last year. "Listen. You know there's nothing I hate more than making a mistake. And leaving you and our family the way I did was truly, honestly, one of the worst mistakes I've ever made. I'll never do that again. I promise you."

"I think I know that now." Jamie sends me a wry smile. "I just panicked in that alleyway. Everyone's been trying to tell me that there might be something going on with you and Jeremy all summer, and I didn't want to hear it. There was this part of me that was just so freaked out you were hiding things again." He shakes his head. "But we're here. Eating creemees. And we just got sort of kicked out of a library together. It seems like everything's going to be okay." He crooks an eyebrow at me. "This thing with you and Jeremy. It's really just for the summer?"

"Yeah." And I try not to let my heart twist in my chest as I say the word. "But even if we weren't, I said some pretty horrific things to him after you left the alley today."

Jamie frowns. "Jeremy's been different this summer," he says quietly. "You, too. You've both been different. In a good way. Maybe you should talk to him. See if . . . ."

"No." I shake my head. "I wish that were the case. There are things you don't understand though, Jamie. Things I can't tell you. It's not my place."

"I know." Jamie frowns. "Lexy and I have always thought there are things Jeremy holds back from us." He sends me a small smile. "For what it's worth, I'm glad he told you. Whatever it is he's hiding."

I am too. Even if Jeremy never shares another secret with me— and right now it sure doesn't seem like he ever will—the fact that he shared his family's struggles with me will always feel like one of the most powerful and important gifts someone has ever given me.

I'm thinking about that when Jamie's phone and mine both buzz with messages at the exact same time. He looks at me curiously as he unlocks his.

The message is to the two of us and Lexy, and it's from Briar.

> **Briar:** *Jeremy just announced to V and V that he's going to Connecticut because he's a reformed rake. Any of you know what he's talking about? Should I leave work and go find him?*

"Oh, shit," I whisper to myself as I read the message a second time.

Jamie frowns. "This is bad, right? It has something to do with what he's not telling us?"

"Could be bad. Or this could actually be a good thing." I slide my phone back into my pants pocket. "Either way, we need to find him. He needs us—well, he needs you and Lexy and Briar. His best friends. Trust me."

Jamie finishes the last of his cone in one bite and chucks his napkin into the trash. "Probably. But I'm pretty sure he needs you even more than he needs us, Aaron."

Jamie's wrong about that—I'm sure of it. But I follow him up the street and back to our cars anyway.

23

THAT TIME JEREMY NEARLY DROWNED SOMEBODY

I'm standing on the bow of Dad's boat, pacing, when the cavalry shows up. I had a feeling they'd make an appearance eventually. Briar looked pretty shell-shocked when I said I was going to Connecticut. My friends have all gotten used to the fact that I never go back home. The only time I've seen Connecticut in three years was for Briar's ocean trip, and they all know it. While we were on that trip, Jamie asked if I was going to show them where I grew up. I said no, and I must have said it *with feeling* because he didn't ask again. So, it's not all that shocking that Briar sent up a smoke signal after I said what I did in V and V today.

I'm not sure how they knew to find me here, though. I figured they'd look for me at The Pink Monstrosity first, and that's why I came right to Dad's boat after I finished throwing some of my stuff into a suitcase at the apartment. I tried to drive directly onto I-89 and start the trip south, but I couldn't. It was like my Audi refused to go in that direction. And instead, I ended up here, pacing back and forth the way Lissie does when she can't get a chord progression right on her guitar. Except that Lissie always seems to figure out the damn song, and right now, I'm wondering if I'm ever going to be able to get in that car and actually drive to Connecticut.

"Jeremy?" Jamie appears at the edge of the dock with Briar and Lexy next to him. "What's going on, man?"

"How'd you know where to find me?" I squint into the sun—must have left my sunglasses back at the apartment, dammit—as I turn to face him. He looks . . . sad? Worried? Maybe confused?

Lexy clears her throat. "We had some help," she says quietly.

And then I see him: right behind Briar is Aaron.

I take a step back without even thinking about it.

"What are you all doing here?" I blurt out. "I mean, I'm fine. I'm going to Connecticut. Why wouldn't I? My fucking parents live there, okay? I can go to Connecticut if I want to!" I go back to pacing, my sneakers slipping slightly beneath me on the boat's deck.

"Jeremy," Lexy says gently, "you want to tell us what's going on? What's really going on?"

"No. Nope. Nope, I definitely do not." That much I know for sure. I do not want to talk about Connecticut and degenerative diseases and DNA testing, and I *definitely* do not want to talk about how many years I've spent avoiding sitting in a room with a man who was once my entire world and now doesn't even know my fucking name. I very, very much do not want to talk about the fact that I've probably fallen in love with Aaron this summer even though I'm not allowed to be in love with people.

I very definitely do not want to talk about any of that.

"Look," I tell them. "I know everyone thinks I'm just a worthless rake—"

"We don't think that," Jamie interrupts.

"Even though I fucked your brother?" I whirl around to face him again as he winces. "Even now? Why'd you take off when you found out about us, then?"

"That had nothing to do with it!" Jamie shouts. "You have to know I didn't run off because of that. I ran off because Aaron was keeping secrets from me again, and you know exactly how that ended the last time. But Aaron and I worked all that out, and I don't care if you and Aaron are a thing. Hell, I *like* you and Aaron as a thing! He makes you come to fireworks shows with us. You keep him from working all night."

A rush of relief pours through my body. So Jamie really was just upset about the secret, and not about me and Aaron hooking up. And he's not mad anymore. That's all excellent news. But still . . . .

"Aaron and I are not a thing," I murmur. Aaron's standing mostly behind Briar, and I can't really see his face as I say those words. I wonder if he looks happy that I've said that. Or if he's upset.

Not that it matters. It's not allowed to matter.

"Whatever," I mutter. "Either way, I need to go to Connecticut. You guys don't have to worry about me. I can do this on my own."

"What? That's ridiculous, Jeremy." Aaron suddenly appears from behind Briar and comes all the way to the end of the dock, until he's standing just at the edge, a quick hop away from where I am on the boat. "Why are you doing this to yourself? Why are you trying to take on all this alone? You don't have to do that, don't you get it? You have friends who want to help! I want to help!"

My eyes sweep back and forth across Delia's Dream as I think of the times I spent here with my father. The hours we spent cleaning this thing. Prepping it for sailing adventures with Dad as the captain.

I've never wished so hard that I'd learned how to sail back then. Because right, now all I want to do is pull up this anchor and disappear across Lake Champlain.

"Why would you want to help me?" I ask the sky. "I don't care about anything, remember?"

Aaron shakes his head. "I shouldn't have said that. We both know it isn't true. I'm sorry, Jeremy. I know you care. If anything, you care too much. And we care about you—please, just let us help you."

I want to say yes. Because the truth is that I don't want to go to

Connecticut alone. I don't want to deal with seeing my mother by myself. I don't want to deal with her ultimatums and my uncle's voice giving me news I'll never, ever be ready to hear.

I don't want to sit in that room by myself and face the reality I've been running away from for three years.

But then I'll have to tell them. I'll have to say all the words out loud. All the words I haven't said to anyone in years.

Anyone except Aaron.

Who, right now, is moving his foot like he's about to step onto the boat with me.

"What are you doing?" I demand.

"I'm coming over there!" he calls. "I know you're mad at me, and you have every right to be, but you need help, Jeremy!"

"Aaron, I don't want to talk about this!" I move fast toward the docking area, like I'm going to somehow stop him from getting on, and I shift the entire boat slightly with the weight of my quick movement at exactly the same time Aaron goes to step onto the boat.

Then physics happens. He moves one way, the boat shifts another, and he loses his balance. And he falls right over the side of the boat and into the lake.

"Aaron!" I jump in after him just as Aaron comes up from beneath the water, sputtering and spitting it out.

I grab onto his arms while I tread water, and I don't even think —much— about how very definitely ruined my favorite fuchsia Nikes are. I'm just so glad to see him above the water and breathing. "Are you okay?" I ask.

He pushes his wet hair out of his eyes and looks at me. And then, in the waters of Lake Champlain, he wraps his arms around me as we both tread water together. "I really am sorry," he says. "I know I can't take back what I said. But I'll never stop being sorry I said it."

I let myself relax into the comfort of his arms. They're wet and slightly chilled against the heat of the sun, but they're . . . Aaron. "Me too," I tell him. "Me too."

We end up back at The Pink Monstrosity. Two showers and a few ice teas later, we're all sitting in Aaron's apartment.

And I've finally told my friends everything. Everything from my father's diagnosis to the reasons I picked Moo U over Yale to the text I got today about my father's hospitalization.

"You got into Yale," Lexy murmurs into her glass. "I always had this weird feeling you were a hidden genius."

"More like a legacy admission with a decent GPA and a good SAT coach," I tell her. I've got no delusions about how my family's privilege helped me get an acceptance letter to Yale.

"So you're ready to do it?" Briar asks quietly. "You're finally ready to go back home?"

"Maybe? I mean, I was this afternoon." I play with the fringe at the corner of the old blanket I'm wrapped up in. "I don't think I'll know for sure until I'm there . . . when I can finally walk into his room and stand in front of him. Have a conversation without running away." The room is quiet as I add, "and I was sure I could do that when I left Vino and Veritas today. But then I tried to drive onto the highway, and I chickened out. That's how I ended up back at the boat." I shrug. "Maybe I can't go home. Maybe I'll never be able to. Maybe I really am just a selfish fucking asshole."

"No, Jeremy," Aaron reaches over to squeeze my hand, and I let myself lean into the calm that washes through my body the minute he touches me. "You're not a selfish asshole. You never were. I know that, and we all know that." Everyone else in the room nods. "The problem is that you've been trying to do all this alone. Listen." He leans forward and grabs hold of my other hand. "If there's one thing I've learned in the last two years, it's that the future is so much more terrifying when you're facing it by yourself. You're a big part of the reason I finally stopped facing my future alone. It's my turn to tell you that you need to stop trying to do this all on your own."

Briar stands up. "Time for a road trip?" he asks quietly.

"Let's do it." Jamie stands up next to him.

"Definitely," Lexy adds as she rises from her chair. "Anything for my J-Bear."

"Ugh, I hate when you call me that." I don't, really, and she knows it. I smile as I look at the way they've literally closed ranks on me. Aaron's basically holding me still on the couch, and they're standing around me, circled up like some freaky guards in a movie about royalty.

And now I know I'm going to make it to Connecticut this time. I know that for sure—because I won't be the one driving the car.

It's late in the evening by the time we get onto the road, and we cross the Massachusetts border in the dark. At some point, Jamie and Briar fall asleep on top of each other in the back row of the Barnsby van, which Lexy insisted on borrowing so we could all ride together comfortably.

I never thought I'd love a minivan, but this one is pretty cool. It even has an entertainment system.

Aaron was driving earlier, and now he's crashed out on the bench seat behind me. Lexy and I are in front, and she's driving when she says, almost in a whisper, "I'm really glad you and Aaron found each other."

I turn slightly in my seat so I can look at him. This isn't the first time I've watched him sleep, and I hope it isn't the last—but who knows? The summer's coming to an end soon, and even if it wasn't, things changed between us today. I'm not sure we could ever go back to our summer fling. "Me too," I admit. Then I tell her something I haven't said out loud once to anyone: "Sometimes I wish we could have more."

Lexy frowns at the headlights of a passing truck. "Why couldn't you? So what if he's going back to school? He's only got one more year there anyway."

I hate every word of the answer that comes out of my mouth.

"Because Aaron deserves to be with someone whose future isn't full of blank spaces."

Lexy takes one hand off the wheel to reach over and squeeze mine. Neither of us speaks again until we cross the Connecticut border.

24

THAT TIME AARON TOLD OFF THE ICE QUEEN

I'm not sure what I expected Jeremy's childhood home to look like. I mean, I expected it to be big. I knew his family had money.

But this?

This is not big. This is not even *large*. This is . . . monstrous, maybe?

It's almost midnight when Lexy navigates the minivan through stretches of wooded streets, past houses that seem to be growing in size as the street addresses go up in numbers, and finally pulls up in front of a set of large iron gates. Jeremy sighs and mumbles, "This is it."

Lexy gapes at him. "Uh, I don't mean to sound like an asshole, but are you . . . sure?"

Jeremy sighs again. "Yes, Lexy. I'm sure this is where I grew up. Hit these numbers on the security box, will you?" And then he rattles off a sequence of five numbers at her.

Because there's a security box. Which, of course there is. Because there's a giant gate in front of us.

I turn to look at Jamie and Briar, who are huddled together in the backseat of the van. "Long way from Tiny Acres," Jamie mumbles.

I know he's thinking about all the holidays and weekends Jeremy's spent rattling around with us in our two-story farmhouse. Half the time, our house only has one working bathroom.

The security panel buzzes, and the gates smoothly begin to glide open. Jeremy sits up in his seat, and I can see his shoulders and back tense. I reach up between the driver's and passenger's seats to gently massage the back of his neck.

"It's just a house," he mutters to the windshield. "Right? It's just a house."

I'm not sure if he's talking to Lexy or me, but I'm the one who answers. "It's just a house. One of it, five of us. We're definitely going to win."

Jeremy turns in his seat and gives me a slight smile that sends crackles through every one of my nerve endings. At some point, we're probably going to have to talk about what happened in that alleyway—was that earlier today? It feels like a million years ago. But for now, I'm glad that we're speaking to each other again. I'm glad that I'm here with him as he takes on all the dragons that I know are probably lurking behind the gate we just drove through.

Or ice queens, I guess. Possibly an ice queen and some dragons.

The driveway winds and snakes through trees and perfect landscaping, and then Lexy pulls up to what I would very definitely describe as a mansion. The thing has got to be eight or ten thousand square feet, if not bigger. (As someone who grew up sharing less than two thousand square feet with four other people, I'm not the best judge of house size.) There's a huge roundabout driveway in front of it and what looks like a multi-car garage off to the side. In the dark I see the shadows of a pool on one side of the house . . . and is that a tennis court?

"Okay, look." Jeremy turns in his seat to face us all as Lexy cuts the engine. "I want to warn you all now: I texted my uncle to let him know we were coming. Which means my mother is probably going to be up and waiting for us."

"Okay?" Lexy looks puzzled by this announcement.

"And she can be a real bitch sometimes," Jeremy adds. "Especially when she's upset. Picture our stats professor from first semester mixed with Cruella de Vil, and you might be in the ballpark of what we're dealing with here."

Lexy winces. "Professor Winley?" she asks.

Jeremy nods gravely.

"She's definitely got the same vibes as the Morse's Line elementary school principal," I mutter to Jamie. He grimaces.

"So, we're going to have to go with some covert ops here," Jeremy adds. "We get in, we do not engage, we head to the guest wing."

"Guest wing?" Briar pipes up in a high voice. "Who the fuck even are you, Jeremy? And how is it that you don't mind eating Cup of Noodles with us all the time?"

Jeremy shrugs. "Because Cup of Noodles is delicious. Duh."

We all murmur agreement, except for Lexy, who would never be caught dead eating something as processed as Cup of Noodles. She rolls her eyes.

And then, together, we pour out of the minivan like a group of drunken clowns, pulling quickly packed bags out of the back. Jeremy hoists his backpack onto his shoulder and stares at the outdoor lights illuminating the large, immaculate front door of the house.

"I can do this, right?" he whispers to me.

"Yes, Jeremy. You can. *We* can," I add.

Then I grab his hand and hold it tight as the two of us march to the door together, with Briar, Lexy, and Jamie flanking us on every side.

The inside of the house isn't any less impressive than the outside. Jeremy leads us through an entryway lined with artwork that probably costs more than our entire farm and into a high-ceilinged room decorated in furniture that I'm guessing all came from very, very expensive antique shops. Sitting on a couch in the middle of the room is Jeremy's mother. She's holding a glass of wine and wearing a silk bathrobe tied over silk pajamas. I never thought a person could look menacing in pajamas. Now I know otherwise.

"Jeremy." She sets down the wine and stands up to move toward us, her hands clasped in front of her, and for a moment, I think she's going to try to hug him. She stops short of him, though, as she nods at us. "You brought some friends with you?"

"They wanted a road trip," Jeremy says with a tight smile. "You remember Aaron, right? That's Jamie, his brother, and this is Briar and Lexy."

"It's good to see you again, Mrs. Everett." I consider reaching out to shake her hand, but I take my cue when she just nods at me again and keeps her hands tucked together in front of her.

"I was glad to hear from your uncle that you'd be coming," she says to Jeremy. "You got the news, then? About your father?"

Jeremy nods. "How's he doing?"

"He's had a minor bout with pneumonia. He's much better now." She takes a deep breath, and I'm surprised to hear how much emotion there is in her voice when she says, "I'm very glad you finally came home, Jeremy."

Wow. That seems like a lot from Delia Everett, especially with the rest of us standing here. Maybe it's the wine. Maybe she's really just missed her son that much.

Jeremy grips my hand so tightly it hurts. "Why?" he asks.

Everyone in the room is silent for a minute as Jeremy and his mother stare at each other. Anyone who didn't know them would think they're total strangers finding each other's faces in a crowd for the very first time.

"For many reasons." Delia Everett smiles weakly. "But mainly, I'm glad you're here because I've missed you, son."

Jeremy grips my hand more tightly.

"I have some things I need to say to you," she tells him. "Perhaps we should go in the other room."

It makes sense to me that she'd want to talk to him alone, but

Jeremy shakes his head. "They know our history, Mom. They know everything. If you can say it to me, you can say it in front of them."

For a moment, her eyes narrow, but she schools her expression quickly. "Fine," she says quietly. "If you insist."

Now Jeremy's holding my hand so tightly it hurts.

"I know you often wish I were more like your father . . . was," she goes on, and Jeremy winces at the past-tense. "We both know I never will be, of course. But I have hated to think of all the time we've spent apart now, and I have also hated to think how you might regret things if you weren't able to see him again."

Jeremy looks more and more shaken by each word she says. I move a little closer toward him until my body's pressed just slightly up against his. "But it's not him anymore, right?" he asks softly. "He hasn't been Dad since I left."

Delia Everett scoffs. "He'll always be your father, Jeremy. Of course we miss the man he was. But he's still your father. It's only right that you've come home to see him." She shakes her head, as if that subject's closed—as if whatever trauma Jeremy might have to deal with when he sees what his dad has become isn't even worth talking about. Like it's just something he's going to have to grit his teeth through and bear.

I have a feeling that's how she's been dealing with most of what life's thrown at her since her husband was diagnosed. Now that I'm looking closely at her, she doesn't look nearly as powerful or menacing as she did in the parking lot the day we met. She looks tired. There are lines around her eyes, and there's a sag to her shoulders I didn't notice that day.

And then there's the sadness that seems to linger in her expression as she looks at her son—the glint of regret that sits there every time her gaze moves back to him.

Any hint of sympathy I feel for her goes right out of me, though, when she says her next words: "And of course, we'll need for you to arrange to have that testing completed while you're here."

Jeremy closes his eyes and draws in a long, deep breath. "Mom," he says steadily, "we've been over this. You and I both know that there's nothing taking that test is going to change. There aren't any miraculous treatments they can give me. The test is meaningless."

I practically feel him shaking as he speaks. I can imagine how much just saying these words is taking out of him. *C'mon, Jeremy,* I will him silently. *You can do this. You are doing it. I'm so proud of you.*

Logically I know telepathy isn't real, but something in Jeremy does shift a little just then as he draws himself more upright and looks his mom right in the eye. "I'm not taking the test, Mom. I'm not. The odds are the odds. Uncle Jerry hit the right side of them, and Dad didn't. I don't want that information ahead of time. Not unless there's some reason I need it—some treatment they could give me. Until that exists, I'm not getting that test."

She shakes her head. "I truly do understand why you feel that way, son, but—" Her voice breaks, but she quickly composes herself. "This isn't a conversation for company. We can discuss this more tomorrow."

"They're not company!" Jeremy's almost shouting now. "They're my friends, Mom. The people who care about me whether I do what they want me to or not."

"You think I don't care about you? That's really what you believe?" Now Delia Everett is raising her voice, too. I have a feeling that's not a common occurrence for someone as prim and proper as she is. "Jeremy Everett, I care more about you than anyone in the world, except your father! But you're too selfish to see that!" She shakes her head. "Your father spoiled you. I told him he would, the way he pampered and coddled you. And now here you are, a grown man who still acts like a child in every way! Your father would be ashamed if he knew what you'd become."

Jeremy's face goes paler with every word she says, and suddenly I can't stay silent anymore. Not when Jeremy's mother is throwing bombs like that. "Mrs. Everett," I say in the same voice I used the last time I went toe-to-toe with her. My "don't fuck with me" voice is what Jeremy calls it when I pull it out it in the office. I have a feeling Jeremy's mom will respond better to that voice than me yelling—and she does. It works. She stops talking and looks at me.

"I know you're upset right now," I tell her steadily. "But Jeremy isn't a child. He's been taking care of himself for a long time now. You should be proud of the man he's become. He may not make the choices that you would make, or react to situations the way you do, but he's one of the most thoughtful, supportive, kind, and loyal people I've ever met. And even more than that, he's one of the strongest people I've ever met." Delia Everett is studying me closely, like she's not quite sure what to make of me. "He has the right to make his own choices about his body and his future. Be careful not to say things you're going to regret just because you don't agree with those choices."

Behind me, Jamie whispers, "Wow, bro."

Maybe I'll also start calling this my "don't fuck with me" voice.

Jeremy's mother draws in a long breath and lets it out slowly. Silence hangs in the room. Finally, she says, "I know what is best for my son."

And then she turns and walks out of the room.

The dragon's gone. Or is it the Ice Queen? I'm starting to mix up my own metaphors. Either way, it's clear Jeremy and his mother have a lot more talking to do. But that will have to come later. Right now, Jeremy seems to be frozen in place next to me. Lexy's tugging at the sleeve of his sweatshirt. "Jeremy, are you okay? Holy shit, now I get why you never told us about your family. That was a thousand times worse than our semester in stats. Geez, I—"

She's still talking when Jeremy turns, pulls me into his arms, and presses his mouth hard against mine.

25

THAT TIME JEREMY DID HARD THINGS

"Morning, cuddle bunnies."

I pull a container of freshly squeezed orange juice from the refrigerator and set it down on the marble island as Briar and Jamie step into the large, open kitchen of my parents' house. Briar's eyes are like saucers. "Jeremy, your kitchen could belong to a gourmet chef."

"Yeah. It could," I agree. This kitchen is impressive, even by my parents' standards. An eight-burner gas stove sits below a restaurant-quality hood that's centered between long shiny cabinets and countertops dotted with the highest-quality kitchen gadgets money can buy. The island where I pull out stools for Briar and Jamie is the size of my entire kitchen back at The Pink Monstrosity. I take glasses out of a cabinet. "My dad loves—loved?—to cook." I shake my head. "See? This is why I never told any of you guys what was going on. I can't even figure out what verb tenses to use when I talk about him."

This is a weird problem with conditions like dementia and Alzheimer's. Am I supposed to use the past or present tense when I talk about my dad? He's not dead. He's lying in a bed just a few miles down the road from the kitchen I'm standing in.

But he hasn't cooked in years, and it's a given that he never will again.

I get busy making coffee to distract myself while Briar pours glasses of juice. "I know it doesn't really help," he says. "But I think I understand why you never told us. I never tell people about what a basket case my mom is if I can help it. Jamie was the first person I'd told in a long time." He sends Jamie a quiet smile. "Sometimes, saying something out loud is a hell of a lot more painful than living with something in your head."

And that's . . . pretty accurate, actually. I sit and think about that while I wait for the coffee to percolate—and I watch Briar and Jamie. Jamie rubs at Briar's hair, and then he gently kisses his cheek. Briar passes him some orange juice, Jamie sips at it, and then Briar nuzzles his head against Jamie's neck gently. They kiss. And then they give each other tiny, fast nods.

Sub orange juice in for hot beverages, and they've moved their disgustingly adorable morning routine three hundred miles from Burlington, Vermont, to Wellsford, Connecticut. And I doubt either of them even thought about it once.

I want that. The thought crowds my brain as I quickly turn away from them to take out mugs and start pouring coffee. Suddenly, all I can think of is the routine I'd be following if Aaron and I were back at the law firm right now, where we should be. He usually gets right to work—he never thinks to get water or coffee or anything like that first. So, I interrupt him around 9:30 with coffee and whatever other breakfast treats are kicking around the break room, and then we chat for a few minutes while Benson growls at us, and we make inside jokes about things like Briar and Autumn's newest board game obsession.

I want that. But it's just one more thing on a long list of stuff life keeps reminding me I can't have. And today, it's time to face item number one on that list. Last night I was distracted enough dealing with Mom that I didn't have much time to think about today, but I can't ignore what's coming anymore. For the first time in three years, I'm going to see my father again.

217

The last time I saw him, he was barely hanging onto names and faces. He was still living here, then. Mom had a home health aide for him. The aide stood in the corner of the room, watching us, when I told Dad I was leaving for college.

"Jerry? You're leaving?" he asked. He kept mixing me up with my uncle.

"No, Dad. It's me, Jeremy," I told him. Some things came back to him then: my graduation, my acceptance to Moo U. They came back to him long enough for him to clap me on the shoulder and then hug me tight. *"I'm so proud of you, son,"* he said. *"Always so proud of you."*

I got in my car and cried all the way to Springfield, Massachusetts. I knew the next time I saw my dad there probably wouldn't be any piece of him left that remembered me. And today I'll find out for sure.

"Jeremy?" A voice says behind me. I turn into the comfort of those syllables—into the comfort of the opening sound of a morning routine that I got to have for one summer, at least. Aaron is standing there, holding out his arms. "Come here."

I fold myself into his arms and breathe.

Dad's bout with pneumonia is mostly over, and he's back at the care facility. Mom makes an appearance in the kitchen long enough to inform me that she has to work, but I should be able to see him during visiting hours.

"And then I'll expect you here for dinner tonight," she tells me crisply. "We have things to discuss." She nods to the rest of my friends as she leaves.

"All she needs is a litter of dalmatians and a few more designer coats," I mutter. Aaron hugs me around the shoulders.

The care facility where Mom and Uncle Jerry placed Dad is close by. I know from our brief conversations that Mom visits him a lot. I can say plenty of terrible things about her, but I can never say that she's not loyal. Or that my parents didn't love each other with the same kind of obsession Jamie and Briar have.

"Jeremy, we're so happy to have you visiting," one of the nurses at the reception desk tells me as I sign in. "I've seen your picture in your dad's room. I'm sure he'll be thrilled you're here."

I swallow hard. "Does he . . . remember me?"

She hesitates. "Sometimes," she says softly. Then she glances at the posse of people behind me. "I'm sorry, but I can't recommend that you bring that many people in to see him with you. He can get easily overwhelmed. Maybe just one other person?"

"I'll go," Aaron says quickly. I don't even try to pretend that I'm not relieved as hell I don't have to do this alone. Or that Aaron is the one facing things with me.

We follow the nurse, whose name is Ella, down the hall. She knocks at the door and then opens it. "Doug?" she calls.

And there's my father. In pajamas, lying in bed, with a tube running into his nostrils. He's watching something on TV: *Wheel of Fortune*. It's a show the two of us used to watch when I was a kid. I always complained about how much I hated it, but I secretly loved yelling guesses at the TV whenever I thought I'd solved the puzzle.

Dad looks so much older than he did the last time I saw him. Grayer. More wrinkled. But his eyes are wide and excited as he looks over at us. "Who's here? Visitors?" He says in a raspy voice. "Ah! Visitors! You're just in time to solve this!"

Ella smooths out the covers on his bed and pats his hand while she holds up a cup with a straw for him to drink out of. "Doug," she says gently. "This is Jeremy. You remember Jeremy? Your son?"

Dad frowns as he studies me. "Jeremy . . . Jeremy . . . ," he repeats to himself. "I knew a Jeremy once," he says to me. "My brother! We played baseball together."

Tears are rolling down my face before I can stop them. Aaron grabs onto my hand and holds tightly. "You can do this," he whispers. "I know you can."

I force myself to speak over the mound that's wedged into my throat right now. "I know about your brother," I manage to say. "You're really close. You named me after him. I call him Uncle Jerry. It's good to see you, Dad."

"Dad? Dad's not here." He looks around, confused. "Haven't seen my dad in a long time! Do you think he'll visit today?" He asks Ella.

"Probably not today, Doug. But Jeremy's here now. And his friend."

Dad smiles at us. "Do you want to solve the puzzle?"

I step closer to the bed, one hand still in Aaron's, the other reaching toward my father. This is the man who taught me to ride a bicycle. He held me when I broke my leg in a soccer game. He kissed me on the forehead and told me he loved me no matter what when I came home from junior high one day and said I had a crush on a guy. "I've missed you, Dad. I'm so sorry I didn't come earlier." The tears are flowing freely now. I can't stop them. Dad looks puzzled.

"You're not late," he says gently. "Just in time for the puzzle." He coughs, gently at first, and then more loudly, until the sound is like nails on a chalkboard in my ears.

"It's not that bad," Ella says when she sees the look on my face. "He was much worse off earlier, but he's better now. You're a fighter, aren't you, Doug?"

Dad finishes coughing and looks up at me and Aaron. "Who are you again? Are you here for the puzzle?"

"I'm so sorry, Dad," I whisper to him. "I'm so, so sorry."

I drop Aaron's hand and I run.

Aaron finds me curled up by an emergency exit door, sobbing. The next thing I know I'm basically curled up in his lap, crying into his chest while he rubs my hair. "You did so well, Jeremy," he whispers. "I'm so proud of you. So, so proud."

"I couldn't stay," I mumble. "I couldn't stay. I'm a terrible person. I'm a rake and fuckup and—"

"No! Stop." Aaron grabs my face in his hands and forces me to look at him. "You're not any of those things, Jeremy. Well," he says, smiling, "maybe a reformed rake, but only in a good way. Jeremy, you did an amazing thing today. Going into that room, seeing your dad again." He shakes his head. "I don't even think you realize how strong you are," he says softly.

I tell him the truth. "I couldn't have done it without you."

He wraps me up in his arms again. "You could have," he whispers. "But you didn't need to."

We end up back at the house, sitting around the pool together. Mom's still at work, and the five of us start taking turns practicing our cannonball skills.

And then something happens: I start talking.

I tell Briar and Jamie and Lexy and Aaron stories about the time my dad taught me to do cannonballs. Mom got upset because he was ruining my new haircut, and he pulled her into the pool with us. We all ended up laughing in the deep end together, taking turns dunking each other. It's still one of my favorite memories of my family.

The five of us have a cannonball contest, and Lexy has the best one, because of course she does—Lexy's good at everything. "Dad would be proud," I tell her.

When I start crying again, they all sit with me. Quietly. No judgment, no words about how everything's going to be okay. Just quiet, because somehow they know that's exactly what I need.

And then it's time to face the next gauntlet of the day: dinner. Mom will be home soon.

We all go inside to shower. I'm surprised-but-not-really when Aaron passes right by the door of the room he's staying in and follows me io mine.

He closes the door behind him and stares at me. "I thought maybe you'd want—" he starts to say.

I tackle him before he can finish. I know exactly what I want.

I push him back against the navy blue wall of my old bedroom, shoving my hips against his and pushing my mouth into his so hard it hurts. All I want right now is to forget. I want to forget, for just a few minutes, about everything that happened today. And I know how to do that with Aaron. I know how to lose myself in the way his fingers flicker against my skin, and the way his soft upper lip curves perfectly around mine. I know how to lose myself in the feel of his hard chest and shoulders and the perfect way our bodies fit against each other.

"I want," I whisper into his mouth. "I want you."

It's not like it's been that long since we were together like this —the last time was just a few days ago when he bought me ice cream. But so much has happened since then that it feels like it was years ago, and my body's behaving like it can't even wait five seconds to get off with him again. My blood is rushing, every single nerve ending in my skin is tingling, and my dick is as hard as it's ever been.

Which is saying something.

We don't hurry, though. Even though all I want is to fuck myself onto him as hard and as fast as I can, we don't rush. Carefully, slowly, we pull each other's clothes away from our bodies, until all I feel is the perfect press of his soft skin against mine. He's just as hard as I am as he gently lays me down across my childhood bed.

"Let me take care of you," he whispers.

And I do.

I let him prep me slowly with the lube I keep in the side pocket of my suitcase. (Never leave home without it.) I let him stroke me from the inside out, one finger at a time, until I'm writhing on three of them and begging to have him inside me. I let him tease me with his tongue, which he drags back and forth all the way from my cock to my taint until I'm clutching at the bed and whimpering. "Inside me," I whisper hoarsely. "Inside me, please."

He's so gentle as he carefully lays me down across some pillows and kneels in front of me. And then he hesitates.

"Jeremy, I'm so sorry," he says. "I just want you to know that I'm still so sorry for what I said in the—"

"No." I grab his hands and cut the words off before any more of them can come out. "Aaron, listen. We were both there in that alleyway. We both said things. We both know there's not a lot of time in life for regrets. And I don't want to waste another minute on them." I trace one finger down his cheek. "I just want to be with you."

He grabs my hand and kisses it hard as he pushes inside of me.

He makes love to me slowly, moving in an inch at a time and circling his fingers around my cock with the same perfect precision that he does everything. Then he pulls my knees up a little higher and starts moving a little faster, and I let myself get lost in the movements and the sensations of his dick pressing into the most sensitive parts of my body. The faster he goes, the more my body thrums.

"I'm so close," I whisper.

Just like that, he pulls out of me. But not for long.

He flips us over on the bed so that he's holding me tight in his arms, holding me together, as he thrusts back inside of me. Every inch of his body is wrapped around mine as he moves back and forth, in and out, and all I want is to feel like this forever: protected.

"I don't think I can let you go again," he murmurs into my ear. "I'm sorry, Jeremy. But I'm worried I can't."

"So don't," I tell him softly. And then, as he moves inside me with one more push, I explode across the blankets of the bed I never thought I'd lay on again. Aaron holds my body tight as he shakes and shudders with me.

He's wearing a condom, of course, but I can't help but wonder: what would it be like to have him bare inside of me?

We collapse on the bed together, too worn out to move. For a long time, we lay there.

Eventually, Aaron pulls out of me gently. He takes care of the condom and cleans me up with a washcloth, wiping me down carefully as he kisses my stomach.

He stops for a minute on his way to the attached bathroom. "We don't have to, you know. Stop. At the end of the summer. We can have more if we want, Jeremy." He steps into the bathroom and closes the door.

I look over at the picture that lives on the end table next to my bed. It's of my father and mother on the day I was born. She's holding me, and he's staring at her like she's the most amazing thing he's ever seen. Like he can't believe how lucky he got.

I wonder: if he knew then how things would end up, would he still have done it all the same way?

26

THAT TIME AARON FAILED THE RIGHT WAY

"*This* was where you played as a kid?"

"Why is that weird?" Jeremy frowns as he looks at the gated entrance to Coveted Hills Country Club. He crosses his arms and stares out at the wide-ranging, loudly green golf course that seems to spread out in every direction. The owners probably spend more money on their water bill every month than my dad spends feeding our cows. "They have a pool with some really excellent water slides. My pool at home didn't have a water slide. Duh." He grins at me and winks, and I know we're both thinking the same thing: how far apart our childhoods really were. Jamie and I were probably playing in frog ponds at the exact same time that Jeremy was taking golf lessons from pros.

But none of that matters now as he and I walk through his old neighborhood together. We've got a little more time to kill before the dreaded dinner with his mother, and there were things I knew I needed to say to him after what just happened between us in the bedroom. But I was kind of surprised Jeremy agreed to go for a walk with me.

I made it pretty clear I wanted to talk about feelings. But he didn't even wince. He just pulled on his sneakers.

We keep moving, past the country club and up a perfectly kept sidewalk. Every lawn we walk by is well-manicured, every bush perfectly shaped. The driveways are clean, like they're washed every day. It's as if this is the neighborhood of no mistakes. I say that to Jeremy.

"Yeah. I used to fit into the picture pretty well." He shrugs. "When Dad got sick, and I left for Vermont, I stopped caring about any of that. About the perfect grades or the perfect image or the perfect fucking lawn. That's when Mom and I started fighting for real." He frowns. "The two of us were never as close as Dad and I were. But what you're seeing this weekend . . . let's just say it definitely got a lot worse when I stopped caring about being the perfect son." He sends me a wicked grin. "Man, it's too bad she's probably too far up her ass to get to know you. You're the son she always wanted. Great GPA, Harvard Law, bright future in front of you. Throw in an MBA and you're everything she dreamed of for me."

Visions of Leicester, where the business/law degree combo was common, fill my head. "The perfect son," I mutter.

"Yup." Jeremy agrees. The sun's starting to slowly sink lower in the sky above us, and Jeremy frowns into its light. "In Delia Everett's world, failure isn't an option."

I can tell that just from the lawns.

We walk farther, but we don't speak. I wonder what Jeremy's thinking about. I'm thinking about failure.

I'm thinking about how terrified I was of this summer. How terrified I was of failing again after Leicester.

And I'm thinking something that I can't quite figure out how to say to Jeremy.

I meant what I said to him when he and I were making love in his bedroom. I don't think I can let him go. I don't think I'll be able to fully walk away when this summer is over. Not really.

You always hear people say that there's power in failure. That it leads to change and growth and learning; that's it's a necessary part of life. I'm not sure I ever believed that until this summer. But somehow, Jeremy and I have become a real-life lesson for me in how powerful failure can be.

This thing Jeremy and I have had together this summer—we've done it all wrong. All of it. And yet, somehow, every little wrong moment has added up to the most perfect relationship I could ever imagine having. I know now that I want more—so, so much more. I also know there's a good chance Jeremy can't give that to me. I understand better than I ever have why Jeremy lives his life the way he does.

But I'm ready to ask for what I want now. I'm ready to tell Jeremy how much I want him, and I'm ready to fail trying to get him. Because, for the first time in a long time, I'm starting to believe in the power of failure.

"Jeremy," I finally say, quietly. I stop in the middle of the sidewalk, next to a hedge that's probably measured down to the centimeter when it's cut. "I meant what I said in your bedroom. I don't think I can let you go. I don't want to." I pull in a long, deep breath because I need all the energy I can find to say what I want to say next. "I want more with you. I want something beyond the end of the summer. And I understand if that's not what you want, but I had to say it out loud. I had to. I want more, Jeremy. I want more of you."

Jeremy stops next to me. The laces of his bright blue Converse are untied at his ankles, his shorts dropping at his waist like he's still a kid, but he somehow looks older than ever as he stares at me intently and traces one hand over my cheek. "I can't believe I'm saying this out loud to someone," he tells me, "but there's nothing I want more right now than a relationship with you, Aaron." A jolt of something like fire passes through my veins as he leans forward, like he's going to kiss me—

And then he steps back and drops his hand. The fire fades to coals and embers so quickly that my body goes cold.

"But," he adds.

My body goes a little colder. It knows what words are coming next.

"But we're watching in real-time how a relationship with me can end. I could never do that to you, Aaron. I could never ask you to take that chance on me. You deserve someone with a future as incredible as yours. We both know there's a good chance I can't give that to you, no matter how much I want to."

"Jeremy!" I reach for him, fast, but he steps away from me again. "You don't know what's coming for you. Even if the worst happens, someday, that's not today. Isn't that what you're all about? Living in the moment?"

"Yeah, and that's why I live it alone." He manages to keep his voice level and even, though I can tell from his expression that he wants to scream the words. "Because we're seeing right now what my mother is going through. I can't put you through that kind of pain, Aaron. I can't let you tie yourself to me. I could never do that to someone who means as much to me as you do." He frowns and studies me. "Maybe Mom's right. Maybe I should take the test. And then if it comes back negative for the gene—"

"No!" I practically do shout, my voice loud and out of place in the perfectly still and silent neighborhood. "No. Not unless you want to, or there's a real medical reason to do it. The test doesn't matter, Jeremy. It will never matter. I want every moment I can have with you, whatever the future holds." I take another step, and I wish harder than I've ever wished for anything that he'll just stay still this time—that he'll let me reach him.

He doesn't, though. He takes another step back. "I wish that's how things worked," he whispers hoarsely. "But I know what I'm talking about here, Aaron. I know better than anyone. And I can't take that kind of risk with you. I just can't."

He turns fast and starts jogging down the street, away from me, like he's racing someone—or something—I can't see.

Jamie meets me at the door when I get back to the house. "Did something happen with you and Jeremy?" he asks. "He looked better when the two of you left, but now he's all pale again and pacing in the sitting area—whatever the fuck a sitting area is. Aaron, what's going on?"

I shake my head. "What's going on is I'm pretty sure I'm in love with him," I mutter to my brother as I kick off my shoes in the hallway entrance to Jeremy's family's kinda-mansion.

Jamie's eyes go a little wide. "Really? It's that serious?"

I shrug. "I think I want it to be. And you know what? I think he does too. But he's convinced we can't have that. Because . . . ." I let my gaze move to the giant portrait on the wall at the front of the hallway. The one of a ten- or eleven-year-old Jeremy, flanked on both sides by his parents. His father's eyes are lively and smiling and every bit as blue as Jeremy's.

Jamie sighs. "I know I was an asshole when I found out about you two. But you are great together. I see it now. I see why it works. If that matters."

"Yeah. It matters. A lot." I take the hug Jamie offers, and we're still holding onto each other when Lexy appears in the hallway.

"Time for dinner," she says in a low voice. "And you two better hurry up, because there's no way Briar and I are enough backup for Jeremy right now."

I square up my shoulders. If I'm ever going to need my Don't Fuck With Me voice, it's probably tonight.

Lexy leads us into a dining room, where a long table is decorated with settings fancier than I've probably ever seen in someone's house. I hope I can remember which fork and knife to use with which course. Jeremy appears in the doorway and sends me a weak smile while someone dressed in what looks like a maid's uniform—and I didn't know people actually wore those, but apparently they do—starts setting large bowls and plates out on the table.

Delia Everett appears in the doorway, looking perfectly put together in a pantsuit and understated jewelry. She nods at us. "Sit, everyone. I've been looking forward to eating with you all.

I'm very excited to know Jeremy's friends better." She passes Jeremy a tight smile, but he doesn't return it.

At first, things go okay. Jeremy's mom seems to have decided to forget everything the two of us said to each other last night, and she's almost overly cordial to me. She is, as Jeremy predicted, impressed that I go to Harvard. She's even more impressed that I worked at Leicester last summer. I decide not to mention how badly it ended. "What on earth are you doing at that tiny firm in Vermont?" she says. "I'll need to introduce you to some friends of mine before your 3L year. Certainly, I can help you find more suitable places to work after your graduation."

Jeremy rolls his eyes and opens his mouth, but I manage to answer her first. "Actually, I've learned a lot this summer," I tell her easily. "I'm very happy at Sprysky and Gentry."

Or I was, I guess. For all I know, I don't even have a job there anymore. I sent Iris and Tom an email letting them know I needed some time off, but I've been so preoccupied with Jeremy that I haven't even checked to see if either of them answered.

That says a lot about how my priorities have shifted, I guess. But I'm still trying very hard not to think about how I may have thrown away everything Iris and Tom gave me.

We talk about Briar's job at the bookstore, which doesn't impress Delia Everett at all, and Jamie's career goals, which don't do the job either. I guess librarians and booksellers don't list high on the Everett categories of Very Important People. Lexy's plans to attend med school get some accolades . . . and then we get to Jeremy.

"And you, darling?" she asks him. "Have you given any thoughts to your plans after graduation?"

Across the table from me, Jeremy's moving the same three tiny potatoes around his plate. He shrugs. "Nope, not really."

She sighs. "Jeremy, honestly. I wasn't going to bring all this up in front of your friends, but it's clear you keep nothing from them anyway, so we may as well have this conversation now. It's also clear they all have plans in front of them. Goals. When are you finally going to start thinking about your future?"

Jeremy's fork clatters to his plate. "Seriously, Mom? You want to do this now? Fine. Then you, of all people, should know why I don't make plans. Because what's the fucking point?" He throws his hands up in the air. "You and Dad made plan after plan for years, right? And look how that turned out."

Delia Everett sets her fork down sharply on her plate. "Your father and I had no choice! We didn't have the medical knowledge in front of us then that you do now. Your father and I had no way of knowing what was coming. But you do! Jeremy, you have an opportunity your father never had—to know your own future! To plan for it. But you refuse that knowledge! You refuse to take the test!" There are tears in her eyes now, "Don't you know?" she says, and I can hear those very same tears in her voice. "Don't you know that I want you to take that test because I love you so very much?" She pulls in a deep breath. "If you have that gene, I need to make sure I can do everything in my power to help you. I need to be able to fight for you, Jeremy. I need you to fight for yourself. I need to make sure I don't lose you the way I'm losing him."

And then she drops her napkin onto the plate and leaves the room. Again.

And the five of us sit there, in silence.

Briar finally breaks it.

"So," he says. "Is someone gonna tell me why I needed three forks for this dinner?"

Jeremy's the first one to start laughing, but it isn't long before the rest of us join in.

27

THAT TIME JEREMY WAS DEFINITELY NOT A SELFISH RAKE

I'm not exactly the kind of guy who second-guesses my own choices a lot. That was part of the deal I made with myself when I promised my dad I was going to live every moment of my life to the fullest. No regrets. No second-guessing. No looking back.

That's what living in the moment is, right?

But right now, staring at the doorway of Dad's room at the care center, I'm definitely second-guessing a lot of my own choices.

I didn't sleep very well last night. Aaron's words hung heavy in my head, and my mom's wouldn't stop playing on repeat over top of them. I was always so sure I'd made the right choice not to get the test. Since my father was first diagnosed, we've always known that the gene he has, the one that he may or may not have passed onto me, is something doctors can only test for. There aren't any preventive treatments. If I've got the gene, I've got it. That's it. All that test will do is give me an idea of how much time I've got to mark.

I'm not sure why my mom thinks she could do so much more if we had those results. But listening to her last night was a harsh reminder of what she's gone through alone since I left. I was able to run away from this room for three long years because I always knew my dad was being taken care of. I knew she'd never abandon him. My mom may not be perfect, but I never once doubted that she'd be there for my father.

I don't think I ever thought much about how hard these last three years have been for her. This trip has been a tough reminder that I really am just a selfish fucking asshole sometimes.

Another reminder of that sad fact is standing next to me right now, his eyes darting back between me and the doorway.

If I cared about Aaron as much as I now realize he cares about me, I would take that test. Wouldn't I? Because then I'd know for sure. Then I could either walk away, or I could try to be the person he deserves.

But I don't want to take that test. I don't want to live with the knowing. Still, I want Aaron. I want him more than anything. And maybe that does make me the most selfish rake that ever lived.

Who knew rakes could fall in love? Romance novels, I guess. Maybe there's more truth in those things than people give them credit for.

"Jeremy?" Aaron says my name incredibly softly, like he's afraid the word might break me in two. "Are you ready to go inside? Say goodbye?"

We're leaving today, as soon as this visit is over. We all have lives to get back to in Vermont. Iris and Tom were great about giving me a few days off to deal with my "family emergency," but a small firm like theirs needs its people back. I'm sure they're struggling without Aaron.

I still can't believe he took time off from work to come to Connecticut with me. Except no, scratch that. I one hundred percent can believe it. Because he's not a selfish asshole like I am.

"Yeah." I straighten my shoulders, trying to borrow Aaron's "power up" position. "Yeah. I'm ready." I sigh. "Whatever happens now," I mutter to myself, "maybe Christmas Eve will at least be better this year."

Aaron shoots me a confused look. "You never come to our

house for Christmas Eve," he mutters. "Jamie invites you every year, but you only ever come for Christmas Day."

"It's my dad's favorite day of the year." I close my eyes as memories flood my brain. Memories of my father playing the piano and singing carols and making cookies for Santa Claus with me. "He loved it even more than Christmas Day. I've never been able to spend it with other people. So I spend it alone." Well, usually, I spend it with a bottle of vodka, but now doesn't seem like the best time to mention that.

Aaron grabs onto my hand and squeezes it tightly in his. "Oh, Jeremy," he whispers.

"Now you know all my secrets. For a while, I had Lexy and Jamie convinced it was one of my traditions to spend Christmas Eve in a strip club."

Aaron snorts, and I send him a half-smile. "Thanks again for, well, all of this. Coming to Connecticut with me. Visiting Dad with me." I sigh as I look back at the doorway of Dad's room. "I know people say things like 'I couldn't have done it without you' all the time, and they never really mean it. But honestly, Aaron . . . ."

"You don't have to thank me," he says quietly. "Whatever you and I end up being—or not being—I'm glad I could be here for you like this. Thanks for letting me."

And *this* is why Aaron Morin is just too fucking good of a person for a selfish rake like me.

I lean over to turn the knob of the door, trying to ignore the way my heart starts pounding more loudly in my chest. I don't know how my mother does these visits multiple times a week.

Somehow, I manage to get the knob turned all the way. I push the door open and step inside, with Aaron holding my hand.

Dad's in bed, monitors and plastic tubes still hanging around him. He looks better than he did last time, though. There's more color in his cheeks, and his eyes are brighter. Today a rerun of *Jeopardy!* is playing on the TV screen. Dad and I used to love to watch that show together too. We were never as good at it as we were at *Wheel*, though.

"Oh, hi there." Dad tries to sit up in bed, and I quickly rush over to help him lay back down.

"You need to rest," I remind him. "Where's his nurse?" I ask Aaron anxiously.

Dad cocks an eyebrow at me. "Nurse? I don't need a nurse. Feel fine. Who are you? Good to meet you." He holds out a hand to me, and I do my best to ignore the vice that clenches around my entire chest when I take his hand in mine and shake it.

"I'm . . . Jeremy," I say hesitantly, determined not to let the tears that are sitting at the corners of my eyes start to fall. Dad looks happy this morning. He doesn't need to have some person he doesn't even remember crying all over his bedside.

"Jeremy . . . ." Dad's eyes drift back to the TV screen and then to me again. He has a distant, wistful smile on his face. "I have a little boy named Jeremy," he tells us. "Good boy, that one." He frowns. "Haven't seen him in a bit. I wonder if I'll see him today."

My breath is catching in my throat now, and there's no way I can speak. Luckily, I don't need to. Aaron steps in. "Your son Jeremy sent a message with us," he says calmly. "He told us to tell you he loves you. He's doing really great things, Jeremy."

I'm barely holding back tears now as Dad beams excitedly at Aaron. "Of course he's doing great things!" He coughs slightly, and Aaron and I both rush to plump the pillows around his head and help him sit up. I find a cup of water with a plastic straw in it and hold it for him while he drinks. For a long time, the only sound in the room is Alex Trebek asking questions that are answers while contestants give answers that are questions.

Dad smiles at the TV. "Jeremy and I watch this together sometimes," he says. "We do okay. We're better at *Wheel*, though."

"Sometimes you get all the answers on *Wheel* before the contestants do," I reply softly.

"That's right!" Dad beams at me. "Jeremy and I are good at

that game. He's always been a good boy, my Jeremy. You know the best thing about him?"

Neither of us answer. I can't speak, and even Aaron seems frozen by Dad's question.

"My Jeremy cares about people. Wants what's best for 'em, you know that? One time not that long ago, this boy he played with on a soccer team kept getting bullied. Other kids would push him down. Shove at him. Just because he was smaller than them." Dad shakes his head. "And my Jeremy, you know what he did?"

I'd forgotten all about this story. I was little then, and honestly, I don't remember it all that well—just flashes of it. But I remember my dad telling this story. He told it over and over again to friends and family members for years after it happened.

"He stopped playing right in the middle of a game one day. He was the best player, and his team needed him. But he just stopped playing, crossed his arms, and said he wasn't going to move again until everyone stopped pushing the other kid around."

"I believe that," Aaron says softly. "Jeremy's one of the kindest people I know."

"He's going to make a great man someday," Dad agrees. "Going to make someone very happy. Whoever my son falls for— that's one lucky soul." Dad yawns loudly. "I'm a little tired. You boys mind turning off the television? Think I'd like to take a nap."

I'm still standing there, frozen to the floor by my father's words, as Aaron moves around me, doing something with the TV and the nurse's call button. None of it is registering, not really. Nothing except the words Dad just said.

Whoever my son falls for—that's one lucky soul.

I turn away from his bed, dazed, and see my mother standing in the doorway of the room.

She's crying.

She and I end up outside at a picnic bench on the back lawn of the care center. Her pantsuit is probably getting dirty, but she doesn't even mention that as she sits down.

"Your uncle would like to see you before you go," she says calmly.

I'd like to see him too, I guess. Maybe. Only maybe I wouldn't. He'll always look and speak so much like my dad. He'll always be a reminder of what I don't have anymore.

But I'll do my best to pretend it doesn't physically hurt to hug him. Uncle Jerry's a good guy.

Mom clears her throat. "There are some things I need to say to you, Jeremy. I know I haven't always been the best mother." She shakes her head. "Your father . . . he was the more naturally nurturing one. It was easy for me to let him take on that role with you." She smiles. "I used to treasure watching the two of you play together. You adored each other."

"We did." The words crack through my throat, and now I know there's no way I'm getting through this conversation without crying. I've probably cried more this week than I have in my entire life.

"Jeremy, I promise that I love you far more than you'll ever know. I just need to make sure you have the best chance possible to be the man I know you can be. That's all I want for you." She draws in a deep breath and shakes her head. "That's all I've ever wanted. That's why I want you to take this test."

For a minute I'm ready to dive back into the same pattern the two of us have been in for three years: I tell her I won't do what she wants, she gets angry, I yell, she walks away, and we don't talk for months.

But my patterns aren't the same anymore. They've been changing all summer. And I think they just changed again as I was listening to my father explain to me who his son is.

"Mom," I say, and I do my best to keep my voice even and steady. "Do you trust me? The way Dad has always trusted me?"

She purses her lips. "I want to," she says steadily. "But Jeremy, some of the choices you've made since your father was diagnosed . . . it's like you have no regard for your future."

That's a fair statement, and I know it. So I take a deep breath, and I tell her the truth.

"You're right."

She looks up at me, surprised.

"The last time I saw Dad, before I left home for college, I made him a promise. I told him that I'd live every moment I could to the fullest from then on—for him. I thought that's what I was doing for the last few years. And maybe I was. But now . . . ." I glance over, toward the side of Dad's building. Aaron's standing there, waiting for me. I can see his broad shoulders shadowed in the mid-morning sun.

"I think I've finally figured something out. I think I can live life that way, the way I promised Dad, and still look forward. It doesn't have to be one or the other. I understand that now." I stare directly at her as I say my next words. "I think I'm finally ready to build the best future possible with whatever time I have. No test is going to change that. And Dad would understand why this is what I want."

She gulps. "But what if—"

"Listen. I promise that if things change with the science, and there's suddenly a chance this test could change things for me, I'll get it. Right away. But for now, this is the choice I know I need to make. This is what I want to do. I'm trusting myself to make this choice, and I need you to trust me too."

Mom shakes her head. "I wish I knew what your father would say," she whispers. "But the one thing I know for certain is that he would hate what you and I are to each other right now. He'd be horrified by what we've become."

"I agree. So help me fix it, Mom. Please? I need you to respect this choice I'm making. I think I'm finally ready to come home more now. Maybe not as much as you want, but I promise I'll try. Maybe we can both do a better job of enjoying the time we have together."

She starts crying then, again, in a way I'm not sure I've ever seen my mom cry before. It isn't long before I am too, and eventually, we both end up on the same side of the bench, hugging each other.

Finally, we separate. She wipes her eyes with a Kleenex as she says, "You've changed, son. Does it have anything to do with that young man who keeps following you everywhere you go?"

Aaron's still by the side of the building, pretending he's not watching us. I send him a quick wink, and he smiles.

"It has everything to do with him," I tell Mom.

———

Aaron and I go to the soccer field. The one where I supposedly stood up to a bunch of bullies before my voice even changed. The one my father still remembers, even though he's forgotten so much else.

"Well," he says quietly. We're sitting on the bleachers, looking out at the grass. It needs to be cut. "That was . . . a lot."

I snort. "You think?" I turn to him. "Listen. I'm not going to get the test. Mom knows that now."

He nods. "Good for you, Jeremy."

I lean my body against his until he's holding me upright on the bleachers, and then I say the words that are harder to get out. "I thought it would be selfish for me to want you . . . because we're never going to know how all of this will end up. But I want you, Aaron. I want this. I want the present and the future and everything else."

Aaron tightens his arms around me slightly. "Yeah? Are you sure, Jeremy? I know this has been a hard few days, and I don't want you to feel like—"

I turn in his arms and cut him off by kissing him as hard as I can. I make every inch of his mouth mine until I'm sure he knows how much I mean what I'm saying to him right now.

"I'm not really a selfish rake at all," I tell him when I finally let him come up for air. "Dad said so, and I believe him. So, I want this. With you." I flash him a grin. "Who else are you going to find with YOLO tattooed on their ass?"

Our next kiss is probably the best one that we've had yet, but I'm determined to top it. Someday.

In the future.

28

THAT TIME AARON HAD ACCIDENTAL THERAPY

"You just walked out of the office? You didn't even tell Iris you needed to cancel your meeting yourself? You asked *Benson* to do it?"

Jeremy's words as he follows me into the bookstore side of Vino and Veritas are probably the loudest ones that have ever been said in this space. He's almost as loud as he was when we got into that fight in the alleyway.

I wince as I think about how badly that fight could have ended. Except it didn't—in fact, if it wasn't for that fight, I'm not sure Jeremy would be standing behind me right now in the self-help section.

"Shhh," I remind him. "People are trying to read."

He glances around us at the near-empty store. "I think we're safe," he mutters. "Don't change the subject. You walked out of the firm? And you didn't officially clear your time off to come with me to Connecticut? What the hell, Aaron? Even I did that!

I sigh as I turn around to face him. I knew the entire time we were driving back from Connecticut that eventually I'd have to deal with my impromptu exit from Sprysky and Gentry. Then we got home and *eventually* became *now*.

And now I have to try and explain to Jeremy why I, Mr.

Perfect, left the job I was obsessed with and disappeared to Connecticut with him with nothing but an email to our bosses. Only I'm not sure how to do that because I'm not sure I really understand it myself.

"Listen," I tell him. "I know it's weird, what I did. But you know what's even weirder? I don't have a single regret. Me! I second-guess everything, Jeremy. I'm the guy who's still second-guessing whether I made the right kind of potholder in the second grade."

Jeremy laughs.

"But this? Leaving the way I did? I haven't regretted it once—not really—since it happened. That conversation Benson and I had . . . ." I shake my head. "It was an eye-opener. I don't want to become him, Jeremy."

Jeremy scoffs. "You could never be anything like Benson Lewis."

I shrug. "I wish that were true, but it's not," I murmur. "I could. I saw it the day we had our fight, and I had to stop the cycle. I had to make sure I had my priorities right."

Not that I have any idea what comes next. I've still got a year of law school to go, and that's going to end with a giant student loan bill. And now I've got a failed internship *and* a potentially failed clerkship to my name. It's going to be awfully hard to pay those student loans off if I can't even get a job when I graduate.

Normally I'd be panicking right now. Normally I'd be questioning every single decision I've ever made in my entire life and emailing Iris and Tom every five minutes with apologies and imagining all the scenarios for how my life will probably go wrong and I'll disappoint every single person who's ever loved me. Normally.

But right now, with Jeremy Everett standing next to me, all I can think of is how fucking *lucky* I am to be with him and have him in my life. I wouldn't give up this feeling for any law firm or any clerkship. And whatever happens, I know we'll handle things. Together.

"I still can't believe you walked out," Jeremy mutters as he pulls a book called *Finding Your Inner You* off a shelf. "What else did you do while we were fighting? Join a cult? Get a tattoo?"

"Yup," I tell him seriously. "Giant tiger, right on my left ball. I can't believe you haven't noticed it yet."

Jeremy arches an eyebrow. "You can joke all you want," he says. "But I would have believed you got a tattoo on your left ball before I would have believed that *you,* of all people, left the firm in the middle of the day without even talking to our bosses. Seriously, Aaron. I mean—"

"Hang on." I hold up one hand to stop him as my eye lands on something . . . or someone, actually. A person, sitting on one of the easy chairs in the area of Vino and Veritas where Briar's book club normally meets.

Someone I know very well: Peter.

"What the hell is he doing here?" I whisper to myself.

"Who are you talking about?" Jeremy asks just as Peter looks up. Our eyes meet, and he cringes slightly. Then he sends me a small, unenthusiastic wave.

"Huh," I say to Jeremy. "Maybe I'm not the only person in the middle of a career shift."

Peter and I go next door to the bar. It's pretty clear whatever conversation is about to happen between us is going to require alcohol.

"What's going on? Why didn't you tell me you were in Vermont?" I ask after we both have bottles of cider and baskets of truffle fries in front of us.

Peter sighs. "Um, well. It's sort of a long story."

"I've got time."

"Okay, maybe it's not that long." He shrugs. "California was terrible. I hated LA. Everyone in my new office was awful. I hadn't even passed the bar yet or started officially working there, and I already hated it. I didn't have anywhere else to go, so I came back to Vermont. I'm studying for the Vermont bar."

"So not everything you told me was a lie," I say wryly. "Why the hell have you been avoiding me, then?"

Peter laughs dryly. "Aaron. Look, we're close. But we both know what this relationship is. I give advice; you take it. I'm the sage here, remember? The one who got into law school first and graduated already. The one who's supposed to have my shit together. There's no way I was going to tell you that I'm about two minutes away from either working for my godmother or opening up a law office in a barn somewhere." He groans and shakes his head. "I failed, okay? I failed, and I didn't want to admit it. I always swore I'd get the hell out of Vermont the first second I could, and here I am studying to pass the Vermont bar. I couldn't face you. You'd never crap out on a law firm the way I did."

I stare at him. "You're . . . kidding me, right? This is a joke. Jeremy's making a video of this for his TikTok or something?"

Peter blinks at me. "Uh . . . no? I mean, not that I know of. I'm not on TikTok."

I stare at him a little longer. I shake my head.

And then I start laughing.

I laugh and I laugh and I laugh, until finally Peter starts to look concerned. "Aaron, are you okay? What's going on? People are looking at us."

I manage to get myself under control long enough to take a sip of water. "Last summer," I tell Peter, when I can finally get a breath in. "That internship I had? I got a terrible review. They told me I lacked *intellectual capacity.* It crushed me, hard, and it's been crushing me all year. And I was too embarrassed to tell you."

"Oh." Peter looks stunned. "So that's why you wanted to come back here," he mumbles.

"Yeah. Just like you." I raise my bottle of cider to him in salute. "And it gets better! A few days ago I walked right out of my job at your godmother's firm in the middle of the day. Totally crapped out on her and possibly destroyed my future career completely." I shrug. "We're just two failures lying to each other. But at least my family and I are good again. Oh, and I may have fallen in love." I send a little wave over to Jeremy, who's hanging out at the bar with Murph, the bartender on duty.

"You've had quite the summer." Peter runs his hands through his hair. "Well, okay. I'm going to need some more details on this whole 'falling in love' thing, but right now, I think it's time we both owned up to some stuff. Let's go." He stands up and throws cash down onto the table.

"Where are we going?" I ask as I scramble to find my wallet.

"My godmother's house."

"Peter! What are you doing here? I thought you were in California!" Iris Sprysky looks just as surprised to see Peter as I was. She wraps him up in a tight hug, her bright magenta dress enveloping most of his body.

"Yes, um, change of plans. I've been staying with Mom and Dad. I asked them not to tell you." Peter straightens up as she releases him, pulling awkwardly on the polo shirt that's tucked into his khakis. "I, um, had a little hiccup out in Cali. Today I ran into Aaron, and I decided—"

"Aaron!" Iris whirls around to face me. "Thank goodness you're here!" She grabs my hands and clasps them between hers. "Tom and I have been so worried!"

My face goes red. "Yes, about that. Listen, I really do want to apologize. I never intended to leave you and Mr. Gentry in the lurch like that."

"Tom," she corrects me calmly. "His name is Tom. And I'm just glad to see you. We were both quite concerned; Tom especially. The firm has reeked of patchouli since you left." She wrinkles her nose. "Will the both of you come inside? I have brownies."

"Did you or Tom make them?" Peter asks warily.

"As if I'd ever give you brownies Tom made! We'd never finish our conversation. We'd probably never even start it!"

She leads us through a house designed with the most eclectic décor I've ever seen. There's actually a full suit of armor in the dining room right next to a tie-dye painting. Soon Peter and I are in multi-colored armchairs at the dining table with pots of tea and plates of brownies in front of us.

She points at Peter. "I'll deal with you in a moment. Imagine not even telling me you were back in Vermont! But you first, Aaron," she adds as she turns her gaze on me. "How are you? Benson insinuated you'd had some sort of a breakdown."

Of course he did.

"It wasn't a breakdown. Not really. It was more of a realization. About my work habits, I guess."

She nods and pours more tea, silently waiting for me to go on. I know I could tell her something simple and vague about an emergency. She'd understand, and she probably wouldn't ask for more details than that.

But I want to tell her. I think I need to. If I'm going to learn how to be the kind of lawyer—and person—I want to be, then I'll need to learn from people like her.

"This is hard to explain. Do you mind a long story?"

"I love a long story." She sits back in her chair, and I try to figure out where to begin.

I decide it's best to start with the farm—Tiny Acres. And I do. I explain how I left, and how hard Harvard has been but how much I've loved the challenge . . . and then I tell her about what happened at Leicester.

She nods sympathetically. "I'm afraid Tom and I have plenty of war stories of our own like that," she says. "Someday, I'll have to tell you about the time I was laughed at in the middle of a courtroom in front of all my colleagues."

My eyes widen. That's . . . horrific. "Are you serious?"

"Aaron. I'm a Black woman who went to Harvard Law and now practices in a state where very few people of color practice law. That's not even the tip of the iceberg of what I've seen in this field."

My face burns again. Wow. Talk about being inside your own little bubble. It's never occurred to me to wonder what it's taken for others I work with to get to where they are today—or how much I'm protected in ways that they all aren't. "I'm really sorry that happened," I finally say quietly.

She nods. "It's interesting how many people in the world choose to use shame as a means of wielding power," she answers.

Shame. I never attached that word to it, but now I know that's what I felt last summer—and what I've felt ever since. "I felt really ashamed after that review," I tell her quietly. "I never even told Peter until today."

Iris passes me another brownie. "Yes. I know that kind of shame, Aaron." She frowns. "And so I must ask: were you feeling that same kind of shame here at our firm? Is that why you left the day you did? I'm horrified to imagine we might have created an environment like that. Tom and I have always resolved that our firm would never be that kind of place."

"You and Tom weren't the reason I left," I rush to assure her. "Me walking out like I did had nothing to do with the firm, not really. I think I was just questioning everything. Whether I could really do this work. The farmstand case was the first time I really felt invested in a career in this field again. Then I failed the firm and the case, and all that shame came rushing back, and I didn't like the person I saw myself becoming when that happened."

There's more to it, of course. There's more to why I took so much time off after I left. But that's Jeremy's story to tell, not mine.

Iris leans across the table. "I think I understand," she says. "Aaron—and Peter, I'll include you in this too because I have a feeling from the way you've been hiding that you're dealing with your own particular brand of shame right now—please hear me. If you want a career in this field, you need to start remembering right now that failure is inevitable, but it's not permanent. You need to remember that every day. It's part of the job. One of the first things I had to learn early was that failure would always be there, and I could never allow myself to attach it to shame."

"How do you do that?" I ask.

"Well, it helps to share an office with someone who believes firmly in the practice of meditation *and* makes excellent brownies."

Peter snorts.

"Truly, though, that's something that you'll have to figure out yourself. I think the answer is different for everyone. But Tom does like to say that the antidote to shame is self-love. I've found that to be very true."

Self-love.

I think about how different the world's felt since I've had Jeremy in my life, reminding me what I'm capable of and pushing me to believe in myself.

"Aaron." Iris's voice is a little firmer now. "Have you enjoyed the work you've done here?"

"Absolutely," I blurt out. "It's the first time I've felt like I could see what I wanted my future in law to be, you know? I really enjoy helping family farms and other small businesses. I like the idea that I'm making the community I grew up in better. Stronger. It feels good." I frown. "Everyone in Boston thought it was strange I wanted to come up here for this clerkship, but I really do love this work."

"I'll tell you this, then." Iris smiles at me. "It can be quite difficult at times to find employees who enjoy working with small businesses and farms. If that's what you want to do, Tom and I will be excited to talk to you about a long-term future here. We won't be able to pay you what some of the firms in Boston will, but we can make sure you have what you need to pay off your loans and enjoy a life in Vermont. If that's really what you want."

For a minute, I can't even answer—all I can do is blink wildly at her. "Did you just offer me a job? After I walked out on you and Tom like that?"

Iris puts another brownie onto my plate, even though I haven't finished the last one. "I am confident you'll make up for that one incident quite successfully before you need to go back to school. I know potential when I see it, Aaron. And I don't make mistakes." She holds out a hand for me to shake. "Are we in agreement?"

I almost destroy a brownie hurrying to shake her hand. "Definitely. Yes. Absolutely. For sure."

"Wonderful. Now, you!" She turns to Peter. "Do I need to intervene in your future as well?"

Peter coughs. "Honestly, Aunt Iris, I'm not sure what I need right now." He looks miserable. I wonder what happened to my usually confident and self-assured friend. This is the guy a mock trial judge once called "unflappable." Right now, he looks like a light breeze could knock him on his ass.

"Okay then. You know where to find me when you figure it out."

"Well." Peter clears his throat. "If you're looking for ways to help, maybe you could get me some of Tom's brownies?"

———

I'm still in a daze when I walk through the door of the office I share with Benson the next day. I can't quite believe Iris was ready to forgive me so easily, and I'm not the only one. Benson looks up at me in shock. "What the hell are you doing here? You haven't been here in days! I thought you quit!"

Jeremy saunters into the tiny room and closes the door behind him. "Need any coffee?" he acts innocently. Like the two of us didn't stay up late last night celebrating everything there was to celebrate.

We celebrated Jeremy standing up to his mother, and me keeping my job, and we celebrated adding yet another person to our ever-growing friend group: Peter, who spent a few hours meeting our other friends and hanging out with all of us at V and V. He's still not saying much about what exactly drove him back to Vermont, but that's okay. I know he'll talk about it when he's ready.

"Coffee would be great." I grin and sink into my old rolling chair—well, *current* rolling chair, I guess. "I took some time off," I tell Benson. "Now I'm back."

"Are you serious?" Benson slams down the coffee mug he's holding. "This place is a fucking joke. If you pulled this shit at any other firm, you'd never work again in the field. They'd blackball your ass."

"You're right," I agree. "I think that's why I want to work here."

Benson opens up his mouth. Then he closes it again.

The impossible has happened: I've left Benson Lewis speechless.

Benson shakes his head as he turns back to his laptop. "Unbelievable," he mutters. "I work my ass off, and all I get is offers to meditate at ass o'clock in the morning. You take off in the middle of the workday without even telling anyone, and somehow you're still the firm's golden boy. Story of my fucking life."

Jeremy and I glance at each other, and I know we're both thinking the same thing: *we actually feel sorry for Benson Lewis.* I'm about to say something about how I'm sure all his hard work will eventually pay off when he starts talking again.

And completely ruins the moment.

"I'm out of here the second I get a decent review from this place," Benson says. "What a fucking waste of time." He shakes his head. "At least I've got a month to show Iris and Tom that I'm the clerk who should have gotten into Harvard. And you can be damn sure I'm going to do it."

Jeremy opens his mouth—to defend me, I know—but I get there first.

"Listen, Benny," I tell him calmly. "Spend this summer however you want. I'm not going to walk around this firm terrified of making mistakes. I will make them, and that's okay." I glance over at Jeremy and smile. "Failure isn't permanent. Did you know that?"

Benson groans. "You sound like Tom. I can't listen to this crap anymore. Just leave me alone and let me do some work, okay?"

"Touchy, touchy," says Jeremy. "C'mon, Aaron. Let's get you some coffee."

Benson rolls his eyes. "I can't believe I have to keep working with you two! A quitter and a fucking playboy. This office really is the biggest joke on the planet."

"I prefer the term *reformed rake* to playboy these days," Jeremy tells him. "But you know, Benson, if you're having a hard time appreciating what life has to offer, I'm happy to teach you a few tricks. Have you ever done karaoke in a strip club?"

The look on Benson's face as we both leave is probably the best thing I see all day. Well, besides the mental image of Jeremy doing karaoke in a strip club.

Obviously.

29

THAT TIME JEREMY WAS QUITE POSSIBLY A CHARACTER IN A ROMANCE NOVEL

"Where are you taking me?" Aaron peers out the window as we wind around the sparkling shores of Lake Champlain. It's no wonder he has no idea where we could be going. I'm taking us on the longest route possible to get from Burlington to Morse's Line, and we've been in the car for hours more than this trip would ever normally take. So far, we've stopped to pick strawberries at a farm in Franklin and had one of the best steak sandwiches I've ever eaten at a little snack bar on the lake. The day's been everything I wanted it to be. But I'm still not giving away the ending of it.

"You'll just have to wait and see." I lift my sunglasses for a moment to flash Aaron a grin and then drop one hand off the steering wheel so Aaron can wrap his around it. His callused fingers rub gently against my palm, and the warmth sends a bolt of energy through me.

We only have two weeks left together before he goes back to law school, and I'm determined to make the most of every second of it. After living in each other's back pockets the way we are now, it's going to be so hard not to have him nearby almost every moment of the day.

Because that's what I have now. And sometimes it's even more ridiculously fucking adorable than what Jamie and Briar have.

I've basically moved into Aaron's apartment; it's bigger than mine. Every morning we get up together, and we usually start the day off right by messing around in the shower (it turns out Aaron is a morning person in more ways than one). Then Aaron makes us egg sandwiches for breakfast while I make coffee, and we just . . . sit there. Eating together. Talking and laughing, and there's usually some cuddling that could definitely compete with Jamie and Briar's.

He almost always drives us to work, and I get him more coffee there. Our lunch routine depends on what kind of case he's working on and whether he can get away, but we have lunch with Briar and Autumn a lot. Sometimes Lexy or Jamie if they're free. After work we . . . .

Well, it's taken me a long time to finally realize what we do in the evenings. But I get it now. We *date*. We actually date.

I, Jeremy Everett, have almost nonstop dates with the same person. Every single night.

We see outdoor movies and show up for open mic night at V and V. We take walks on the Rail Trail. We go out for ice cream. We play board games with Jamie and Briar. We go to dinner at the Morins'.

And I never, ever get tired of it. When Aaron leaves in a few weeks, I know I'll feel like there's a small hole inside of me where he's supposed to be—every morning in the shower, every day at lunch, and every single evening.

Aaron squeezes my hand slightly. "It's going to be okay," he says softly over the background noise of the radio.

It should probably scare me how easily he can read my mind. It doesn't.

The song on the radio is a Taylor Swift one Briar likes a lot, and it used to get played at club nights I'd go to. I've never listened to it much before, but now I let the words wind around me as I think about what they mean. It's a duet between two people who are talking about what hot messes they both are . . . and how that's exactly why they're perfect for the other person.

Or something like that. Deciphering the meaning of poetry and song lyrics is more Jamie and Briar's thing. But I think I've got this song figured out.

"I'm really glad you wanted a hot mess like me," I blurt out.

Aaron laughs. "Same, babe. You think anyone else would put together an office picnic for a chronic workaholic?" He lifts my fingers to kiss them. "I hope you know how much I'll miss you when I'm in Boston," he says softly.

"Yeah," I mutter. Boston and Burlington aren't that many hours apart, but this long-distance thing is definitely going to test our relationship. Aaron's going to be busy as fuck with his last year of law school, and I'm not under any delusions that my senior year at Moo U will be a cakewalk.

But it's just one year. And after that, Aaron's already got a job lined up here at Sprysky and Gentry, and me? Well, I'm finally starting to color in some of the blank spots that I was always so sure made up my future.

I've decided that I want to take the LSATs this year and apply to the Moo U law school. There's no guarantee I'll get in, of course. My grades are sketchy AF, and they may tell me to take a hike. But I'm staying on part-time at Sprysky and Gentry this year, and Tom Gentry already offered to write me a recommendation. He's an alumnus there, and he thinks I have a chance.

And if that future doesn't work out? That'll suck, but I'll figure it out. I always do.

And this time, I won't be doing it alone.

"Speaking of Boston," Aaron says quietly. His hand is gripping mine again, and it's a little tough to maneuver some of these curving roads one-handed, but I wouldn't let go of him for anything.

Well, maybe if a deer ran out in front of me. But definitely not anything else.

"Yeah? What's up?" Aaron's tensing up next to me, and I can't figure out why. We've made a lot of hard choices together in the last few weeks. What could be left after all that?

Aaron pulls in a long breath. "Look, I just want to say that I meant what I said back when we first got together. I understand that monogamy has never been your thing, and I trust what we have. I really do. But I'm thinking we should talk about boundaries before I leave for Boston. Maybe if we make a list of what we both want and need, we can—"

I start laughing so hard I really do almost miss a curve. I swerve fast to take us away from a tree. "Aaron, stop. First of all, can I just say how much I love that your idea of figuring out how to have an open relationship with me starts with making a list?"

"It's just a logical way to—"

"Okay, no, you're right." I rub his palm and send him a smile. "Your brain just never stops amazing me, that's all. But listen . . . if you want an open relationship, yeah, we can figure that out. You know I'm all about consensual adults doing what makes them happy. But actually? I haven't slept with anyone except you all summer."

Aaron jerks his hand out of mine and turns in his seat to stare at me. "What did you just say?"

I shrug. "Yeah. Maybe I'm more monogamous than I used to think. I haven't wanted to mess around with anyone else since we started hooking up. So I just haven't. And I don't really want to right now. I don't think I'll want to when you're gone either. But I would like to put some time into practicing phone sex," I add, because there's no way I'm going to be able to go weeks at a time without getting off with Aaron Morin.

Aaron's still staring at me. "Really, Jeremy? Are you sure? I don't ever want you to feel like I've pressured you into anything."

I keep my eyes on the road while I reach over to softly rub his cheek with my hand. His five o'clock shadow is rough against my skin. "Aaron, all you've ever done is make me feel safe to be what I want. Who I want. I don't see that changing anytime soon."

He blushes into my hand and then squints as he looks out the window.

"Wait a minute. Are we in Morse's Line?"

"Yup." I turn onto a dirt road a few miles from the Morin farm, and the car bumps and jostles against the uneven surface below us.

"Where are we going?"

"You think I'm going to ruin the surprise? You'll just have to wait and see."

Aaron studies the farms we're driving by carefully. "Wait a minute. We're close to the Tursky Farmstand."

"Nope. We're at the Tursky Farmstand." I pull into a small driveway and shut off the engine of the car. I shove open the driver's side door and step out of it, calling, "C'mon!"

The farmstand is still closed. Right now, it's just an empty set of wooden booths covered in plastic, with the giant sign labeled TURSKY in faded red letters hung up on strings between them. Behind the booths, a series of fields and an old barn are silent and still.

Aaron steps up beside me. "It looks . . . ."

"Sad." I quickly agree with the word he hasn't said yet. "Yeah. I know."

"I still wish I could have done more for the owners." Aaron frowns.

"You did everything you possibly could, Aaron."

"I know. But still . . . ." Aaron looks over at me, puzzled. "Why are we here, anyway?"

"Um, well. See. I kind of did a thing?"

"A thing?" Aaron crosses his arms.

"Yeah. And I know you'll say it's extra, and Jamie and Lexy will say it's extra, but I'm okay with that! I like being extra, okay? I think you like me being extra." I'm babbling now, but I can't seem to stop.

"Jeremy, what are you talking about? What extra thing did you do?"

"IsortofboughtthefarmlandfortheTurskys," I say in a rush.

Aaron's eyes go wide. "What the hell?"

"I mean, I didn't buy it myself! I told my mom about it, and she found some investors who talked to the Turskys about getting behind their business, and technically the investors bought it, and now they own it with the Turskys, and they're reopening next year."

Aaron just stands there. Staring at me. "You . . . bought me a farmstand?"

"Well, no. Not exactly. Like I said, I didn't buy anything. I just made some calls and put the Turskys in touch with Mom's people, and she was actually happy to help. She seems to have decided she likes you. I mean, as much as she likes anybody."

Aaron grabs me in his arms and kisses me so hard I can barely breathe.

I legit gasp when he finally pulls away. "Wow. I mean, I was pretty sure you'd be happy. I didn't know you'd be *that* happy, though."

"Yes, you did." He laughs and grabs onto the belt buckle of my shorts, pulling me closer against him. "I can't believe you did this," he murmurs. "Jeremy. You saved the farmstand."

"I know how much it means to you. And I really want you to be happy. Always."

"Jeremy Everett." He wraps his arms hard around my neck, holding me tight against his body. "You are the most extra human being alive sometimes; you know that?" He sighs into my skin happily. "And please don't ever try to be anything else. I . . . ."

I tense up as I feel the words he's about to say echoing in the air between us. There was a time not that long ago when I would have dreaded hearing these words come out of his mouth—

because I couldn't say them back, and I knew I'd never be able to say them back.

But right now, standing in the middle of an empty driveway on a humid day when the air of Vermont is gluing my skin against Aaron Morin's, all I want is to hear him say those words.

"I love you, Jeremy Everett. I love you so much."

Who knew I could cry again after all the crying I've done in the last few weeks? But right now, the tears that are running down the sides of my cheeks are the kind of tears I always thought only existed in Jamie and Briar's books.

I'm actually crying because I'm *happy*. Who knew that really was a fucking thing people do?

"Geez, Aaron." I wipe the wetness away from the corners of my eyes before I lift his head in my hands and hold him there, steadily, so I can stare right at him when I say, "I love you back. So much."

And then we kiss. Obviously.

Every kiss with him just seems to get better. I guess practice really does make perfect.

It's a few hours later, when I'm on the boat with Aaron, that I find myself thinking about my dad.

We're lying together on a cushion I hauled up from below. Aaron's stretched across it, and I'm basically wrapped around his body. I found a thin fleece blanket to cover us against the cool breeze that's coming off the water, and a clear night above us is broadcasting stars and a perfect crescent moon.

Aaron rubs gently at my hair. "You okay?" He whispers.

Somehow, he knows I'm not—not exactly. His ability to read my mind seems to know no bounds. "I was thinking about my dad," I say, as the boat rocks gently below us. "About the time he tried to teach me to sail."

"You never did tell me why you didn't learn how."

I sigh into his chest. "Well . . . he tried, and it didn't happen."

Aaron's quiet for a minute. Then: "Tell me about it," he says.

I snuggle more closely into him as I speak the words into the night. It's been so long since I thought about that day. "I was maybe ten? Dad and I had been coming up here every summer for a few years, and I was so excited because this was the year he was finally going to let me sail the boat. I thought I was such a fucking badass. I kept telling all my friends at school about it."

Aaron laughs. "I bet you were the cutest ten-year-old."

"I was adorable. Naturally," I agree. "Anyway, the entire drive up here, we'd been going over what I needed to do one step at a time. I'd been watching him for years, so I was sure I'd be able to do it too. But then I stepped on the boat, and he said, 'Okay, Jeremy, what do you do first? This is your show,' And I just . . . ."

"You panicked?" Aaron asks softly.

"Kind of, I guess. But it was more like I just wasn't ready to do it alone. I couldn't imagine not being his co-captain. And then I felt terrible because I'd been so excited to sail the boat all by myself for the first time. But I just didn't want to anymore."

"What happened?"

I blink into the soft, yellow moonlight as I think about that moment. "Dad told me that it was okay if I didn't want to sail the boat. He said I didn't have to do anything I didn't want to do, and he told me it didn't matter if I could sail the boat by myself or not because he'd always be there to do it with me. He . . . he promised that," I add in a whisper. "He promised me that."

Aaron pulls me tightly against his chest. "It was so much easier to stay away," I say. "It was so much easier to stay up here and pretend I wasn't losing him. You know? And I know this is better. Going home to see him more often will be better. But right now . . . ."

Aaron tilts my head up so that I'm looking directly into his eyes. "Right now, you only have to take this one day at a time. Right now, I'm here anytime you need me. Anytime you need to talk or be pissed or be happy or be sad. You're not on this ship alone, Jeremy. Not anymore. I promise you that."

I sit up just enough to press my mouth against his, and I lean all the way into the warmth of his body.

"I love you, Aaron Morin," I whisper.

"I love you back," he murmurs into my ear. Then he lowers me all the way back down onto his body and pulls the blanket up farther across our chests with one hand as his other hand snakes down to push at my shorts. "I love every inch of you," he whispers against my ear lobe as his hand finds its way into my boxers. He brushes it against the top of my dick, and my entire body jumps against his. "I love every inch of your brain and your heart, and I definitely love every inch of this guy."

I laugh against his chest. "Aaron," I say. "Have you ever bottomed?"

He's still brushing his hand against my dick, which makes it even harder to concentrate when he answers, "Yeah, a few times. It's not always my thing, but I'd love to try it with you, Jeremy. I'd love to have you inside of me."

I move so fast I almost roll the two of us off the boat deck.

Somehow, we make it below deck without losing all of our clothes in a place where our boat-neighbors might be able to see us. By the time we crash onto the boat's tiny bunk, we're both naked and clutching at each other. I've never wanted anyone more than I want Aaron Morin at this moment, and I'm starting to worry I'm not even going to make it all the way inside of him before I fall apart in his arms.

He finds condoms and lube in one of the bedside tables. "Maybe we can lose these soon?" he says as he passes the condoms to me. "If you're sure you want to keep going with the whole monogamy thing . . . ."

The idea of my skin against the inside of Aaron's body, no barrier between us, and vice versa, has my dick so hard it hurts. "I very, very much want that," I tell him as I pour lube into one hand. "Fuck, Aaron."

He sits up to kiss me long and hard, circling his tongue around mine. "Yeah, that's the idea," he says against my lips.

I prep him slowly, easing one finger in at a time, watching every single reaction to make sure I'm not hurting him. It's killing me to go this slow, but I'd rather die than make this painful for Aaron. For someone who hasn't bottomed much, it doesn't take long before he's writhing against the bed, grabbing at the sheets with his hands and begging me. "Inside, please," he says. "Now, Jeremy."

"Are you sure?" I push one finger in a little farther, pushing against the spot that I've been teasing mercilessly, and—

"Now!" he yells out. "Inside me, now!"

That's all I need to hear. I slip the condom on, raise his legs a little higher as I kneel in front of him, and I make sure I'm looking right at the expression on his face when I push inside of him.

I go slow at first. Aaron's got his eyes closed and he's clutching gently at the sides of my waist as his body adjusts to me. I keep moving slowly until I feel his body relax against mine. Then I begin to move just a little faster, a little further, until I hit that spot again.

Aaron gasps. He calls out, "More!"

I move in and out, pressing back and forth in a way that ensures he feels every inch of me against the places that make him cry out and grab at my body as he ruts into me, begging for more. We move faster and faster together, until it almost feels like we're perfectly synced, in rhythm, and I know we're both close. I reach for Aaron's cock, rubbing and teasing at the sensitive head as I whisper, "Come for me, Aaron."

"Jeremy!" he yells out into the tiny hull of the boat, and I lose myself in him while he loses himself in my hand.

We land together with him spooning me. I manage to take care of the condom, and then he pulls the covers around us as he wraps his body around mine.

"Well." Aaron kisses my neck. "I don't know if I want to do that every day, but I definitely think we should add it to our repertoire."

"Yeah?" I grin.

He grins back. "Yeah." He looks thoughtful. "And one more

thing," he adds. "I think we should take sailing lessons," he whispers. "Together."

I turn to look at him. "Really? You want to learn to sail?"

He smiles as he traces a hand across my cheek softly. "No, Jeremy," he whispers. "I want to learn to sail *with you.*"

The boat rocks below us as we kiss, and my future has never looked brighter.

EPILOGUE

THAT TIME AARON TOOK A WEEKEND OFF

"Aaron!" Jeremy comes running at me from the end of Church Street like he's about to jump into my arms in front of the crowds surrounding us. I laugh and hold them out, my laughter growing even harder when he stops short to hug me around the neck. "Fuck, I missed you!" he says, and then he crushes his mouth against mine. "It's so good to see you," he adds when we both finally come up for air.

"So good to see you," I murmur. That's an understatement. This long-distance thing is no joke, and I'll honestly be glad when it's over at the end of the year. It's only October, and I'm already dreading the end of every weekend. Sunday nights are my nemesis: those are the nights when Jeremy and I kiss each other goodbye and one of us starts the long drive home away from the other. But I'm not going to think about the impending doom of Sunday night right now. I've been working my ass off all week so I could take this entire weekend to enjoy myself with Jeremy, and I'm going to make sure we take advantage of every minute of it.

Tomorrow we're going to Lissie's guitar recital with my family. Sunday we're spending the day in bed. And right now we're starting the weekend off right with drinks at Vino and Veritas, and all of our friends will be there. I'm determined not to even think about school for the next forty-eight hours. Monday can wait until Monday.

I suspect I'll always be the kind of person who looks ten steps ahead of where I am, but I'm getting better at enjoying my present. Jeremy makes it easier to remember that life is what's happening in front of me. After all, how could I possibly ignore what's in front of me when Jeremy Everett is the one who's standing there?

"I'm so glad you're home!" he says excitedly as he grabs hold of my hand. "You remember me talking about Scott, right?" He gestures at a taller guy standing next to him who's wearing a pink cravat with a paisley-print button-up. I like him already.

"Of course," I say as I shake Scott's hand. "Jeremy's told me a lot about you."

"That sounds dangerous," Scott replies cheerfully.

"Not really. Mostly he just tells me about your adventures in thrift store shopping. Thanks for teaching him T-shirts can cost less than fifty dollars."

"You won't believe the last place Scott took me to!" Jeremy exclaims excitedly. "I got this killer pair of vintage Levi's for a dollar. A *dollar*, Aaron!"

Scott and I send each other quick grins. "Wait until he finds out thrift stores have sales," he whispers to me.

That's going to blow Jeremy's mind for sure.

"Let's go," Jeremy urges. "The crew's meeting us at the bar."

"I texted Peter and told him to come by. Hope that's okay."

"Of course it is," Jeremy replies easily. "The more the merrier. We've been inviting him to game nights. Sometimes he shows up."

Good. Peter and I have been talking at least once a week since I went back to school, and it's clear he's not very happy being back in Vermont. The more friends he makes here, the better.

We make our way up Church Street while Jeremy and Scott talk about Scott's current job hunt. "I'm just not sure if I'm clown material," Scott's telling us as we step into Vino and Veritas together. The two of them keep moving, but I stop for a second. I stop and take it all in.

Tiny Acres, the farm where I grew up and became the person I am today, will always be my home. But over the last year or so, a few other places have begun to feel like home. The Pink Monstrosity. Jeremy's sailboat. Spysky and Gentry. And Vino and Veritas, the bar where Jeremy and I have spent so much time together over the past few months.

Briar's at the bar talking to Tanner, who's pouring drinks. Lexy and Mindy are swaying together in front of the stage as Jon plays a soft, sweet melody on his guitar. There are hints of garlic and onion in the air, and I wonder what Joss's dinner special is tonight.

"Aaron! Jeremy!" Autumn sees us first and waves to us from a table where she's sitting with Peter and someone else I don't recognize. Jamie's with them, too, and I'm not surprised when we pull up chairs at their table and find them all talking about farming.

"I don't know," Autumn's saying. "Bowen and I really want to move the hemp farm into marijuana because it's the wave of the future, but we're having so many problems with getting zoned for it. Maybe we should give it all up and move into dairy."

"Naw," says Jamie. "Dad's holding his own with dairy; don't get me wrong. But the milk prices are all over the place. It's hard to see what the future holds there."

"Exactly," says the guy sitting next to Autumn. He smacks the table and manages to land his hand right in a bowl of tartar sauce. "Ooops," he says as Jamie hands him a napkin.

Thank goodness Jeremy and I finally got our shit together. It's nice not to be the person dumping condiments all over everything right now.

"Aaron, meet my brother, Bowen," Autumn says. "He's not normally like this, I swear. Sometimes he barely even speaks. But you get him talking about farm work and he can go on for days."

"I'm not that bad. Nice to meet you, Aaron."

"Hi, Aaron. Good to see you," says Peter. "The commodities market for dairy is highly uncertain right now," he goes on, and I almost do a double-take. Since when is Peter researching the dairy markets? We've got some catching up to do this weekend.

"Hey, babe." Jeremy nudges me. "Scott and I are going to the bar. Want a cider?"

"Sure do," I tell him. He passes his lips across my cheek in a gentle kiss as he stands, and a quick shudder runs through my body.

I don't think there will ever be an inch of me that doesn't react to having Jeremy Everett against my skin. I don't think there will ever be an inch of me that doesn't love this life we're building together, here, surrounded by people who I hope I know the entire rest of my life.

The entire rest of *our* lives.

"I'm heading to the bathroom," I tell the table. "Be right back." I'm lost in thought as I walk through the bar, imagining a world where Jeremy and I have our own apartment near Briar and Jamie —or maybe a house just outside of Burlington—and I work at Iris and Tom's firm and he goes to the law school at Moo U. Maybe we could get a dog? I haven't owned a dog in years. I wonder if Jeremy likes dogs. Do dogs go sailing? I need to do some research. I'm so busy thinking about dogs and apartment pet fees and sail-boats that I don't even notice I've run right into someone.

"Whoops, sorry." I look up to see who I've just smashed into near the back of the bar . . . and standing there is Benson.

"Oh. Aaron." He clears his throat. "It's, um, good to see you."

"Sure, Benson. Good to see you too." That's not totally a lie. Benson and I ended our time together this summer on a decent note. We both got good reviews, neither one of us killed the other, and he even came out for drinks with me and Jeremy once in a while. I wouldn't exactly call us *friends,* but he's definitely not a nemesis anymore either. Jeremy started calling him our *frenemy.* "I'm sitting over there if you want to join me."

Benson glances over at the crowd of people currently

surrounding the table I'm pointing at. "I'm heading out, actually. Just finished meeting with a study group here."

I can't figure out if he's telling the truth or not. Benson remains hidden inside of himself. He's never seemed all that interested in getting to know any of our friends. "Maybe another time. How are things at Moo U going?"

"Good. Fine. How's school going for you, Harvard boy?"

"Hard as fuck," I tell him cheerfully, knowing he'll never admit the same thing. And he doesn't. He just shrugs.

"Well, you're welcome to join us if you change your mind," I tell him. "I'll see you around, I guess." I start to move past him, but he grabs hold of the sleeve of my shirt.

"Can I ask you something?"

"Uh, sure. Why not."

He frowns over at the bar, where Jeremy's standing next to a short blonde woman. She's holding a book, and he's talking to her excitedly. Objectively, she's very attractive. She's got short hair that angles down in front of her face, soft blue eyes, a runner's build, and she's laughing at everything Jeremy says.

"How can you be with him?" Benson asks. "How can you trust him? You know who he was. Who he is."

They seem like strange questions given that Benson watched me and Jeremy fall in love with each other in real-time. But maybe that's why he's asking them. I suppose Jeremy and I will always look like a confusing couple to anyone who doesn't know us well personally.

Jeremy's laughing hard now at whatever the woman's saying. He turns to find me in the crowd, and I know the minute he spots me. His blue eyes turn the shade of the lake on a perfect summer day, a smile takes over his face, and everything about him softens. He gestures at me and then starts walking over. The woman follows him.

"Well," I say. "That's easy. He makes me more than I could ever be without him."

Benson just stares at me. He looks more confused than Jeremy probably did the first time he walked into a thrift store.

"Benson!" Jeremy crows as he reaches us. "I'd say it's great to see you, but we both know I'd be lying. It's okay to see you, I guess."

"Jeremy." Benson gives him a short nod.

"Aaron, guess what. Shara and I met at the bar. She's joining Briar's book club, and you won't believe what book they're reading next."

"I just picked it up next door," Shara says cheerfully as she holds a novel up. "I'm hoping my wife will join too. We've been reading more romance novels together." She flips the book over so we can all see the front cover: *The Reformed Rake.*

I snort-laugh while Benson wrinkles his nose.

"Right?" Jeremy says. "This is hilarious. We have to find out if this was Briar's idea or Jamie's."

"Briar's," I say just as Briar and I make eye contact from across the bar. He raises his glass to me and winks. "Definitely Briar's."

"Well, I can't wait for our first meeting," Shara says. "You should come, Jeremy! Especially if you really are a real-life reformed rake like you say."

"Oh, he is," I tell Shara as Jeremy moves to stand next to me. He pulls me closer against him and I let his body relax into mine.

Shara says goodbye after she and Jeremy agree to find each other on some social media site I've barely heard of. Then Jeremy and I are left standing there with Benson.

Benson studies me curiously. "This is really what you want, huh?" he asks. "A dinky law firm in Vermont? This maybe-reformed playboy?" He points to Jeremy as he says it, and his tone makes it clear he's only half-joking.

"Awww, Benson, I didn't know you cared," Jeremy says sweetly.

I turn and wrap my arm tightly around Jeremy's waist. I trace my finger down his cheek and across the top of his sweater.

"Yeah, Benson," I murmur. "This is what I want. And you only live once. Jeremy's ass says so."

Jeremy bursts out laughing, and the lyrical sound echoes in my ears like it was meant to be there.

In his laughter, I hear the sound of all the perfect moments that lie ahead of us.

ACKNOWLEDGMENTS

So many people supported me in bringing this book to life. Many thanks are in order, and I apologize deeply if I forget anyone here.

First of all, huge, huge thanks to Sarina Bowen for letting me play in your True North universe again. I am so grateful to have worked with you and your team on this project. Jane, Jenn, and Natasha—you're all rockstars. Working with the four of you has been an honor and a privilege from the start.

Charley Descoteaux, there's no way this book exists without you. Thanks for keeping me writing when I wanted to quit, for giving feedback on this manuscript so many times, and for loving Jeremy and Aaron at every step of this journey.

Thanks to my intrepid beta readers/cheerleaders who've been with me from the very beginning: Karen Bradley, Shantel Schonour, and Riley Stouffer. I owe you three so much.

To the entire World of True North author team: I've learned so much from each and every one of you! I am very grateful for your wisdom and friendship. Thanks to Victoria Denault, Rachel Ember, Laurel Greer, Regina Kyle, Garrett Leigh, Leslie McAdam, and L.A. Witt for all the wonderful feedback on early drafts of this manuscript. Andi Burns, thanks for the pep talks (and for being Aaron's earliest fan).

Kari McPherson Shafenberg, my editor and friend: you make me a better writer. I'm so grateful to have you as my co-pilot on my writing journey.

Team COMMA, aka Charley Descoteaux, Rachel Ember, and Leslie McAdam: thanks for the laughter, the learning, and the chats about everything from grammatical errors to blurbs. Best writing salon ever. Leslie and Rachel, thank you for the hours you put into helping me with the legalese in this book. #teamcommaforever #commaanarchy

Mom, Dad, and AK, thanks for your endless and unconditional love and support. Travis, thanks for being the reason I believe in romance. And for making me stop to eat when I lose track of time in my writing cave.

And, last but certainly not least, thank you to every single reader who's followed me on my writing journey. Thank you for your kindness, support, and encouragement. Every word in this book is for you.

Printed in Great Britain
by Amazon